What's a tux got to do with it?

Struggling actor Rick wears the tux on a gig
as a hired escort for—surprise!—perennial
bridesmaid Frankie Raimoni, the tomboy
who was gaga over him in high school.

Rafe's undercover work cost him Maria Castillo,
the only woman he'd ever loved.
Now it leads him to a senator's party—
wearing that damned tux—and there's Maria.
Widowed…and five months pregnant.

En route to his daughter's Christmas dance,
Rob donates all the money in his pocket
to a very enticing reindeer collecting for charity.
But the "reindeer" isn't impressed with the
fifty-seven cents—or the hot guy in the tux!

**Kristine Rolofson,
Muriel Jensen
and Kristin Gabriel
send three brothers on a…**

Date
With
Destiny

Kristine Rolofson has worked as a seamstress, secretary, wallpaper hanger and waitress, but her passion has always been writing. Married for almost thirty years and the mother of six, she began to write when two of her children were still in diapers. Winner of the Holt Medallion and the National Reader's Choice award, this author of over thirty bestselling books attracts readers wherever she goes.

Muriel Jensen is the award-winning author of over seventy books that tug at readers' hearts. She has won a Reviewer's Choice Award and a Career Achievement Award from *Romantic Times* magazine, as well as a sales award from Waldenbooks. Muriel is best loved for her books about family, a subject she knows well, as she has three children and eight grandchildren. A native of Massachusetts, Muriel now lives with her husband in Oregon.

Two-time RITA® Award winner **Kristin Gabriel** lives in rural Nebraska. The author of almost twenty books, her first, *Bullets over Boise,* was made into the TV movie *Recipe for Revenge.* Kristin met her husband in college, then made the bumpy transition from city girl to farm wife, providing plenty of fodder for her stories. A busy mom with three active teenagers, Kristin divides her time between writing and attending school activities. Her hobbies include reading, dieting and procrastination.

KRISTINE ROLOFSON
MURIEL JENSEN
KRISTIN GABRIEL

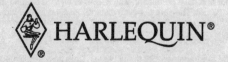

Date with Destiny

HARLEQUIN®

TORONTO • NEW YORK • LONDON
AMSTERDAM • PARIS • SYDNEY • HAMBURG
STOCKHOLM • ATHENS • TOKYO • MILAN • MADRID
PRAGUE • WARSAW • BUDAPEST • AUCKLAND

ISBN 0-373-83561-2

DATE WITH DESTINY

CONTENTS

TRANSFORMING FRANKIE

Kristine Rolofson

PROLOGUE

"MAYBE I'VE DONE something wrong," Carmen Perez told the granite stone etched with her husband's name. "I've spoiled them, taken care of them, cooked for them. No wonder they're not looking for wives."

She sighed and readjusted the clay pot filled with tulips so that it wouldn't tip over on the freshly cut grass. "I'm not getting any younger and neither are those boys. They don't understand how fast life goes. One minute you're young, and the next you're…well, getting gray hair and ready to retire."

Carmen paused to compose her thoughts. She didn't want to complain too much. A woman with four healthy, handsome sons had no right to complain, of course. But three of those healthy sons needed wives. Daughters-in-law were such a blessing.

Carmen took a tissue from her pocket and wiped her eyes. Anyone walking past the cemetery would see a small, wiry woman huddled in her raincoat, shivering in the wet spring wind that everyone who lived in Seattle was accustomed to. Her black and silver hair was short, her glasses concealed the lines around her dark eyes and her thick shoes protected her from the damp grass that covered her beloved husband's grave.

But nothing could protect her four grown children from Carmen's worried interest in their lives. She figured it was her duty to worry. They were her sons, after all, and she would hold their best interests to her heart until the day she joined Jose in the graveyard.

"It's not right for them to live the way they do," she declared. "They need their own families, like Tomas has." She omitted complaining that her eldest lived too far away with his wife and son. "They need to settle down, to be happy."

And she didn't mean the kind of "happy" that came from Rick's wild social life or Rafe's mysterious charm or Rob's talent for making furniture. But she didn't have to explain that to Jose. He would know what she meant. He always had, right up until the day he died.

Carmen patted the headstone and reached into her pocket for a tissue. "Oh, I know you think they have plenty of time, those boys of ours. But time is precious when you get to be my age, though fifty-five is still middle-aged," she added. "And I try to keep myself up, not that it's easy."

You always look good to me.

Yes, that's what her husband would say. He would also tell her to mind her own business— their sons would be just fine and she should stop worrying.

You worry too much. All the time, worry, worry, worry, he would say. And then he would distract her with a kiss or two. Not that kisses worked for long. All the Perez men knew that Carmen was a formidable force when she wanted to accomplish something.

"I want daughters-in-law," she told her husband's headstone. "And more grandchildren to baby-sit and spoil. Rob's two, Maggie and T.J., need a mother, and Rafe should stop traveling around, and Lord knows Rick needs a nice girl to make him listen to reason and stop—"

The crackle of lightning high in the sky overhead ended Carmen's weekly plea for heavenly help. She made the sign of the cross, patted the smooth granite of the stone one last time and turned toward her car as thunder boomed in the distance.

A sign, she decided, smiling a little as the rain pelted her head. Her prayers would be answered.

CHAPTER ONE

"I AM ABSOLUTELY SURE I'm making the biggest mistake of my life." Frankie Raimondi unlaced her mud-splattered work boots and kicked them away from the front door of her small apartment before she stepped into the living room, where her sister waited to pounce.

"Isn't the bride the one supposed to say things like that?" Rosa handed her a tall-stemmed glass filled with a bright blue liquid. "Drink up, you'll be fine."

Frankie grimaced as she reached for the glass. "Is this another one of your weird martinis?"

"Of course. Try it."

She did, though she knew from past experience that it was a good idea to sip, not gulp, her youngest sister's alcoholic concoctions.

"Now sit," Rosa said, pointing to the sofa that was covered with a blue sheet in deference to Frankie's dirt-covered jeans and shirts. "I think Katherine's idea was brilliant."

"That's because you want your wedding to be

perfect.'' And Rosa, Little Miss Perfect, expected everyone to be paired off neatly. The wedding, a tribute to perfect planning and high expectations of grandeur, was going to go off without a hitch because Rosa wanted it to. And Rosa, the youngest of three sisters, most definitely got her way.

Always. It was enough to make a perfectly sane construction worker drink blue alcohol.

''No,'' her sister was saying. ''It's because Donny doesn't have any unmarried friends in the wedding party.''

''I can't believe I'm going to drag some stranger to your wedding.'' Frankie sank onto the couch and rested her feet on the battered coffee table she'd found at a job site. Her apartment was small but functional, though one of these days she was going to give the walls a fresh coat of white paint and hang up some curtains over the miniblinds.

''You're not dragging anyone. You're simply hiring an escort,'' Rosa countered. She brushed imaginary sawdust off the seat of their grand-mother's wing chair and then lowered herself gracefully onto the red velvet cushion. ''It's perfectly acceptable and done all the time now. Katherine said so.''

And Katherine was another person who was difficult to argue with, especially since Frankie considered her friend to be a woman of sense. Most of the time. "She found someone?"

"Yes."

Frankie closed her eyes and prayed for the wedding week to pass quickly.

"Stop looking like a martyr," she heard her sister order, so Frankie opened her eyes and stared into the bottom of her martini glass instead while Rosa continued the conversation. "It's better than going alone. Can you imagine the aunties trying to fix you up with their neighbors or dentists or that funeral home director—I can't remember his name—the way they did the last time?"

Yes, she could imagine. Humiliation had been the theme of that weekend, when one of her cousins finally wed her longtime live-in boyfriend. The bridesmaid gown had been a strange nauseating shade of yellow and designed for the more physically endowed maids. Frankie remembered the yellow push-up padded bra that had seemed to have a life of its own.

"What if this escort is gay? Or what if he thinks I've hired him for sex? Is that what guys like this think?" Not that there was anything wrong with sex, but Frankie couldn't remember the last time she'd shaved her legs in anticipation of a hot date.

"I imagine you can handle it," was Rosa's response. "No one messes with you."

Unfortunately. Frankie worked in the midst of lots of men, none of whom she would ask out. Or would ask her out. She was almost as strong, almost as tough and always as stubborn as any of the guys who worked for Raimondi Construction. An object of lust she wasn't, never had been and never would be, even if the yellow bra emerged from the closet and volunteered to try again.

"I don't need a man," she said, but she didn't even convince herself, much less her sister.

"Have some more." Rosa lifted the glass pitcher and refilled Frankie's glass. "It will relax you."

"Okay." A twenty-five-year-old construction worker who had to pay a man to go out with her could at least hold her liquor. "Look, why don't we forget the whole 'escort' thing? I'll be on my best behavior, I'll walk back up the aisle with one of Donny's married college buddies, and I won't wear my work boots with the bridesmaid's dress, I promise." The picture of that made Frankie smile, especially when she imagined the expression on her mother's face. Her father would never criticize, because Frankie was the son he'd never had and, as he liked to say when he bragged to his cronies, his "right-hand man." "I promise to give up my jeans on the big day, even if I look ridiculous in pink."

"Rose," Rosa corrected. "An antique rose silk top with spaghetti straps, long twirly skirt and high-heeled sandals—"

"Another problem," Frankie added before she took a big gulp of her drink. "Walking in heels." She couldn't imagine herself in a "twirly skirt" either, even after several overlong fitting sessions at Marcella's La Boutique, but the other women in the Raimondi family had drowned out all of her objections.

"You need to practice, that's all. You'll look lovely, Francesca." But even Rosa didn't sound convinced. "Tina will do your hair." Tina was their married sister.

"She won't have time, not with the kids to dress." Frankie yawned. "Are you sure I have to go to this thing tonight?"

"Donny's sister wants us all to get to know each other. Wear something…nice."

"How nice?" She closed her eyes and pictured the contents of her closet. The dark blue bridesmaid's dress she'd worn to Tina's wedding was the closest thing to "nice" that she owned, and it was zipped inside a plastic bag and would never again see the light of day.

"Not jeans," Rosa said, and reached inside the Nordstrom's shopping bag at her feet. "In fact,

Mom sent you something. I helped her pick it out."

"You didn't tell her about my, uh, date, did you?"

"Do I look crazy?"

"Not after a couple of martinis." She eyed the ivory tube of fabric that Rosa dangled before her. "What is that?"

"A dress. It's stretchy. You have to wiggle into it."

"I do?"

Rosa handed her a flat package. "Panty hose. The underwear is part of the panty hose so you don't have any lines or bumps."

"I'm going to look like a hooker. A hooker with a gigolo boyfriend." She put the packet and the so-called dress on the coffee table.

Rosa ignored her. "Thirty-four B, smooth cups with a tiny bit of padding," she said, and pulled a small cream-colored bra from the bag. "Cute, huh?"

"No." As the least-endowed Raimondi female in three generations, Frankie didn't think padded bras were cute at all. "But tell Mom I said thanks."

"You'll look fabulous." And then Rosa glanced at her watch. "Oops, I've got to go home and get ready. You know where you're going?"

"Casey's. Eight o'clock."

"Don't forget the man. Katherine arranged it so he'd meet you there. The escort service is called For Women Only, and your date will be wearing—"

"A condom? A penis-print tie? A paper bag over his head?"

"A carnation," she said, trying not to laugh. "In his lapel."

"How original."

"Hey, you might get lucky." Rosa stood, revealing the curvaceous body that had made the boys in their neighborhood act like idiots since she turned thirteen. Five feet tall, petite and extremely feminine, Frankie's younger sister was used to turning men into obedient drones.

"You mean you could call this whole thing off and elope to Paris?"

Rosa only waved and let herself out of the apartment, leaving Frankie alone with the rest of the blue martini mix and a padded bra.

CHAPTER TWO

RICK PEREZ ignored the For Sale sign posted in front of the building on Sandringham Drive and took the stone steps two at a time to the door, which he unlocked with a practiced motion. With any luck his mother wouldn't find a buyer for the old brick building in the near future. The trendy Belltown location suited Rick perfectly, as did the low rent of his second-floor apartment. An aspiring actor needed all the financial breaks he could get, even if business was picking up and he'd had two callbacks for a movie that was going to be filmed next winter.

"Hey," he heard his brother Rob shout from the open door of his apartment on the first floor. "Rick?"

"Yeah." He stooped to pick up a large package leaning against the stairs to the second and third floors before he walked down the hall to his brother's kitchen. The writing was unfamiliar, though the package was addressed to "R. Perez" at 10 Sandringham Drive, Seattle. Which could be any one of the three brothers, though none of them was known for mail-order shopping. Rick tossed the package on the kitchen table next to Maggie's crayons, then raised his arms and pretended to be a monster.

Maggie screamed, as she always did, and tried to run away, but Rick was fast. He picked up his niece by her waist and pretended that he was going to hold her upside down. She screeched with delight. "Who's your favorite uncle?"

"Uncle Rafe!"

Rick growled and tipped her over a few more inches. "Wrong, Miss Maggie. He's much too serious. Let's try again—who's your favorite uncle?"

She giggled again. "Uncle Tom?"

"Wrong again, my pet." He narrowed his eyes and looked menacing, but of course the five-year-old wasn't fooled one bit. "Tom lives too far away. You have *one more chance.*"

"You are," she screamed. "Uncle Rick is my mostest favorite uncle in the whole wide world! Cross my heart, Uncle Rick!"

He lifted her high off the floor until they touched noses. "And I'm the most handsome uncle. And the youngest. And the—"

"Loudest." His brother shot him an exasperated look. "Among other things I can't mention in front of the kids."

"I've been taught to project my voice." He winked at Maggie before he set her down, then reached for his nephew, a chubby two-year-old who held up an orange truck. He stopped before lifting him and ruffled his hair instead. "Hey, T.J. You've got something in your pants that doesn't smell too good."

"He never smells good," his older sister declared, wrinkling her nose.

Rob picked up his son. "Geez, T.J. You're getting too big for diapers."

Rick opened the fridge and helped himself to a beer. "Mom says he'll figure it out when he's ready."

"Grandma's gonna get him some big boy pants," Maggie informed them, returning to the kitchen table and her coloring books.

"I brought a package in from the hall." Rick flipped the beer cap into the garbage can and took a sip from the bottle. "Maybe Mom ordered them from a catalogue."

Maggie shook her head. "She said she was gonna go to the mall tomorrow and I could go with her after church."

"Must belong to Rafe then," Rob said, carrying his son around the corner to the bathroom.

"Then we'd better not open it, I guess." It sure looked tempting. There was no return address, but that didn't mean it wasn't a package from his agent with some new scripts to read.

"Open what?" Rafe stood in the doorway and panted. Sweat rolled down his forehead and he swiped at it with the arm that wasn't encased in a grubby sling. "Geez, it's hot out there."

"This."

Rafe stepped closer. "It's not mine." He eyed the beer in his brother's hand. "You'd better not have taken the last one, kid."

"Nope, there's plenty. How far did you run?"

"Six miles. Maybe more. Hi, Mags." He ruffled the girl's curls on his way to the refrigerator.

"Hi, Uncle Rafe." She looked up from her coloring. "You can go in my swimming pool if you want."

"Thanks for the offer, honey, but I'll settle for a beer and a shower."

"Yeah," Rick said, winking at her. "Me, too."

Rob returned to the kitchen, T.J. under his arm. He dropped him in Rick's lap. "Got a date tonight, little brother?"

"More like an acting gig." He set the wriggling boy on his feet and watched him return to his truck.

"What's that supposed to mean?"

He should have kept his mouth shut. Rob was looking at him as if he'd just announced he was dancing in a strip club. "I'm, uh, doing a gig as an escort."

"You have to act like you're on a date?" Rob shook his head. "I don't get it. You're getting paid for this or doing it for free?"

"Paid. Don't knock it till you've tried it."

Rafe smiled, which he didn't do often. "Now I've heard everything. Someone's paying our little brother to take her out. Anyone want to order a pizza?"

But it was Rob who couldn't let the conversation drop. "And you've done this kind of *gig* before, Rick?"

"No, but how bad could it be?"

"Bad," his brother declared, but then again Rob, a widower with two kids to raise, wasn't the most adventurous guy in the northwest. "*Really* bad."

"Hey, it's done all the time. And my, uh, date is supposedly in her twenties. She might not be bad-looking. You never know."

"Yeah, right." Rafe shook his head. "Your dream woman, alone and lonely on a Saturday night, waiting for you, Prince Charming, to take her money and take her out. Get real."

Rick shrugged. "Hey, at least I'm going out. With a woman. Which," he said, grinning, "is more than I can say for either one of you."

"I'd rather stay home," Rob declared. "No sh—kidding." He bent over and took a crayon from T.J., who had decided to eat it like a French fry.

"Not me," Rick said, though he wouldn't admit to his older brothers that he was having second thoughts about the whole thing. He'd agreed to do a favor for a friend of his, and now he'd turned into a gigolo and a prime source of amusement to two men who never forgot anything, especially if it involved their little brother's humiliation.

"Shut up and open the box."

"Wait." Rafe took the package and headed for the door. "We don't know what's in here."

"That's why we're opening it."

"It could be anything." Rafe didn't like surprises. He was used to giving orders, and right now he looked like an injured Rambo Santa, standing there holding out the package as if it contained a ticking bomb.

"We'll know who it's for when we see what it is," Rob said, ducking his head into the refrigerator. "There'd better be another—yeah, here's one." He shut the door and met Rick's eyes. "He's taking it *outside?*"

"I guess he thinks it could explode. He's spent too much time in the jungle," Rick muttered, but he joined the rest of the family and followed Rafe out to the backyard. He watched his brother carefully open the package while holding it above the pool, only to discover that the mysterious box held clothing.

"It looks like a tux," Rafe announced, tossing the empty box onto a lawn chair. He held up an expensive-looking black tuxedo and a diamond-patterned silver vest. Matching pants and a dress shirt dropped to the grass, where Rick retrieved them.

"Perry Ellis," he said. "New. No one remembers ordering this?"

"Buttons?" Maggie held up a bag.

"Cuff links," her father said. "They look brand-new, too."

"Well," Rafe said, handing the jacket and vest to Rick. "It sure as hell isn't mine, though the size is right."

"We're all the same size," Rick reminded him. "And it's not mine, either."

"You take it," Rob told him, grabbing T.J. before he climbed into the wading pool. "Wear it to the Oscars someday."

"Yeah." Rafe shot him a disgusted look. "Or you can save it for the next time some woman pays you to go out with her."

Rick winced and took the matching pants from

his brother. Maggie giggled, so Rick tossed her over his shoulder and headed for the house, but not before he hollered, "This is the last time I tell you guys anything."

CHAPTER THREE

"MAYBE THE DRESS was a mistake." Rosa looked Frankie up and down.

"What's wrong with it—never mind," Frankie said. "Forget I asked." She headed toward the bar, her sister following close behind.

Rosa caught up to her before Frankie could try to perch on one of the leather-covered bar stools. She wasn't sure if her dress would stretch enough to let her do anything but stand around and look stupid. She decided against the bar stool. No way would she risk splitting the seams and having a crowd of people watch her thighs pop out of the fabric.

"I'm sorry. The dress is…fine. At least you wore the right shoes."

"Contrary to popular belief, I can dress myself, Rosa. I do it every day." She turned to the bartender, a Tom Cruise look-alike who gave her a sympathetic smile. "Jack Daniel's. Straight up, please."

"You got it," he said. "And don't worry about the dress. You've got the legs for it."

Frankie looked down at her legs at the same time Rosa did.

"I told you," her sister said. "The panty hose do the trick. It's hard to impress bartenders."

"Nah," the guy said, winking at Frankie. "We're easy."

"Thanks." Frankie felt strangely comforted. "I'll remember that the next time I'm not wearing—"

"Stop," Rosa hissed, her hand on Frankie's arm. "You can't tell the bartender you're not wearing underwear or get drunk in front of Donny's family."

"He started it," Frankie pointed out. "And I *don't* get drunk." She took a sip of the whiskey and prayed for patience. Then she gave her sister a look of warning. "But don't tempt me."

"I never should have made those blue martinis," Rosa said. "You're usually more cooperative."

"A few hours ago you were telling me that martinis would relax me enough to pretend I wasn't dating the male version of a hooker."

"Frankie, *please* keep your voice down. Remember the word 'escort'?" Rosa smiled and waved at someone on the other side of the room.

Frankie hid a sigh as she recalled that brides—even obsessive compulsive perfectionists like her sister—became nervous ninnies the week before the wedding. Tina had broken out in hives.

"Okay, I'll be quiet. Point me toward the future sister-in-law who planned this event, will you? I know I should remember her from the shower, but Donny's sisters all look the same." She took another sip of her drink and thought about kicking her shoes off. She'd have to wait until she was seated at a table, though. And before she sat down she had to find a man wearing a carnation. Sometimes life was much too complicated.

"There's a strong family resemblance." Rosa flipped her long hair, styled stick-straight and gleaming from expensive gel, off her shoulder. Her short dress was pale blue, her perfect fingernails were painted the palest pink and her eye makeup was nothing short of spectacular. Frankie had watched her sisters do their makeup for years, and yet the skills had never rubbed off on her.

"I hope my daughters look like Raimondis," Rosa whispered. Frankie smiled, nodded and kept sipping her drink while the groom's sisters welcomed her to the party. She made her escape by pretending to head to the ladies' room, and then she moved back to the lobby and hovered near a stack of tourist brochures. She had a good view of the entrance and a good grip on her drink.

Frankie saw Rick Perez first, the flower stuck on his lapel second and the amazed expression on that familiar, handsome face third. He had seen her, recognized her, walked toward her. Which meant Frankie had to slink out of the bar before he realized she was his date for the evening.

Or, she thought in a panic, did he already know? It wasn't as if her name was Jane Smith or Ann Johnson. No, she had to have the memorable mouthful *Francesca Raimondi.*

Humiliation, Frankie decided, seemed to be inevitable, because Rick was walking through the mirrored foyer and heading her way. There was a puzzled smile on that handsome face, a flash of recognition in his dark brown eyes. Oh, yes, Frankie sighed. He remembered her. And she'd know that face and that smile and those eyes anywhere.

Even in a place as dimly lit and crowded as Casey's.

He stopped in front of her, forcing Frankie to stare directly into the white carnation before she lifted her chin and met his amused expression with a casual smile. "Hi, Rick."

"Frankie?" He put his large hands on her shoulders and the warmth immediately spread down her arms and turned her fingers numb. She wondered if she was having a stroke. "Or should I call you Francesca? That's the name I was given—"

"Frankie is fine," she fibbed, having intended to ask her escort to call her by her more sophisticated given name. "I didn't know you were going to be my..."

"Date?" He grinned. "Yeah, I'm it. Disappointed?"

She'd loved him since she was ten, kissed him once when she was eighteen. Disappointment wasn't the word she'd use to describe how she felt. "This is really embarrassing."

"Yeah. You've gotta believe me. This is the first time I've done anything like this. I wasn't given the client's last name and I never think of you as Francesca." He slid his hands down her arms. "Look at you. In a *dress*."

"It's not a dress," she muttered. "It's a tube sock with ruffles."

Rick laughed, gave her hands a squeeze and then released her. Frankie took the opportunity to start for the door.

"Hey," he said, blocking her way. He was devastatingly handsome. Black slacks, white shirt, silk sports jacket, all worn with a casual air that made him look like the movie star he would be someday. "Where are you going?"

"I can't do this. If I'd known it would be you, I never would—oh, no."

He frowned. "What?"

A familiar dark-haired dynamo hurried toward them. "Frankie! And little Ricky Perez? Is that really you?"

"You remember my younger sister, Tina?" It was an unnecessary introduction, because Tina was already hugging Rick and telling him she'd seen him on the History Channel last year when he'd played an escaped convict. She asked how his older brothers were doing and said that the old neighborhood missed them, but she saw his mother at the grocery store once in a while.

Frankie eased closer to the door. She would make a break for it now and make her apologies tomorrow. The bar was so crowded that no one would miss her anyway.

But Rick was quick, grabbing her hand before she could take two steps back. His fingers held hers tightly as he pulled her closer to him, keeping his voice low. "Frankie, babe, don't leave me."

"I—I need some air," she stammered.

"Tina, we'll catch up later," he told her sister, who gave Frankie a thumbs-up sign before she returned to the crowd surrounding the bar. Then Rick led her across the foyer, through the glass doors and outside. "Nice sunset," he said, the breeze ruffling his black hair.

"How do you do it?" She leaned against the brick wall and shivered a little, despite the tight sleeves of her stupid-looking dress.

"I told you, Frankie, this is my first time. It's a favor for a friend who got a TV commercial and couldn't—"

"No," she interrupted. "How do you look so perfect? You were the cleanest kid in elementary school. Even when you played football in high school, your uniform was never dirty."

"That's because I was so lousy the coach hardly ever played me." He grinned down at her. "Were you a cheerleader?"

"You've got to be joking."

Those gorgeous eyebrows rose. "Why?"

"My sisters were cheerleaders. I built the sets for the drama department." Which meant she got to watch Rick rehearse. He was the star of every production, of course, and always surrounded by admiring girls.

"Ah." He shoved his hands in his pants pockets and asked her the question she'd been expecting. "So, Frankie, what am I doing here? You trying to make an old boyfriend jealous or you needed a date for the company party or what?"

"Rosa's getting married."

He looked surprised. "You Raimondi women marry young. My mother said Tina has a baby already."

"*Two* babies."

"Geez."

"This week is going to be matchmaking hell," she informed him, folding her arms in front of her chest as if she was surveying a building site. "Every aunt, cousin and family friend is going to ask me when I'm getting married and who I'm dating and if I have a ring yet. It happens at every wedding, holiday and funeral."

"So you've hired someone to pretend to be your boyfriend." He looked impressed. "Way to go, Franks."

"Do *not* call me Franks. That's even worse than Frankie."

"It's hard to think of you as anything else," he said, smiling down at her.

"Try." He was tall, tall enough to make her feel almost petite despite the three-inch heels she wore. Not that she was tall, but even at five-seven she was the tallest female in her family.

His smile deepened. "Do I have to promise not to tease you, too?"

"Never mind," she said. "This isn't going to work."

"What, you mean the gig?"

"The *gig,* as you call it, is not just for tonight," she told him. "It's for next Friday night and the wedding on Saturday. You have to wear a tux. And you have to act as if we've known each other a long time."

"We have."

"You know what I mean."

"Lucky for you I'm out of work right now, so I'm free if you are." He leaned closer, bracing one hand next to her shoulder on the brick wall. She barely heard the nearby chatter, because Rick Perez had bent forward to nuzzle her ear. His breath was warm against her skin, his scent so delicious she thought she might just give up trying to stand. "Look happy," he whispered. "We have an audience."

She closed her eyes and felt his lips against her cheek. She hoped with all her heart that her cousins were watching this. They would be on their cell phones to their mothers within the hour.

"Okay." He withdrew a few inches and glanced toward the door. "That was a good start."

"Yes." She cleared her throat. She tried to remember that sex was completely overrated. "A good start."

"Frankie, babe, you're not going to cry, are you?"

"Of course not. My feet hurt, that's all."

He looked down at her size 9s, encased in white pumps that felt two sizes too small. "Not exactly construction boots, are they?"

She shook her head and watched the way the corners of his eyes crinkled when he smiled. Russell Crowe had better watch out.

"Well," he said. "Shall we do it?"

"Do it?"

"Get a drink. Mingle. You can tell me what this party is all about while I hold your hand and fend off your old boyfriends."

"One of Rosa's future sisters-in-law wanted to throw a party so we could all get to know each other before the wedding."

"And since I'm your date for the wedding, it made sense for me to meet everyone tonight." He took her hand and tugged her toward the entrance.

"This wasn't my idea," she confessed, hoping he wouldn't think she was desperate for a boyfriend. "Rosa and a friend of mine ganged up on me."

He gave her fingers a squeeze. She was sure he meant to be reassuring. "I'm glad I could help."

"You're not," she muttered under her breath. He was only going to make things worse. Rick Perez was the last man on earth she wanted to pretend to be in love with.

He opened the door for her. "Relax, Frankie. We're going to have a good time."

Frankie hid a sigh. Relax? When Rick Perez was whispering in her ear, kissing her neck, holding her hand? She'd be lucky to survive this night without blisters, a hangover and heart palpitations.

RICK WASN'T SURPRISED to be having a good time. After all, he'd grown up with the Raimondis and they had mutual friends. Once he talked Frankie out of running home, he set out to make sure she had more fun than she thought she would. He got a kick out of seeing her again, even though his pride was a little dented from her less than enthusiastic reaction to him being her date.

Come to think of it, Frankie had never been too impressed with him. Not like the other girls he'd gone to school with. Except for that one time, right after graduation.

"Rick?" She'd walked up to him after graduation, away from the crowd gathered in the parking lot behind the school. She'd worn a white graduation gown and her hair had been sticking up all over in a frizzy kind of halo. She looked ready to run and yet somehow determined.

"Yeah?" Oh, he'd been so cool. His buddies had snickered and one elbowed him in the ribs.

"Hey, Franks," one of the guys drawled. "Is Tina still goin' out with Walt?"

Frankie shrugged, but her gaze had been on Rick. She swallowed hard and stuck out her hand. "Congratulations," she'd squeaked. "I hear you got a scholarship."

"Yeah." What a brilliant conversationalist he'd been back then. "I can't wait to go."

"Well," she'd said, hesitating. And then, before he could brace himself, she'd leaned forward and kissed him. Right on the mouth. It was over before he'd had a chance to react, but the guys had roared with laughter.

"Franks," he'd called, because she'd turned really fast and run away. "Hey, Franks!"

And now, naturally, she was a pretty good-looking woman who didn't want to be reminded of her old nickname. And didn't want to be kissed, either.

Rick drank a beer, tossed the silly flower onto the bar and stuck close to his date when the party moved into the larger room with the dance floor and the band. Casey's was dark, crowded and noisy. He avoided some flirtatious looks from a bridesmaid and a cousin, endured a barrage of questions from Tina's husband, Walt—a suspicious-looking ex-football player from Washington State—and had to inform a hovering cocktail waitress that no, he had no interest in meeting her after work. He kept Frankie next to him, within reach, and watched her switch from a margarita to ginger ale after thirty minutes.

"Frankie," he whispered, leaning closer. He wished he could tuck her hair behind her ear so he could see her profile. She didn't turn toward him, which made him drape one arm over her shoulder. "Really, Frankie, you're not doing your part."

"What?" Now she turned to look at him.

"We haven't danced yet."

"We don't—"

"Yes," he said, taking her drink out of her hand and setting it on the table. "We do."

Rosa's future husband, a tall guy who looked pretty happy with his life, agreed. "Come on, Rosa. We haven't danced, either."

Rick led Frankie onto the dance floor and took her in his arms as the band played a slow rendition of some song he remembered from college. Lady something. "So, let's get our stories straight. How long have we been going out?"

"A few months," she answered. He pulled her into a close embrace. "But we're crazy about each other."

"Do we live together, too?" He'd never danced with a woman with calluses before. Her hands were small, her unpainted fingernails filed short.

Her body was slim, but not skinny. She was all muscle, he realized, which made sense, considering her job.

"Absolutely not. No one would believe that one."

"Why not?"

He felt her sigh, and his hand tightened on the waist of the bizarre dress. Ivory wasn't her color. Ruffles didn't suit her either, he mused, though he liked the way the low neckline tantalized him with all that smooth skin. "Why not?" he asked again.

"I'm...independent."

"You always were." He remembered what a tomboy she'd been growing up. They were the same age and had shared the same neighborhood and gone to the same schools, but while Rick had been a hellion as the youngest of four brothers, Frankie Raimondi had never backed down from any of his challenges. "Remember when I dared you to climb on the roof of your house?"

"That was an easy one."

"I didn't know you climbed up there all the time to get away from your sisters. I was so damned impressed." He chuckled. He'd had to pay her five dollars, too, because she'd won that bet. Come to think of it, she'd won a lot of bets those years. And now she was in his arms, but he wouldn't exactly say she was having a good time. "Frankie, can you at least pretend you're enjoying this?"

"I majored in business," was the stilted reply, "not in dance."

"We'll have to dance at the wedding." He leaned back to look down at her. She was prettier than he remembered, the kind of woman who could wear jeans and a T-shirt and look sexy as hell. "I'll teach you."

"I can't afford it."

"Dancing lessons are included in my fee," he teased. "It's a package deal."

"Please tell me that's all that's in the package." She'd gone pale and those brown eyes gazed up at him with an expression close to horror. So, Frankie thought that anything intimate between them would be the stuff of nightmares? He was a little insulted and told her so.

"And," he said, "I don't hire myself out for sex."

"Could you please keep your voice down?" She glanced around them as if the other dancers could hear above the music.

"But dancing? Frankie, you've got yourself an expert."

"It's hopeless," she said. "Forget dancing. Just act like you're crazy about me."

"Yeah, I understood that the first time you said

it." He tightened his grip on her hand. "You're wobbling."

"It's the heels."

"It's not my incredible sex appeal?" Her answer was a very unladylike snort. "You know, you're going to hurt my feelings."

"Your male ego will survive," she muttered, but she relaxed against him a little bit more. They danced without speaking for a long moment, until Frankie broke the silence. "You must really need the money."

"There you go again. Those shoes are making you cranky. Do the Cinderella thing and kick 'em off."

"I'll keep my shoes on, thank you. I'm not exactly Cinderella and you're not—"

He looked down at her and grinned. "Prince Charming? Come on, I'm doing my best. Are you always this mean to your dates?"

"Only the ones who put worms down my back."

Rick sighed. Trust a woman to remember every little offense.

CHAPTER FOUR

"FRANKIE, WE HAVE A PROBLEM." Katherine shut the door to the pink-tiled ladies' room and looked around to see if they were alone. "I should have been here early to help you, but I was in a meeting and it ran late. I'm sorry."

"It doesn't matter." Frankie had been too busy trying to act like Rick's girlfriend to notice how late it had gotten. "Have you seen Rosa?"

"She told me you were in here, but she didn't say how—or who—your escort was, except to smile and fan her face as if he was pretty darn hot."

"She's busy being a bride and torturing Donny. She keeps pouring margaritas and telling me how nice I'll look in the bridesmaid's gown." Frankie dried her hands on a paper towel and turned back to the mirror. "I need an opinion. Tell me the truth, how bad is this dress?"

"It's not terrible, but it's not exactly you."

"My mother bought it." Frankie attempted to

redistribute the shirred fabric so that it didn't bunch around her waist.

"You have to stop wearing clothes that your mother thinks are perfect," her best friend declared. "We could go shopping sometime—anytime—if you didn't break out in hives at the sight of a mall."

"I'll think about it." She'd have to do more than just think, especially now that she would be spending so much time with Rick. She attempted to smooth the tightly pleated fabric over her hips, but it wasn't easy. A pair of pliers would come in handy right now.

"We'd have fun. And I'm not your mother." Katherine smiled at her in the mirror. "No ruffles, I promise."

"I don't think I want to wear this again. From now on I'm going to country-western bars so I can wear jeans and tank tops."

"It's dark out there. No one will notice if ivory isn't your best color. And besides," Katherine added with the diplomacy that made everyone love her, "the dress does make you look sexy."

"Sexy?" She eyed herself in the mirror. Long dark hair, dark eyes, pink lips. Nice enough, but definitely not sexy. "Sexy is definitely an improvement. The bartender told me he liked my legs."

"Look, Frankie, forget about being sexy. I'm

sorry I brought it up.'' She lowered her voice when another woman entered the ladies' room and went into a stall at the far end. ''The man you're with is *not* the man I hired. That man you were dancing with is *not* Paul Bunyan. He's more like Cary Grant.''

Frankie laughed. Katherine was a big fan of classic movies. ''No, it didn't work out the way—''

''Oh, good Lord.'' Katherine, a usually unflappable preschool teacher, looked as if she'd been told none of her students were toilet-trained. ''He's from the agency, isn't he? He wore a white carnation and showed you the agency's card and his driver's license and the official contract?''

''Not exactly.''

Poor Katherine looked as if she was ready to haul her out of Casey's ladies' room and into her car, so Frankie hurried to explain. ''I've known him all my life, so it's all right.''

''You know him? What happened to Paul Bunyan?''

''He got another acting job, so Rick filled in. Come on, you can meet him and see for yourself.'' They walked out of the ladies' room and down the dimly lit hall to the dance floor, which had grown more crowded in the past hour. The room seemed filled with beautiful people in their twenties and thirties, the kind of people who knew how to dress and didn't wear hardhats to work. "Maybe I should start wearing lipstick. Or get my navel pierced. What do you think?"

"I think," her friend said slowly, "that lipstick is a good idea."

"I've got some."

Katherine sighed. "Is he an old boyfriend or something? Is that why you want to go shopping?"

"I didn't say I wanted to go shopping, I said I'd think about it. And no, he's not an old boyfriend."

"But you wanted him to be," Katherine guessed. "You have that same look on your face that you had when you came across that garage full of old wooden doors."

"They were beautiful doors. The workmanship was—uh-oh, he's watching. Don't look like we're talking about him."

The tables that held Rosa's party were in the far corner, but Frankie spotted Rick right away. He stood next to Rosa's fiancé and appeared to be listening to something Donny was saying, but he was watching the crowd. As if, Frankie thought, he was looking for her. Waiting for her. Waiting a little impatiently, maybe.

Oh, now that was romantic nonsense.

He smiled when he saw her and Frankie smiled

back, much to Katherine's shock. "You've known him all your life?"

"Just about."

"And you've kept him a secret."

"We're old friends, that's all."

"Which is why your fists are clenched."

Frankie concentrated on relaxing her fingers. "You know I'm not good at things like this."

"Which is why a professional escort was a good idea," Katherine said. "Not a gorgeous childhood friend you have a history with."

"There's no history. Come on." Frankie led her over to the crowd. "I'll give you the official introduction and you can judge for yourself."

"Is he gay?"

"No. I even kissed him once, when I was eighteen. It goes under the heading of My Most Embarrassing Moment, because I wasn't his type. Rick Perez dated all the really hot girls in our class. There was even a rumor that he slept with one of the student teachers."

Katherine muttered something under her breath, but Katherine never swore. Rosa, more than a little tipsy, came over to join them.

"I would never, never…" she gurgled, hanging on to Frankie's arm. "Never in a million years would I b'lieve that Rick Perez—*the* Rick Perez—

had become a—'' she lowered her voice to a stage whisper ''—*male escort.*''

''He's doing a favor for a friend of his,'' Frankie explained. ''He doesn't exactly work for—''

''Not that he wouldn't be good at it,'' Rosa said, taking another sip of a margarita from a glass the size of a fishbowl. ''I'm sure he's very good at—''

''He's not an escort,'' Frankie hissed. ''He's an actor.''

''Holy sh—''

''Rosa,'' Katherine said. ''Do you want some coffee?''

''*Your* male escort,'' Rosa added, staring at her sister. ''You should have put on mascara. Makes your eyes look bigger.''

''Coffee,'' Frankie said, taking her sister's arm. ''Or I'll tell Donny you tried to elope with Bobby Cristofaro when you were sixteen.''

''You wouldn't.'' But Rosa went willingly over to the table with her sister and didn't say a word when Frankie asked their waitress for black coffee.

''Sit,'' Frankie said, pointing to the empty seat beside Rick. ''And don't say anything.'' She didn't want Rosa embarrassing Rick in front of everyone, and she certainly didn't want her sister spilling the truth about Frankie's ''date'' with the best-looking guy in Seattle.

''Good going,'' Katherine said, picking up her

glass of white wine. "But there's a lot to this story that you're not telling me."

"I can't," she said. "It's not all that interesting."

"I don't believe you." Katherine smiled as Rick changed places with Rosa and stretched his arm out behind Frankie's chair.

Frankie didn't tell her friend that for years she'd dreamed of going out with Rick. Dancing with him—well, maybe not dancing, but having his arms around her and holding her hand and whispering in her ear. Those dark eyes gazing down at her as if he couldn't bear to look away, the caressing touch on her back, the sexy smile that promised all sorts of wonderful things to come.

But in the dream she hadn't had to give her Visa card number to a dating agency, either.

"I'LL TAKE YOU HOME."

"That's not part of the deal." They were in the parking lot again, only this time Frankie stood under a streetlight next to her small pickup truck, her keys dangling from one hand.

"Yes, it is," Rick insisted. This area of Seattle was well-known for its nightlife, but that didn't mean it was safe for a lone female. Hell, anything could happen, whether it was midnight or not. "I don't let my dates drive home alone. Ever."

"You're being ridiculous." She looked at him with those huge dark eyes and he couldn't figure out what she was thinking. Frankie had always been hard to figure out. She could be tough as nails when it came to standing up for herself against the school bully, yet heartbroken and crying over a broken robin's egg an hour later.

He tried again. "I promise I won't put worms down your dress."

That made her smile. "It's so tight you couldn't even if you tried. I'm going to need scissors to get out of it."

That gave him an excuse to look lower than her stubborn chin, down to the expanse of smooth skin above her breasts. Her squished breasts. He wondered why she'd worn a dress that flattened such a lovely part of her body. He also wondered what it would be like to slowly peel that dress off her and kiss some of that soft-looking skin underneath those ruffles. And then he felt a flash of guilt. This was Frankie, after all. He didn't have those strip-her-clothes-off fantasies about the only girl in tenth grade who beat him at arm wrestling.

"I can't leave my truck here," Frankie said. "But thanks for the offer."

"Look, at least let me follow you home. You know I'm not a serial killer or some kind of pervert."

She laughed. "Okay. I'm not too far from here. I have an apartment near Pioneer Square."

"It's on my way," he fibbed.

"Okay, then," she said, opening the door of her truck before he could do the gentlemanly thing and open it for her. "Try to keep up."

Leave it to Frankie to get the last word.

FRANKIE PARKED her truck in the private gravel lot behind the building she and her father had spent almost a year renovating. A labor of love, her father called it, because he'd gone over budget making certain the 1892 brick house was restored to its former glory. A ritzy antique store and the Silver and Gold beauty salon occupied the first floor, Frankie shared the second floor with a rare-book dealer, and a trio of modern artists rented the entire third story and sold paintings that cost as much as a new car.

Rick played his part right to the end, pulling his car next to hers in the lot and switching off the engine.

He opened his car door at the same time she got out of her truck. "I'll walk you to your door."

Frankie pretended not to be pleased, but it was rare to have a man make sure she arrived home safely. When had Rick become so protective? It was his job, she knew. It was written in the contract somewhere, right above the lines that said, *Make your date feel special. Hold her hand in such a way as to convince her that you are thrilled to be breathing the same air with her. And, should the situation arise, use a condom.*

He gazed up at the three-story building as they walked to the back door. "It's an Elmer Fish, isn't it?"

"Yes. How did you know?"

"I live in one of his homes, too, in Belltown. My mother has it up for sale now, but we're not in any hurry to move out."

"We?" She pictured a co-ed group of actors— all with perfect skin and perfect hair—having wild sex on futons in between acting jobs.

"Rafe and Rob. We each have our own apartment."

The wild actor sex vision faded, especially since she remembered that Rob was married. She imagined Rick's mother delivering casseroles to her sons and making sure they behaved themselves. "You live alone?"

"Yes." They were at the door now. The glow of the porch light illuminated his perfect, handsome, future-Oscar-winner face. "Do you?"

"Well, I've thought about getting a dog." She gulped as he leaned his arm against the wall again, the way he had a few hours ago when he'd convinced her to go back inside Casey's for the evening.

"What kind?"

"What?" He was too close. She couldn't quite remember what they were talking about.

"What kind of dog?"

"Something big, I guess." Something to keep her company.

"Good night, Frankie," he said, frowning a little as he looked at her mouth.

"You can stop that," she told him. "There's no one around to see."

"No," he said. "You're right." But he lowered his head and kissed her anyway. Frankie tried to be prepared for the briefest of kisses, the kind of pecks reserved for lukewarm first dates, the kind that said thanks-for-lunch-see-you-around, but the second Rick's lips found hers, she felt a jolt deep in her abdomen. He stopped and lifted his mouth a fraction of an inch, as if he'd felt her response and didn't know what to do.

Before Frankie could do more than just think about moving away, Rick kissed her again. And this time it wasn't brief, either. His hand left the wall and cupped her face, his mouth slanted over hers and coaxed her lips apart.

He didn't have to coax much. Frankie, swept away in a whirl of dreams-coming-true passion, dropped her keys, opened her mouth and lost her mind. It was long minutes later when he released her, another long moment before either one of them spoke. Her knees were shaking, but she blamed it on the stress of wearing heels for four hours.

"Frankie." He bent over and picked up her keys. "I'm sorry. That was dumb of me."

"That's okay." She took the keys from his out-stretched hand and, unwilling to embarrass herself any further, unlocked the door. Before she disappeared inside, she turned to look over her shoulder, but didn't meet his gaze when she said, "You're fired."

CHAPTER FIVE

TWO MORE MINUTES, she thought, kicking off her uncomfortable shoes before she climbed the back staircase. Two more minutes of Rick's delicious kisses and she'd have peeled off the stupid dress and thrown it—and caution—to the wind. She'd have made a fool of herself the way she had when she was eighteen and she'd impulsively kissed him after their high school graduation ceremony. What had he said then to make his friends laugh? She'd never heard the words, but she'd seen the looks and heard the guffaws.

So much for kissing Rick. She was a smart woman who didn't go back for seconds when it came to humiliation.

No, she decided later as she crawled into bed, the ceiling fan whirring pleasantly overhead. She didn't need this kind of complication, never mind the headache from that one margarita. Rick was fired. He could go back to auditioning for movie roles or television commercials or whatever it was he did. She didn't need him pretending to be her date or touching her back or acting as if he liked the way her mouth felt against his.

Tomorrow she would call Katherine and tell her that she needed some new clothes if she was going to survive Wedding Week. Heck, she needed a whole new wardrobe if she was ever going to get any kind of social life. How pathetic to be twenty-five and so hard up for a date that she would let herself be talked into hiring an escort. And then to have her paid date turn out to be her childhood crush. Well, it was a sign that she needed to make some changes in her life.

Katherine thought she'd look good in black.

Frankie rearranged her pillows and stared at the decorative tin ceiling she'd talked her father into painting instead of replacing. She would go to the wedding events alone, she'd tell her family that she just broke up with her boyfriend—yes, she'd say to the curious aunts, the same young man that she was with at Donny's sister's party. No, she would say to her cousins, she wasn't suffering so much that she couldn't eat a second slice of wedding cake, but she wasn't interested in meeting any men right now, thanks so much.

She needed time, she would sigh when she told her mother and Tina. Time to herself for a while, before she let herself become involved again. In the meantime, there was a particularly hard-bodied

Chippendale dancer who kept calling her for tips
on how to wear a tool belt.

"SO WHEN DID all this happen, you getting a boyfriend and that boyfriend the son of Carmen
Perez?"

"Just a minute, Mom." Frankie moved the
phone to her left ear so her right hand was free to
make pot of coffee. She should have known her
mother would be calling first thing this morning,
immediately after Rosa woke up and reported on
the evening. Dorothy was most likely trying not to
jump up and down at the thought of her ugly duck-
ling having a date with a male swan.

"You and I should talk more," her mother said.
"You spend too much time with your father."

"I work for him," Frankie pointed out. "He's
my boss."

"Does he know who you're going out with?"

"He probably does now, because he's sitting in
the dining room reading the paper and he's heard
everything you and Rosa said."

"Carmen and Jose raised such nice boys." Her
mother sighed. "Which one is Ricky?"

"The wild, insane one," she replied, watching
the coffee drip into the glass carafe.

"Quit your teasing, Frankie. All those boys were

gentlemen. Your father said one of them works in South America now."

"Really." She reached for the aspirin bottle and poured herself a glass of water.

"So what does Rick do?"

"He's an actor. Ask Tina. She said she's seen him on the History Channel."

"Oh, my," Dorothy Raimondi breathed. "An actor? He must be very handsome."

"He is."

"And the dress? You liked the dress? It fit okay?"

"Like a glove," Frankie declared. "The bartender asked for my phone number. Look, Mom, I've got to go. Katherine's coming over and we're going to a movie." She heard her mother tell her father to be quiet, that she couldn't hear a thing and she'd find the *TV Guide* as soon as she got off the phone. "Mom?"

"Just a minute, Frankie. I think Tina just drove up with the kids. Why don't you come over later? I made lasagna."

Frankie could almost taste the sauce. "Okay, but I don't know when, so don't wait dinner for me."

"I'll put a nice big piece aside," Dorothy promised. "We'll have a nice long visit and you can tell me all about your young man."

Frankie winced. "Mom, there isn't anything to

tell,'' she said, but her mother had hung up. Dorothy would expect a detailed romantic story. A description of their first date. An explanation of the relationship. And a timetable so the Raimondis could plan the next wedding.

She wanted to put her head on the kitchen counter and scream.

RICK RETURNED to the scene of the crime late Sunday morning. Not that it was much of a crime, Rick decided. He'd be damned if he was fired just because he'd been stupid and given in to an impulse. He still wasn't sure what had happened, except that one minute he'd been looking at Frankie's mouth—he'd never noticed she had the kind of lips that turned up at the corners and made a man forget he was supposed to be working—and then he'd kissed her. And not long enough, either. He should have made it last, since it might have been the one and only chance he'd get.

"I'm not going to apologize again," Rick told her as soon as Frankie opened the door. She held a portable phone up to her ear and said, "None of your business, Rosa," before she hung up.

This time he tried not to look at her mouth, which was easy, because this morning Frankie wore a white tank top that didn't flatten her small, perfect breasts, and a pair of shorts, the very short nylon kind that rose up at the thigh. And Frankie had a beautiful pair of thighs.

"I didn't come here to grovel."

"In that case," she said, opening the door wide, "you can come in."

"I brought food," he said, willing her to turn around and yet hoping she wouldn't tempt him with another distracting part of her anatomy. Her dark hair was pulled back into a ponytail, she wore no makeup and she even seemed a little sleepy, which made him wonder what her bedroom looked like, before he caught himself. He had no interest in Frankie Raimondi's bedroom or anything else of hers, he reminded himself. He was here as a friend, bringing coffee and pastry and the hope that she wasn't really angry with him just because he'd gotten into his part as a boyfriend.

"Coffee?" She tossed the phone onto the couch, took the paper bag he held out to her and sniffed.

"And cinnamon rolls. There's a bakery near my apartment that makes them fresh every day." He shoved his hands in the pockets of his slacks and looked around the high-ceilinged room. Bright, casual and comfortable, like Frankie herself. Last night's high heels were tossed by a red chair. "Nice place."

"Thanks. I'm going to paint it this summer."

"How long have you lived here?"

"About a year and a half. My father and I restored the building."

He followed her into the kitchen, a surprisingly large room that overlooked a neighbor's garden. Apple-red and white tiles lined the counter, the black and white linoleum floor looked new, and the old-fashioned tall cupboard doors were painted white to match the tiles.

"I like your place," he said, watching Frankie take his peace offerings out of the bag and set them on the red-and-chrome kitchen table. "My grandmother used to have a table like that."

"Mine did, too. Until she gave it to me." She smiled, which meant she'd forgotten to be mad at him. A good sign. "You can sit down."

He pulled out one of the chrome chairs and did just that. "Look, Franks—I mean, *Frankie*," he said as she set one of the rolls and coffee cups in front of him. "About last night—"

"Look, *Ricky*," Frankie said, giving him a glare she probably thought was intimidating, but made Rick want to laugh. "I know you've had a lot of girlfriends—"

"Not that many." He peeled off the plastic lid.

"But if you think a woman enjoys being told that a man is sorry he kissed her, well, you're wrong."

"I'm not sorry I kissed you." Rick took a careful sip of the hot coffee. "I'm sorry you got mad."

"You're just sorry you got fired." She sat down and pushed the sugar bowl toward him. "Do you want cream?"

"No, thanks. And no, I'm not sorry about being fired." Though he wasn't sure what Frankie would do next. Hire someone else, he supposed. The thought made him lose his appetite for the cinnamon roll sitting next to his coffee. "Now you can ask me to be your date for the wedding—and for the other stuff, too."

He noticed that she drank her coffee black, like he did. She set her cup down without taking a sip. "Why would I want to do that?"

"Because you still need me to ward off the matchmaking relatives. You need a guy to dance with, too." He leaned back and saw that she was about to protest. "And don't forget the dance lessons, either."

"I've changed my—"

"One-two-three, one-two-three. That's a waltz."

Frankie didn't say a word. She broke off a piece of the cinnamon roll and proceeded to eat the entire thing, piece by piece, until it was gone. She wiped her fingers with a paper napkin from the plastic dispenser set in the middle of the table and then drank the rest of her coffee.

"You're not talking to me?" he finally asked.

"I'm thinking."

The trouble with women, Rick decided, was that you could never tell if they were thinking or about ready to kick a guy into the street. He thought it best to remind her of his skill. "I can do the fox-trot, too. Slow, slow, quick, quick."

"You learned all this in college?"

"No. When we were kids, my mother made us take lessons. She said we needed civilizing. I think it worked for everyone but Rafe."

"I don't have a lot of free time."

"What, you spend eighteen hours a day pounding nails?"

"I don't exactly pound nails. Next to my father, I'm the boss."

"I should have guessed," he said, which made her smile. "But even the boss gets time off. Just let me know, okay?"

"Okay."

It was as much of a commitment as he was going to get. He pushed his chair back and stretched, looking around the kitchen. "Why is your ruffly dress hanging out of the garbage can?"

She blushed, which surprised him. "I don't need it anymore."

"Oh." His disappointment surprised him, too. He'd hoped to talk her into dancing. Or a walk in the park and lunch at the Chowder Shed over by the water. She looked at her watch, a bad sign.

"I guess I'd better go. Katherine's picking me up to go shopping."

"Groceries or clothes?" If they were shopping for groceries, he could tag along and carry the bags.

"Clothes," she said, destroying his plan to be helpful. "No more ruffly dresses. I'm making a change."

"Oh." Making a change? Uh-oh. In Rick's experience, every time a woman said that, it meant trouble. He didn't want her to change. He liked Frankie just the way she was.

CHAPTER SIX

FRANKIE WAS VERY, very pleased with herself. She was buying more clothes than she'd intended, of course, but not as many as Katherine wanted her to. She said no to a floral skirt that barely covered her rear, but yes to a new pair of shoes with heels that didn't look like golf tees, and a strapless bra to go with Friday night's black dress. She even splurged on dangling jeweled earrings.

"No one will recognize me," Frankie said aloud, holding the earrings up to her face while looking into the mirror.

"That's the idea," Katherine said. "As the last unmarried sister at the old age of twenty-five, you have to look above sympathy."

"Right." Frankie handed the earrings to the saleslady, who rang them up on the cash register.

"Wedding or no wedding, it's time you took off the hard hat and put on some mascara and eye shadow," Katherine declared a moment later as she steered her toward Nordstrom's oversize cosmetics department.

An hour and a half later they were seated on the deck of a waterfront restaurant.

"So let me get this straight," Katherine said, leaning across plastic baskets filled with fried shrimp and French fries. "A man you had a crush on eight years ago showed up on your doorstep this morning and offered to take you dancing, and you said no?"

"He said he'd give me lessons, not take me out." Frankie took a sip of her iced tea. "And he only said it because he feels sorry for me, having to hire a date and all that."

"Call me crazy, but I don't understand. Is there something wrong with this Rick Perez, some character flaw that makes him a real jerk in handsome clothing?"

"No." It wasn't fair to hold the worms against him forever. "Except I kissed him once and he laughed about it with his friends."

"How old was he when you kissed him?"

"Eighteen."

Katherine let out an uncharacteristic hoot. "I think it's time you forgave him. It's a stupid age for guys," she pointed out. "You know my brother? He drove us crazy. What about Rosa's wedding? I assume he's going to take you or you wouldn't have bought new clothes."

"Stop laughing," Frankie begged. "He said I

couldn't fire him because it would wreck his escort career before it even began. I think he was teasing, but I couldn't tell because he teases all the time.''

''Please tell me you didn't fire him. He really was adorable, Frankie.''

''I said I'd think about it.'' And she'd eaten the cinnamon roll he'd brought as if she'd just come out of hibernation. She hadn't known what else to do.

''Ah,'' Katherine announced. ''I get it.''

''Get what?''

''You're not over him.''

''This shrimp is really good.'' She made a big show out of dipping one in cocktail sauce.

''It's not going to stop at the clothes and the makeup, is it.''

''I'm thinking of getting my hair done,'' she said, trying to sound casual. ''Maybe.''

''What color?''

''I wasn't thinking of color, just a cut. Maybe some highlights?''

Katherine's mouth dropped. ''You're serious about this?''

She shrugged. ''Anything would be an improvement.''

''You're smart and you're pretty,'' her friend declared. ''But a few highlights wouldn't hurt.''

Neither would a sex life, Frankie thought, but

she didn't really crave a one night stand or even a fling of a month of two. No, she wanted more than that. A man who made her feel feminine and sexy and content. She wanted someone who would wake her with kisses in the mornings and wouldn't laugh when she cried at sentimental television commercials.

She wanted a man who didn't mind that she owned more power tools than he did.

"SO, HOW'D IT GO LAST NIGHT?"

"Fine." Leave it to Rosa to be waiting at the front door. "Why are you whispering?"

"I have a little hangover." Rosa winced and opened the door wide so Frankie could enter the house. In the background Frankie heard her mother scolding her father for having the television on too loud.

"I tried to save you from yourself."

"You lucked out, you know," she said. "Getting Rick Perez to haul you around? It's like a gift from the gods. He'll add a lot to the wedding reception."

"Anything for your wedding, Rosa," Frankie said, but her sister didn't seem to notice the sarcasm. She held out her hands palm down.

"How do you like this color?"

Frankie peered at the perfect oval fingernails,

now painted silver. "Let me guess. You wanted your nails to match your wedding ring."

"It's called Platinum Dream."

"Very appropriate." Frankie managed to get past her sister and head into the living room, where her father, ensconced in his black leather recliner, watched an old war movie. Tina's six-month-old daughter was asleep on his chest. "Hi, Dad."

"Hey, Frankie." Joe Raimondi was still a good-looking man and the adored center of the family. "Come give your old man a kiss. Don't worry about the baby. She's a good sleeper, like her grandfather."

"I see that." Little Josephine was drooling on her grandfather's T-shirt. Frankie kissed her father's cheek and hoped she wouldn't have to talk about Rick. She was a terrible liar, and besides, she didn't want to get her mother's hopes up. Rosa lay on the couch and put an ice pack on her head.

"The bride has a hangover," Joe muttered, winking at Frankie. "Don't tell me you partied too much last night, too. I need you to look at some blueprints for the Seward Park building and let me know what you think."

"Sure. Where are they?"

"On the dining room table, unless your mother put them away." He patted the baby's back. "She's upstairs with Lisa right now. Trying to get a two-year-old to take a nap isn't easy, but your mother's determined.''

"Where's Tina?" Frankie perched on the arm of the chair next to her father. The last thing she needed was her sister babbling on about Rick. Deceiving her parents wasn't something that made Frankie feel comfortable. And yet her mother had been so happy on the phone this morning.

"Shopping, I think," her father said. "There seems to be a lot of things to do right now. Your mother is driving me—"

"There you are!" Dorothy Raimondi, tiny and plump, hurried around the corner of the living room. "Are you hungry, Frankie?"

"Katherine and I ate downtown, but—"

"I'll fix you a nice plate to take home," her mother said. She pushed her dark curls off her forehead. "I hope it's not this hot next weekend. The church isn't air-conditioned."

"I hope it doesn't rain Saturday," Rosa said, shifting the ice pack. "My hair will be ruined."

"We'll spray it," Dorothy said. "Don't worry." She turned to Frankie. "You come with me, Frankie. I've got some iced tea and some lemonade cake and a nice bowl of fresh fruit for you."

"Watch out," Rosa called. "She wants to know when she can expect an announcement."

"Announcement?" Joe looked away from the

television and frowned at his wife. "Frankie doesn't need to make announcements, Dottie. I need her in the business."

"The business," Dorothy scoffed, "can let our Frankie have a social life." With that said, she hustled her oldest daughter out of the living room. "Now," she said, once they were in the back of the house and settled at the kitchen table. "Tell me how long this has been going on with you and the Perez boy."

"Not long," Frankie hedged. "We've been friends for ages, though."

"I saw Rick's mother at the grocery store the other day. She didn't mention you and Rick were going out."

"Maybe he didn't tell her. Where's that lemonade cake you were talking about, Mom?"

"In the refrigerator. Sit right there and I'll get it." The distraction worked. Dorothy loved feeding her family, her in-laws, the neighbors and anyone who dropped by to say hello. Once Frankie had come home from school to find the mailman eating a meatball sandwich at the kitchen table.

"I went to Nordstrom's today and bought a dress," Frankie said, once a glass of iced tea and a slab of cake had been placed in front of her. "For the rehearsal dinner."

"You didn't like the white one I got you?"

"Uh, well, I wanted to wear something Rick hadn't seen already." She filled her mouth with cake and pointed to the list of wedding errands propped against the salt and pepper shakers. "Can I help?"

Her mother smiled and shook her head. "Nah. You just make sure you look real pretty for the wedding, Frankie. How about trying some eye shadow?"

"I bought some," Frankie said, and watched as her mother's face lit up with happiness.

"I knew it," she said, clapping her hands together. "Some day, I told your father, some day our Frankie will meet a man, and then—"

"And then?" Frankie prompted, though she wasn't sure she wanted to hear what happened next.

"Then you would start acting like a *lady*," Dorothy declared. "Love changes things, Frankie."

Frankie forked another piece of cake. "Don't get crazy, Mom. Love doesn't have anything to do with eye makeup."

"FRANK-*IE!*"

"Boss!"

"Hey, Raimondi!"

Frankie's father, seated behind his desk in the center of the trailer they used as an on-site office, looked up from a pile of papers. "Honey, I think you're being paged."

"They want me to go with them to celebrate Joey's birthday." She'd just added up the latest set of figures, tallied the employee payroll and assembled all the paperwork for the company accountant, but she was still dressed in her work clothes.

"Frank-ie-Ray-Mondy!"

"That's Red," she grumbled. "I told him I'd catch up with them at Sullivan's." She stood up and pushed the door open. "*What? I told* you I'd—"

"Hi." Rick stood in the parking lot, Red Richardson beside him, grinning like a fool.

"Boss, you've got company." Red, who was old enough to be her father, winked at her.

"I see." Okay, so her heart skipped a couple of beats when she saw him standing between the company trucks. That didn't mean anything except that he'd surprised her. "Hi."

They were drawing a crowd. At least six of the guys who hadn't left yet stood around pretending they weren't watching and listening, so Frankie pushed the door open and, as if Rick was a casual friend of the family, said, "I'm glad you made it. Come on in and say hi to my father."

Rick grinned at her and walked up the metal steps to the door. "You're a hard woman to find.

I asked around the site, but no one knew where you'd gone.''

"I was finishing up some paperwork." She was also grubby, smelly and covered in dust, and despite having bought enough clothes for a year, she wore dirty jeans, a faded blue T-shirt and a yellow bandanna around her neck. "What are you doing here?"

Before he could answer, Frankie's father stood and offered his hand. "You're one of the Perez boys, aren't you? And how's your mother these days?"

Rick shook her father's hand. "I'm Rick, the youngest. And Mom is just fine. She's talking about retiring."

"Tell her I said hello, would you?"

"I will, thanks," Rick assured him.

Her father gave Frankie a curious glance, which she ignored by looking innocent. As if childhood friends dropped by the office trailer every Monday at five o'clock.

"Well," he said. "What are you two up to tonight? Another wedding party?" He ran his hand through his hair and sighed. "Tell you the truth," he said to both of them, "I'll be glad when all this is over and the house can get back to normal. I hear we're going to see you Friday night at the rehearsal dinner."

"Yes, sir. I'm looking forward to it."

Frankie ignored her father's wink. "Um, Rick, why are you here?"

"I'm here to try to talk Frankie into having dinner with me."

She looked down at her dirty jeans and mud-crusted boots. "You're kidding, right?"

"You can clean up first," he said. "If you want."

"Go on, Frankie," her father said. "I can finish up here. Give me those invoices and I'll see that Dorothy gets them in the morning."

"Well—"

Her father smiled. "Go. You don't have to hang around and keep me company. I'm going to stay here and hide from the wedding for a while longer. Your mother seems to have a lot of things for me to do before Saturday."

"All right." She picked up her backpack and her thermos and kissed her father's cheek on the way out the door. "See you tomorrow."

"Bye, honey. Take good care of her, Rick."

"Yes, sir."

The parking area was empty, much to Frankie's relief. She walked over to her truck and tossed her things inside before turning toward Rick. "What are you really doing here? And how did you know where I was working?"

"Rosa told me. I called your house."

"You're not going to turn into a stalker, are you?"

"It was a simple invitation to dinner, Frankie."

It was a chance to wear her new sundress and look like a woman. It was a chance to practice walking in her new sandals.

"Okay," she said. It was another chance to show Rick Perez she was all grown-up, not someone to be trifled with. And that she had forgotten all about that kiss Saturday night, too.

"I'll pick you up at what—" He looked at his watch. "Seven?"

He thought she needed almost two hours to get ready? "Six-thirty," she said. "I'm starving."

"See you later."

She climbed in her truck and resisted the urge to look at herself in the rearview mirror. She didn't care, not really. What difference did it make if Rick Perez saw her in her work clothes?

And yet, the thought of the blue-striped sundress hanging in her closet made her step on the gas pedal.

In case you change your mind about dance lessons, Katherine had said holding the dress up by its hanger. *Because I don't think Rick is going to go away, even if you fired him.*

THE DRESS STUNNED HIM. She could tell by the way his eyes widened when she opened the door to greet him. Katherine had said it was perfect for summer evenings, but Frankie had taken some convincing. She didn't often wear dresses, especially short ones with little straps and a built-in bra. She felt half-naked, and it wasn't a bad feeling at all.

"Uh…" he said. "Wow. I like this better than the tube sock dress."

"Thanks."

His gaze dropped to her feet, encased in flat white sandals. "Good. I hoped you wouldn't wear the shoes that made you topple over."

"I threw them out." She grabbed her purse and slung the strap over her bare shoulder. "Where are we going?"

"An Italian place called Capella's. Do you know it?"

"No." She locked the door behind her and walked beside him down the stairs. "I thought you would live in California."

"Not as long as I can get work here, though it hasn't been as much as I'd like." He took her hand and held it as they walked outside into the warm summer air.

"How do you survive?"

He shrugged. "I wait tables when I have to. And sometimes I work for my brother. Rob makes furniture and he always needs extra help. There are a few things he lets me do, like sanding boards.'' He smiled down at her. ''I'm not especially good with my hands.''

She blushed as his fingers touched the bare skin beneath her shoulder blades in order to guide her toward his car. Rick Perez was flirting with her.

CHAPTER SEVEN

"YOU CAN DO IT," Rick said, taking Frankie's hand and walking her to the center of his living room. A waltz played on the stereo and he'd programmed it to repeat itself. "It's not hard."

"Easy for you to say." But she let herself be led, allowed him to take her in his arms. Her fingers were light on his shoulder, her right hand was warm against his palm. She was the same woman he'd known for years—and yet she wasn't "good old Frankie" at all. It was the dress, he decided. It was all those blue stripes and that short skirt and the expanse of smooth skin that made Frankie look different to him. Her dark hair was pulled back into a familiar ponytail, and except for rose lip gloss, she didn't have on any makeup. She was still the Frankie he knew and liked.

Liked a lot. As a friend, he reminded himself, careful not to hold her too close. He'd enjoyed the past two hours. She'd eaten pizza with the gusto of a person who'd put in a full day's work. They'd shared a decanter of Chianti, laughed at his stories about acting in a movie in Vancouver last winter, split a dessert of triple-fudge chocolate cake.

And then she'd agreed to dance, giving him an excuse to touch her.

"Now," he said, enjoying the feel of his hand against her bare back. "One-two-three, one-two-three. Just relax and follow me."

"How?"

"Step forward—that's one—step to the side, then bring your other foot to meet it."

She did as she was told, though too slow for the music. He guided her through the basic pattern of the box waltz until she relaxed her painful grip on his hand.

"Don't look down," he said, which made Frankie look up at him and frown.

"I have to," she said. And stumbled against him when he took a step backward. "Sorry."

"Wait," he said, and led her over to his couch, a brown leather relic he'd claimed when his mother would have donated it to the Salvation Army.

"I told you it was hopeless," she said, sitting down with such relief he wanted to laugh.

"Not so fast, Frankie." He sat on the coffee table and faced her. "Give me your feet."

"Why?"

"Just do it."

She shrugged and lifted one foot and then the

next to rest on his thighs. He unbuckled the strap that crossed her arch and her ankle, then tossed the shoe to the floor. "You have cute toes."

"Great. An escort with a foot fetish."

He ignored her and removed the other shoe. The short skirt revealed a nice set of legs, and the feel of his hands on her ankles made him want to smooth his hands higher, to her calves, past her knees, to sweep underneath the hem of that dress and feel what he was certain was a pair of warm, satiny thighs.

But this was Frankie. He couldn't go around groping Frankie, who trusted him to teach her to waltz.

He set her feet on the floor and removed his own shoes and socks while she watched.

"I hope you're not going to take off anything else," she said.

"Not unless we polka. I get a little crazy when I hear 'Roll Out the Barrel.'" Rick stood, took her hand and led her back to the center of the enormous living room. The music, still repeating The Tennessee Waltz, surrounded them, but this time when he began the steps, his toes touched Frankie's. "See? Less painful."

And more erotic, he realized. He'd never danced barefoot before and he liked the experience so far.

Frankie's toes were warm. He imagined them trailing up his leg while he—

"Your floor is very clean."

"Thank you." He wasn't going to admit that he'd washed it this afternoon because he hoped she would come over tonight. "I do my best."

"You're a man of many talents."

"Another compliment, Frankie?" He heard her sigh against his shoulder. "What's the matter? You don't like men who mop?"

"Your bookshelves aren't level."

"No?" He liked the feel of her body against his. The wooden floor was warm and smooth under his feet, her toes brushed his again and made him wonder what it would be like to be horizontal. In bed. Touching toes and other places.

"They look like they could fall down any minute." She turned her head and the ponytail brushed across his face. "What'd you hang them with?"

"A hammer. Nails. The usual." He twirled her so she would have to hang on to him. "See? I told you this was easy."

"Did you hammer into the studs?"

"I can't remember." What he did remember was how Frankie's long legs looked in this dress, that she wasn't wearing a bra, that her skin was soft and smooth and that he'd liked kissing her a couple of nights ago.

She tripped, swore under her breath and fell against him. He held on to her and stopped dancing. She was laughing when he lifted her right hand to his shoulder. His hands dropped to her waist and held her to him as firmly as he dared. After all, Frankie was known to kick, and he hadn't forgotten fifth-grade recess.

He kissed her, of course. He was only human and here was a desirable woman tucked against him in the privacy of his apartment. She tasted sweet, like chocolate frosting. Her lips were warm as he urged them apart, and after a second's hesitation, she responded with a quick passion that took his breath away. When her hands curled around his neck, when her tongue teased his, when he wondered if they would both fall on the floor and keep kissing for hours, Rick couldn't hide his surprise. Or his physical response. He took a deep breath and told himself to go slow.

"Don't expect me to apologize again," he whispered, his lips against the corner of her mouth.

"No," Frankie said, her voice low. "This is good practice."

"Practice?"

"For the party on Friday and the wedding on Saturday." Her hands slid slowly down his chest and she patted him in a friendly way. "We have to act as if we're lovers. As if we make love every night." She smiled. "As if we can't stop thinking about being together. You're a good kisser."

"Thanks."

"Practice," she sighed. "You've had lots of that, haven't you?"

"Well, uh, I suppose." He wanted to practice a while longer. He wanted to practice—hell, no, he wanted the real thing. He wanted to lead Frankie into his bedroom and do a lot more that he didn't intend to apologize for.

"This has been nice," Frankie said, giving him a smile and a quick peck on the cheek. "But you'd better take me home. I have to be at work at seven."

Nice? The word haunted him for hours, long after Frankie had been delivered to her door and Rick returned to his quiet apartment. Nice was a platonic word, something to describe the weather or lunch with his mother. *Nice* didn't apply to kissing Frankie Raimondi.

"THE DRESS WORKED," she told Katherine, having promised to call her when she got home. "Rick looked really impressed."

"How impressed?"

"His mouth hung open."

"I like that in a man. What else?"

"We danced. We kissed. He brought me home."

"And he left?"

"Yes." To her disappointment he'd left a little too quickly. With no kiss good-night. He'd only nodded when she'd said she'd see him Friday.

"Good. Don't sleep with him, Frankie. Not before the wedding."

"I'm not going to sleep with him at all," Frankie said. "I just want him to look at me as if I'm a grown woman, not a tomboy who beat him at arm wrestling."

"Are you sure?"

"I want him to *think* about sleeping with me," she admitted. "But I think even that is a little far-fetched. He's just being nice."

"Maybe," her best friend said. "But don't forget he's an actor. They're good at acting nice if they want to. You *hired* him to act nice."

"So far, so good," Frankie said, thinking of that kiss. Her lips felt full and warm, but she wasn't going to tell Katherine that she could close her eyes and still feel his mouth on hers, his tongue teasing her tongue, and his body—such a hard, solid body—against hers.

"Be careful."

"I will. Nothing can happen at the rehearsal dinner."

"The black dress will torture him, though," her friend pointed out. "Your mother is going to be thrilled when you walk in with him."

"Eighty-seven Raimondis are going to be ecstatic," Frankie declared. "And I might even be a little giddy myself."

"Keep within sight of the wedding party," Katherine said. "And no matter what happens, stay vertical."

"No problem," Frankie promised. "I've forgotten how to have sex anyway."

"COME FOR JUST a small family dinner," her mother said on the phone Tuesday. "Nothing fancy, but wear something decent and fix your hair."

Frankie should have guessed something strange was going on, but she was at work, in the middle of calculating costs for a job in Bellevue, and wasn't really paying attention.

"Sure," she'd said. "Six o'clock is fine." And then she'd gone back to her figures and blueprints before heading outside to check how the installation of the roof was coming along. Hours passed before she remembered her mother's dinner invitation, and that was only because her father complained that he had to leave work early to stop and buy the wine.

"I'll be glad when this wedding is over," Joe Raimondi told his daughter. "It's like your mother's obsessed."

Frankie tried not to smile, but her father's exasperated expression didn't leave her a choice. "Mom's very enthusiastic."

"Yeah, well, we're gonna need a vacation after we get Rosa married. Maybe a nice cruise." He sighed and opened the trailer door. "I'll save you a cold beer."

It never occurred to Frankie to refuse the invitation, not only because her mother was one of Seattle's best cooks and Frankie hadn't shopped for groceries for a long while, but because not attending a family dinner was like stabbing her mother in the heart. There was something about Italian mothers that made them oversensitive about empty chairs at the dinner table.

But, Frankie discovered, that wasn't going to be a problem tonight, because seated next to Tina and helping himself from the platter of antipasto was Rick Perez.

"Frankie!" Her mother waved her into the dining room. "You're late, but that's all right. Sit down." She pointed to the seat across the table from Rick, but Frankie found it hard to move her feet. Her brown cargo shorts were clean and her white T-shirt ironed, but her outfit wasn't guaranteed to excite lust, like the blue sundress. Heck, she wasn't even wearing perfume. She hated perfume. She wished her sandaled feet would move. Any direction would be fine.

"Look who I met in the drugstore this afternoon," Tina said, lifting her wineglass for her father to refill. "We were both buying Pull-Ups."

"Pull-Ups?" Frankie didn't believe this story for a minute. Tina and Mom had set this whole thing up.

"Hi, honey," Rick said, giving her one of his charming smiles. "How was your day?"

"Fine, sweetheart." Frankie sat down and tried to act as if dinner with Rick was something that happened every Tuesday. She scooped some of the Italian salad onto her plate. "And yours?"

"I tried out for a part in a Toyota commercial."

"Pull-Ups are training pants like diapers but without the sticky tabs," Tina explained. "Rick has a nephew who's having trouble with potty-training, too."

"T.J. has a long way to go," Rick agreed. "My brother's tried everything."

Dorothy passed Rick the basket of bread. "He's only two. Sometimes the little ones just have to decide for themselves."

"There are lots of things people should decide for themselves," Frankie said, staring at Tina, who only smiled back instead of looking ashamed to have orchestrated Rick's introduction to the family. "Where's Rosa?"

"On the phone." Joe pushed the meatball platter toward Rick. "Eat up, son. Dorothy's meatballs are the best you'll ever taste."

"The jeweler lost the wedding rings," Frankie's mother said. "And Donny's trying to figure out what happened."

"Uh-oh." Frankie finished the last of her salad and waited for Rick to pass her the meatballs. "I'll bet she's not happy."

"Happy?" Rosa, a cell phone plastered against her head, popped out of the kitchen. "Do you know how long it took us to pick out the perfect rings?"

All of the Raimondis nodded. This wedding had been planned for two years. The stack of bridal magazines next to Rosa's bed was four feet high.

"Rick?" Rosa looked from their guest to her oldest sister. "Frankie? You brought him *home?*"

"Tina did."

Rosa finally remembered to close her mouth, and then her attention went back to the telephone. "No," she wailed. "I don't *want* any other ring. I want *my* ring, the one that matches my *diamond,* the one that we picked out *together.*" She disappeared into the kitchen again.

Joe shook his head. "Looks like Donny's in for a long night."

"So," Tina said, turning to their guest. "Did you get the part?"

"I won't know until next week." He grinned at Frankie and took the basket of bread Tina passed to him. "We'll have to celebrate if I do."

"Sure," was all Frankie could reply. She knew she wasn't going to see Rick Perez after the wedding, unless he was on the cover of *People* magazine or giving an interview on *Entertainment Tonight*. It was all a game, but suddenly it felt silly and sordid and not very nice. Her father winked at her, her mother beamed as she set a platter of meatballs and spaghetti in the middle of the table. Tina started chattering about her kids, and Rick—always the actor—looked as if he fit right in.

It got worse when Walt arrived with Lisa and Josephine and Rick ended up with the baby in his arms. She cooed and kicked, but Rick held her as casually as if he'd fathered a dozen kids. He even managed to eat Dorothy's special tiramisu without a spoonful dropping on him or Josephine.

Frankie didn't know if she was relieved or disappointed when he left shortly after dessert. He thanked her family, complimented her mother's cooking, handed the baby to her grandfather and tugged Frankie to the front door for a quick kiss good-night.

"Nice," Rick said, and left. Frankie stood at the door a long time after he'd driven away. Life wasn't fair, obviously. Rick Perez was perfect.

Too bad he was hers for only four more days.

CHAPTER EIGHT

"HEY, THERE'S THE STUD-FOR-HIRE."

Rick winced at the bottom of the stairs and turned to see Rob standing in the doorway to his apartment, with T.J. tucked under his arm like a football. "Hey."

"How's it going? You want a beer or something?"

"I'm going out," Rick said, but he walked over to his nephew and tickled him under his chin. "What's the kid done now?"

"He's getting a bath." Rob backed up and Rick followed him into the apartment, where Maggie looked up from her Barbie dolls and let out a screech of excitement. She ran over and threw her arms around his knees.

"Uncle Rick!"

"Hey, Mags. What's up?"

"We're goin' to see Grandma tonight. Wanna come?"

"Can't, honey, but tell Grandma I'll be over on Sunday."

"Please?" Maggie begged. "You look nice and Grandma likes it when we look nice."

Rob laughed. "Uncle Rick's all dressed up because he's got a date. Come on," he told his younger brother, so Rick had no choice but to follow him into the bathroom and watch him set T.J.—fully clothed—into the empty tub.

"You sure take strange baths down here," Rick said, leaning against the wall by the sink. The bathroom was long and narrow, with black and white tiles that reminded him of Frankie's kitchen. He watched his brother strip the little boy's dirty clothes off, toss the wet diaper in the trash and reach for the portable shower head. "You invent this all by yourself?"

"You wait," Rob warned, adjusting the water temperature while the dirt-coated toddler jumped up and down as the spray hit his round belly. "When you have dirty kids of your own, you'll be undressing them in the tub, too. That way you wash the clothes and the kid at the same time and keep the floor clean."

"How'd he get so dirty?"

"Rafe dug a hole in the backyard and filled it with water. They played in the mud all afternoon."

"Sorry I missed it." He took a step sideways so he could avoid T.J.'s splashing. "I did a men's cologne ad at Nordstrom's."

Rob shook his head. "I think I'd take the mud hole myself."

"Yeah. The mud probably smelled better."

"Where are you going tonight? Another hot date with a paying lady?"

"Nah." He debated about telling Rob the truth. "I can't take her money."

"No? T.J., turn around. What is she, a charity case or old enough to be your mother?"

"I'm serious, Rob." He sighed. "I know her. You know her. Frankie Raimondi."

Rob made T.J. sit down before he turned toward Rick. "Frankie Raimondi? Was she the one who arm wrestled you or the one with the big—"

"The arm wrestler."

Rob grinned. "What does she look like now?"

"Pretty damn good," he admitted, remembering Frankie's legs in those little shorts Sunday morning. And the way her dark eyes crinkled when she laughed, and the feel of her skin and the way her lips moved under his. "Her sister's getting married. Rosa, the youngest."

"And you're the official wedding date?"

"Yeah."

"You don't seem to mind too much."

Rick folded his arms across his chest and tried to act nonchalant. "It's a favor for an old friend. And I get to wear the mysterious tux Saturday night."

"Don't eat the soap," Rob muttered to T.J., then turned back to his brother. "Did you ever figure out how it got here?"

"No, but I've been busy." He looked at his watch. "I've got to go. I've been invited to crash the bridesmaids' party."

"Sounds like a good time. Hand me a towel, will you?"

Rick took one from the stack folded neatly behind the toilet and handed it to his brother. "How old were you when you and Susanna got married?"

"Twenty-six. Which seems pretty young now." He wrapped the little boy in the towel and lifted him onto the bath mat. "Why? You thinking about making Mom happy and settling down with a nice girl?"

"Hell, no." He just wanted to see more of Frankie Raimondi. Rick didn't add that for two days he'd been trying to figure out a reason to see Frankie again before Friday night's rehearsal party. For some reason, ever since that dance lesson, he'd been a little crazy. But that didn't mean he was ready to walk down the aisle himself.

"YOU'LL BE NEXT," Tina announced, taking a frozen strawberry margarita from the waiter and waving the glass in Frankie's direction. "Dum, dum, dee, dum," she sang before handing her sister the drink.

"Thanks," Frankie said. "But let's get Rosa married first. I'm not in any hurry."

"Not when you're dating Ricky Perez? Please," Tina giggled. "How long has this been going on?"

Not long enough was the answer Frankie wanted to give her sister, but she sipped her drink and kept her mouth shut. She didn't want to think about Rick right now. She'd spent the last two days thinking about him, and now it was Wednesday— finally—and she'd see him in less than forty-eight hours. She planned to resist his charm, was determined to get a bill for his services and promised herself to stay away from his mouth.

"You're wearing eye makeup, Frankie," Tina said. "It looks good, too. Does that mean you're having sex with him?"

"It means I went to the Lancôme counter at Nordstrom's," Frankie replied. "It cost me a small fortune, too." And too much time spent practicing in front of the bathroom mirror before she looked presentable.

"I'm wearing a red lace thong," Tina, mother of two, announced. "Do you have one of those?"

Frankie didn't answer, not because she didn't

have thongs, but because she didn't want the waiter to know about her underwear.

"You might want to kick back on the tequila," Rosa told Tina. "Aren't you breastfeeding?"

"I'm fine. The baby's getting a bottle and Mom's baby-sitting all night. The limo will take us home, so drink up." The waiter—a bare-chested muscular guy wearing nothing but a pair of denim shorts—finished setting the drinks on the table, collected the money and winked at Rosa.

"You're the bride, right?"

"I sure am."

"Are any of you ladies single?"

They pointed to Frankie, who sat at the other end of the table in her new silk top and matching miniskirt, and to Katherine, serene and beautiful in a beige sundress. "They are."

"Cool," was all he said, but the grin on his face made Frankie blush. He was the California surfer type, with a perfect tan and perfect muscles. The other waiters were dressed as scantily as possible and, Tina explained, danced with the customers whenever they were asked.

Rosa lifted her glass. "To the best sisters and girlfriends a bride ever had! Here's to Girls Night!"

"What's the name of this place again?" Frankie sipped her second drink and watched two of Rosa's married girlfriends flirt with the bartender, a guy who looked a lot like Tom Cruise.

"Balls."

Frankie had thought she was going to a sports bar.

"WHAT THE HELL is this place?" Rick stopped inside the door, right behind the groom, and peered past the bar on his right to the dance floor. A lot of guys had taken their shirts off and a lot of women looked as if they were enjoying themselves while dancing to very loud salsa music. "A gay bar?"

"I don't think so. It's new." Donny gulped. "Rosa said it's the trendiest place in town for bachelorette parties."

"If those guys start dancing and stripping," Walt said, "I'm outta here. I just wanted a cold beer and a night with Tina. And without the kids." He looked around and then met Rick's gaze. "Cripe. Do you believe this? I don't think this is the place for a married man to be drinking in."

"Do you see them?" Rick felt overdressed in his black polo shirt and khaki slacks. "Maybe this wasn't such a good idea."

"They're expecting us to show up," Donny insisted. "Or Rosa wouldn't have told me where they were going."

"I don't know," one of the other guys said. "We were having a pretty good time at Hooters. We could always go back."

"Nah," the groom said. "Follow me. But leave your shirts on."

Rick grinned as they made their way through the crowd lining the dance floor. Frankie wasn't expecting him, but he didn't think she'd mind if he showed up tonight. It was a friendly, helpful thing to do. Like giving her dance lessons.

Of course he didn't expect to see her fast-dancing with a half-naked guy wearing nothing but a leather loincloth and a gold necklace. She'd worn her hair loose and her back was to him, but Rick would have recognized those legs anywhere. Just what did she think she was doing? Leather Nuts looked like a jerk—what kind of guy would wear fringe?—and of course Frankie didn't seem to have a clue as to how beautiful she was. She needed a friend to protect her, keep her safe, hold her electric drill.

Donny's voice brought him back to reality.

"Gentlemen," the groom said, his voice edged with laughter as the music ended, "it's time we claimed our women."

"How long do we have to stay?" Walt asked as his wife waved to him from the table across the room.

"You're on your own," Donny told him. "You, too, Rick. I'm going to see if I can get my bride alone tonight."

"Good luck." Rick thought about what it would be like to have Frankie all to himself again. He didn't want her dancing with waiters, and he sure as hell didn't appreciate the fact that the guy looped his arm around her shoulders and whispered something in her ear that made her laugh. He wanted to grab the guy and tell him that Frankie was—what? His date? His woman? His *friend?*

"Frankie," he called, coming closer to her. "Hey, babe. Sorry I'm late. Did you miss me?" He ignored Leather Nuts and made a show of taking Frankie's hand and pulling her close for a kiss. It was a quick kiss, meant only for show, but the feel of her mouth just about jolted him to the floor. It was like an electric shock, though it felt good.

"'Babe'?" She frowned up at him and the waiter mumbled something and disappeared into the crowd.

"Sorry about that. I thought that guy was bothering you."

"He was, a little. Tina and I were dancing and he came over and started wiggling around." She laughed and dropped his hand. "I thought my sister would faint at some of the moves he was making."

"Jerk."

"It was kind of fun," Frankie said, letting him guide her in the opposite direction of her sisters' table.

"Fun?" She looked different tonight. Maybe because she wore some makeup and a deeper shade of lipstick that made her mouth look wide and inviting. Maybe it was the pale green camisole or the short skirt. Maybe it was because he'd begun thinking of her as a woman he wanted to be with. A lot.

"Well, sure. I probably should get out more." She smiled up at him and he felt his heart flip. "What are you doing here?"

"Donny invited me to have dinner with the guys and then we came here, to crash your party. But I can't stay," he added, forcing himself to sound casual. He didn't want to be here at a bar called "Balls," watching Frankie dance with other guys. If he stayed, he'd act like a possessive jerk, when all he wanted to do was take her hand, take her home, take her to bed.

CHAPTER NINE

"WHAT WAS THAT ALL ABOUT?" Katherine moved over so Frankie could sit in the end chair. "Where'd Rick disappear to?"

"He came with the guys, but he said he couldn't stay." She looked down at her outfit. The skirt was wrinkled, but the mint green color showed off her tanned legs. And Rick hadn't noticed that she'd looked different. At least, he hadn't noticed enough to stay. "I don't think he appreciated my new eye makeup. I'm not even sure he noticed there was anything different about me." If that was true, Frankie figured she'd wasted quite a bit of money.

"He didn't look happy to see you dancing with that waiter," her friend pointed out. "He looked jealous, like he wanted to haul you off the dance floor. That's very encouraging."

"Rick was pretending to be my boyfriend because he thought the guy was bothering me." She pushed her half-empty drink aside and turned to her best friend. "I'll admit that I've been a little in love with him since I was eleven. You'd think I'd be over it by now.''

''Well, when the guy is kissing you and dancing with you and acting like you're his woman, it's hard to stay away from him.''

''The last time he kissed me, I thanked him for practicing for the rehearsal dinner.'' She made a face. ''He comes close and I push him away. What's wrong with me?''

''Absolutely nothing. You're protecting yourself from getting hurt.''

''Yes.'' She sighed. ''I still have my pride.''

''And the black dress,'' Katherine said. ''Don't forget that.''

She would need more than the black dress to get Rick to pay attention to her, Frankie decided later. She was the only one left in the limousine when the driver pulled up in front of her building. Frankie stood staring at the window of the Silver and Gold salon for a long moment before making a decision.

She might as well go for broke and try to make Rick Perez wish he really was her lover, her boyfriend and the man of her dreams. All it would take was time, money, courage—and a pair of scissors.

BECOMING BEAUTIFUL wasn't that easy. On Thursday, during her lunch hour, Frankie begged, pleaded, offered to pay double, build shelves in the backroom and use her truck to pick up a lavender leather sofa before Madame Renoir agreed to give her an appointment at the Silver and Gold salon.

"He must be someone important," the tall forty-something salon owner said, looking up from a gold-edged leather appointment book.

"Yes," Frankie stammered. "It's an emergency, actually."

"And short notice," Madame Renoir observed. "All right, tomorrow. What time is this big date?"

"I have to beat my sister's wedding rehearsal at five-thirty."

Madame Renoir, who knew desperation when she heard it, tapped her pencil on the glass desk and eyed her potential new client. "We'll need plenty of time, darling. When can you get here?"

"Anytime at all. I have the day off." That would be news to her father, but what the heck. Even the boss's right-hand man had to take a day off once in a while.

"Frankie," Madame Renoir said, her gaze focused on Frankie's ponytail. "I'm going to consider you my greatest challenge."

"Is that a good thing or a bad thing?"

"I'll tell you tomorrow. Be here by two and wear a shirt that buttons down the front. No

T-shirts to pull over your head and mess up your hair, all right?''

"Right." Frankie dared a small smile. She felt reckless and brave and a little intimidated, but she wasn't going to back down. She'd walked past the salon for over a year and wondered what magic the beauticians worked inside the small rooms.

"Don't be late and don't wash you hair first. We'll take care of everything."

Madame Renoir wasn't kidding. And her staff didn't fool around. Friday afternoon Frankie appeared at the salon and was taken over by a young woman who introduced herself as Margo. She led Frankie to a row of sinks for a shampoo.

"You must be very important," Margo said, wrapping a towel around Frankie's neck before covering her with a white cape.

"No. This is my first time here."

"Madame cancelled the mayor's wife's appointment this afternoon," Margo whispered. "She told her there was an emergency."

"That's me," Frankie said, starting to laugh. "I work on construction sites and my sister's getting married and I have a date with…well, never mind." She held out her hands, revealing her roughened skin and nails. "Is there someone here who does fingernails?"

Margo bit her lower lip. "If Jerry can't, I'll work on them myself."

"Thanks."

"Lean back and close your eyes," Margo said. "You're about to get the royal Gold and Silver treatment."

"Sounds scary," Frankie muttered, but she did as she was told and lowered her neck into the indentation of the black basin. Margo turned on the water and the magic began.

HE'D BEEN TOLD to meet her at seven at the Mayflower, a downtown hotel known for its wedding parties and elegant receptions. The bridal party was to return from the rehearsal at seven and meet the rest of the family members and out-of-town guests in one of the private banquet rooms.

"I could drive you to the church," he'd offered last night on the phone, but independent Frankie had informed him she already had a ride. She would wait for him in the lobby, she promised.

She was late, but Rick figured rehearsals for weddings took a long time. He'd been a teenager for Rob's wedding, but he could still remember the organized chaos of the wedding events. He saw Tina first, scolding her husband about something as they stepped out of the revolving door. Then

Rosa, wearing something bright pink and flowing, and carrying a wrapped gift. And then—Frankie?

Rick wasn't prepared for the woman who walked toward him. The ponytail was gone, and her hair—highlighted with faint streaks of lighter brown—flowed in soft layers to her bare shoulders, framing her face. Jeweled earrings sparkled from her earlobes, her brown eyes held a touch of mascara and an interesting sweep of shadow, and her lips were dark rose and very, very inviting.

Especially when she smiled at him in such a self-satisfied way.

"Frankie?" He stood and held out his hand for her and was secretly pleased to feel the calluses under his fingertips. This was Frankie, all right.

"Hi." She smiled, a queen dispensing favors.

"Hi, yourself." He kissed her, which was the natural thing to do. He was supposed to be her boyfriend. He was supposed to look infatuated. She smelled like roses, another enticing surprise. "You look beautiful."

"You like the dress?"

"Very much." Narrow halter straps circled her neck, leaving her shoulders bare and revealing an intriguing slice of skin between her breasts. The dress slithered over her curves and skimmed past her knees. The shoes were black, open-toed and heeled, another surprise.

"Since we're not dancing," she explained, reading his mind, "I decided to live dangerously."

"Dangerous," Rick said, "are the ties around your neck. Why do I have the feeling the whole dress will fall off if the knots slip?"

She smiled. "Don't hold your breath for the answer."

"Frankie—"

She slid her hand in his and led him toward the stairs. "We'd better join the others. Are you ready to meet the rest of the family?"

No, he was not. He needed to find the men's room and splash cold water on his face. He needed to loosen his tie and get some air. He also needed to kiss Frankie again, longer and softer this time.

"Sure," Rick said, wondering if she had anything else planned to torture him with. "Lead the way."

"WELL, HOW DO YOU THINK the party's going?" Frankie perched on the empty chair next to her mother after her father left to get another cup of coffee.

"Lovely, Frankie. And I'm so glad Rick is here for you. He's so polite and so *handsome*," Dorothy whispered. "He looks a lot like his father, but then all the Perez boys do, I think."

"Handsome is as handsome does," Aunt Gloria

huffed, seated on the other side of Dorothy. "You'd better watch yourself with that one, Frankie. He looks like the love 'em and leave 'em type."

"That one" was heading in her direction and carrying two glasses of champagne.

"I'll be careful," Frankie promised, though the new haircut made her feel daring and adventurous. "What do you think of my hair, Mom?"

"Very nice. Did Rosa do it for you? I don't know how that girl has the time—"

"No," Frankie interrupted. If Rosa had done her hair it would have been streaked with blonde and piled on top of her head with a flower clip. "The salon at my apartment building had a couple of hours free." Her father returned and set his cup down at Frankie's elbow.

"Are you having fun, Frankie?"

"Here, Daddy, I'll move." She ignored her father's protests and slipped out of the chair. "And I'm having a wonderful time."

"Your hair looks very nice," her mother said. "I always knew you'd be a beauty like your sisters if you took a little time fixing yourself up."

"Thanks. I think."

"Frankie looks beautiful every day," her father declared, giving her a wink as he sat down. "But it's a good thing you don't wear dresses like that to the site. I wouldn't get a lick of work out of anyone.''

She saw Rick hesitate to interrupt, so Frankie leaned down to kiss her father's bald spot. ''We have to go find Rosa. I think Donny's father is ready to give a toast.''

''Have fun with your young man,'' her father whispered. ''He seems nice enough.''

''Thanks.'' Frankie turned to Rick and smiled. ''You're doing great,'' she said, when he handed her a glass. They moved away from the table. ''My father called you 'my young man.' ''

''Your mother's been watching me,'' he said, taking a sip. ''I can't tell if that's a good thing or a bad thing.''

''Mom can't believe my good luck.''

He guided her toward an empty table. ''She asked me if I planned to stay in Seattle for a while or if I was going to move to Beverly Hills.''

''She's going to be unhappy when I dump you.'' Frankie took another sip of champagne and decided this was one of the best nights in her life. She loved her hair, her dress and her lipstick. Her feet didn't hurt. And no one in her family had looked remotely sorry for her.

''You're going to dump me?''

''That's what I'll tell her. I don't want her blaming you for breaking my heart.'' Which was very noble of her, she thought, considering that her heart would surely suffer.

Rick frowned. "I don't intend to break anything."

Frankie thought she'd better change the subject. "The last date my mother met was when I still lived at home. He rode a motorcycle and, uh, was a little overweight. He was partial to black leather."

"Sounds scary." His arm went around her waist and sent little shivers of excitement down her spine.

"Not really. Underneath the leather beat the heart of an accountant with the highest grades in my economics classes."

"Economics?"

"I graduated with a business degree," she informed him. "Who do you think is going to take over Dad's company when he retires?"

"You are, of course." He grinned. "When I'm rich and famous you can build me a house."

"That's a deal." She took another sip of champagne. She could resist him, she really could, despite the magic feeling that surrounded the evening. Dinner had been great fun, since they'd been seated with Tina, Walt and the groom's youngest sister's family. After dessert, three younger cousins looking for boyfriends had shaken their ample breasts in Rick's direction, but he'd smiled politely and hadn't left Frankie's side. And now she was standing here in the elegant Plymouth Room, drinking champagne with Rick Perez while he smiled into her eyes.

It seemed as if he couldn't help touching her.

"I think…" she said slowly, the champagne bubbles tickling her nose. "I think I will change my name to Francesca from now on."

"Your name *is* Francesca," Rosa pointed out, coming up behind her. "Didn't Mom ever tell you?"

"Very funny," Frankie said, and Rick's fingers caressed her side. "I'm ticklish," she murmured, but the sensations his hand created were anything but funny. She wanted to melt into a little black, sparkly puddle at his feet.

"Come on," Rosa said, taking her sister's free hand. "Donny's dad is going to make a toast and then he's taking us downstairs to dance."

"Dance?" Frankie remembered what had happened the last time she and Rick had been in each other's arms. She had run like a scared rabbit, not her style at all. What was she so afraid of? "I thought we were all going back to the house and going to bed early. Doesn't the bride have to get her beauty sleep?"

"The wedding's not until two o'clock." Rosa

grinned at Rick. "You can keep her out as late as you want, but make sure she gets back to the house before dawn."

"I'll do my best," he said, dropping his hand from Frankie's waist as Rosa scooted away. "Would you like more champagne?"

Yes, Frankie decided, she would. She lifted her empty glass and handed it to him. She was going to drink champagne and toast to the bride and groom and dance with her handsome date for as long as her feet held her up.

Which was what she did, until long after midnight. She and Rick were one of the last couples on the dance floor, swaying to an old Sting song, bodies pressed together in such a sensual way that she wondered if this was foreplay. Oh, yes, Frankie decided, her thighs brushing Rick's. This was seductive and tempting and magical. She felt beautiful and desirable and not at all self-conscious.

Before the music stopped, before the other members of the wedding party departed for breakfast at Maria's house, and before Frankie could come to her senses and remember that she wasn't Cinderella in a fairy tale, Rick leaned down, his breath tickling her ear and his lips grazing her skin in soft kisses along her temple.

They barely moved their feet, which was a lovely way to dance, she decided. When the song ended, Rick led her off the dance floor to a private corner table, but didn't release her hand. Instead he tugged her closer and kissed her, briefly, softly, promising much more.

"Francesca," he said. "Come home with me."

CHAPTER TEN

FRANCESCA. Yes, she definitely was Francesca tonight. Her dress felt silky against her bare skin, her hair looked like a movie star's, and her sturdy feet, encased in heeled sandals, didn't wobble in the least.

Nothing could go wrong, not during such a magical evening. She was a little numb from the wine and a little warm from the dancing and, after Rick flagged a cab to take them to his apartment, she was even a little bit shocked to find that kissing Rick in the back of a taxi was almost as much fun as kissing him while dancing. It was as if they couldn't get enough of each other, couldn't imagine the night without being together.

Once they arrived at the house, they tiptoed up the stairs to his apartment, Frankie carrying her shoes in her hand and stopping once because Rick pretended he heard a noise.

"Stop teasing," she whispered, following him to the second-floor landing.

"I can't help it." He smiled and touched her

cheek. "All of a sudden I feel like a teenager who doesn't want his older brothers to catch him doing something wrong."

"This *is* probably wrong," she admitted, feeling her spirits wilt a little.

"No way," he said, reaching for his key. "Why didn't we go out when we were in high school?"

"Because you were mean to me." She watched him unlock the door. He pushed it open to let her enter first. *Because I didn't wear dresses and fancy shoes and lipstick and have my hair done by someone named Madame Renoir.*

"I'm really, really sorry about that. I always liked you, but I didn't think you liked me at all." He closed the door with a gentle click, leaving them in darkness, and then he reached for her.

"I kissed you at graduation and you laughed."

"Not me. I was too shocked." He found her mouth in the darkness and kissed her into silence.

"Then it was your friends who laughed," Frankie whispered. "I was mortified."

"I promise to never laugh when you kiss me, okay?"

"You're laughing now," she said against his mouth. She could feel the upward curve of his smile under her lips.

"Not laughing," Rick said, pulling her closer to

the warmth of his body. "Smiling. Happy you're here."

"Are you going to turn on the lights?"

"No."

"Then how—"

"I'm going to dance you into my bedroom." He put his right arm around her waist and lifted her hand with his left. "Pretend we're waltzing again."

"Without music?"

"Pretend. One-two-three, one-two-three—"

She closed her eyes and let him twirl her around the wide living room and through another door into Rick's bedroom. The tall windows on the other side of the bed glowed from the light of a corner streetlamp. Rick stopped dancing, but Frankie stayed in his arms as his fingers caressed her shoulders, then moved higher to find the ties that held up the halter neckline of her dress. He didn't undo them, not until after he swept her hair from her cheeks and took her mouth again.

And then Rick made short work of the bow. The two pieces of fabric slipped down and revealed her breasts, full and perfect in the dim light. "Beautiful," he said, sliding his hands down her sides and pushing the rest of the dress over her hips. The fabric slithered to the floor, leaving Frankie standing almost naked in his bedroom. His fingers hesitated before plucking the thin side straps of her black thong. There was only so much one man could take in a short period of time, and having Frankie standing in his bedroom was almost as erotic as having a naked Frankie standing in his bedroom.

"You don't like thongs?" She shivered under his hands and Rick cleared his throat and willed himself to slow down.

"I'm overwhelmed," he admitted, as Frankie began unbuttoning his shirt. "You wear these when you're working?"

"Sure."

"Sure?" He wondered how the guys on the job sites got any work done.

"It's a 'Francesca' thing." She pulled his shirttail from his pants and forced the sleeves down his arms. "I like it when you're overwhelmed," she said, pausing to brush a light kiss in the center of his chest. "But could you help me a little here?"

"Gladly." He kicked off his shoes and removed the rest of his clothes in something approaching lightning speed.

"That was fast," she said with admiration in her voice.

"I'm going to try to slow things down before I embarrass myself." He wanted nothing more than to pull her to him and feel that satin-smooth skin against his body, but he resisted. He wanted to take his time more than he wanted to be inside her; he wanted to taste and touch and lick and kiss until he knew every inch of her body. She would taste like honey, he mused, inhaling the rose scent of her hair. She would be slick and open and ready for him when the moment came to enter her.

"You don't have to slow down," she told him. Her voice caught when he took her hand. "I'm not good at waiting."

"Francesca," he said, lifting her fingers to his lips. "Will you come to bed now?"

Her smile was pure female, tantalizing and full of such sweetness that he realized right then and there that he was lost. Frankie Raimondi, the girl who had beaten him at arm wrestling and cried when he'd teased her, had stolen his heart.

THE ONLY THING to do was run. Long after Rick fell asleep, Frankie lay in the bed beside his warm body and decided that tonight she had made the biggest mistake of her life.

Making love with Rick had been more wonderful than she'd ever fantasized. He had been a tender and passionate lover, a man determined to please her. To please Francesca, a woman who wore makeup and sexy dresses and whose plain brown hair had been cut to float like layers of petals around her face, he had joined her in this wide bed and touched her with reverence. He had made her feel beautiful and desired, as if he couldn't get enough of her. And when she was quivering and just about insane with wanting him, he'd slid himself inside her and taken her right to heaven.

Frankie rolled over on her side and looked at her sleeping fake boyfriend. Nothing about last night had been faked, not on her part, anyway. Rick had made sure she was satisfied—twice, in fact, and it made her blush to think about it—before he came deep inside her. He'd used a condom; she'd forgotten her own name and remembered once again that she'd loved him since she was a skinny kid with a secret wish.

She'd wished he would notice her. And now he had. Noticed her so much that she was in this bed, without her dress and her perfect hair and artfully applied makeup. When he woke in the morning she would be Frankie again. After the wedding was over, she'd be Frankie again, with jeans and muddy boots and hair smashed under a hardhat. The reality was not a fancy party or midnight kisses in the dark or waltzing to bed. She couldn't bear to see Rick disappointed and trying not to show it—or worse, feeling sorry for her and pretending to be nice. They had both gotten carried away and she wouldn't hold it against him, but she sure wasn't going to stick around and pretend that making love to Rick had been no big deal.

So Frankie, holding back tears, slid out of bed without making a sound. She no longer needed a date for the wedding, because she'd decided not to go.

"RICK! WOW," Rosa said, standing in the doorway of the Raimondi family home. "You look like a movie star."

"Thanks." The mysterious tux had fit perfectly, much to Rick's satisfaction. He hadn't liked waking up two hours ago to find Frankie gone, but he knew she had to get home and get ready for the wedding. "Why's the bride answering the door?"

"I have a lot of nervous energy. What are you doing here so early? I think you're supposed to meet Frankie at the church at—"

"I needed to see Frankie for a minute." He hoped he didn't sound desperate.

"You can't come in." That's when he noticed Rosa was wrapped in a pink bathrobe and her hair was piled in curls on top of her head, as if she was ready for the prom.

"Could you please just ask her to come to the door?" He gave her his most charming smile. "Just for a minute. I won't keep her long, I promise." He only wanted to say hello to her, wanted to talk to her before the wedding began and she was so busy they wouldn't have time for privacy. And he needed privacy for what he wanted to say.

"She can't. I mean, she won't." Rosa took a deep breath. "She said if you called to tell you she's gone to the airport."

"That's okay. I'll wait," he said, certain that she would return with wedding guests, and he would be able to steal her away. "What time did she leave?"

"Ages ago. She's probably halfway to Italy by now."

He wasn't sure he heard her correctly. "Did you say Italy?"

"Yes. The country that's shaped like a boot. *That* Italy."

"You're not telling the truth, Rosa." Frankie's sister couldn't even look him in the eye. "Where is she really?"

Rosa leaned close and whispered, "I'm supposed to get rid of you. She hasn't stopped crying since she got home. What happened? What did you do?"

"I didn't do anything." Except love her, he wanted to add. "Please, Rosa. Let me come in and find out what's going on."

"I can't." She looked behind her and winced.

"My mother's having a fit about all of this. You'd better go."

Rick stood firmly planted on the front step. "Without talking to Frankie? No way."

"She's not exactly, um, accessible right now, Rick. No one can get near her except Daddy, and he can't get her to come in, either."

"Come in?" Rick realized exactly where Frankie would be hiding in order to stay away from her sisters. "Thanks. I'll see you at the wedding."

"I hope so," the bride whispered, and then shut the door.

Rick didn't waste any time walking around the two-story house to the backyard. He stood by the clothesline and shaded his eyes as he looked up at the roof. Sure enough, a small figure in shorts and a yellow shirt sat perched on a section of roof above a set of double-hung windows. She'd thrown acorns at him from up there about fifteen years ago. He'd lost a five-dollar bet, too. Rick waved.

"Frankie!" he called, but she didn't wave back. He walked closer and saw that she wore sunglasses and had a box of tissues on her lap. "What's the matter? What the hell is going on?"

"Go away," was all he heard.

"No." He'd stay all day, if that's what it took to get Frankie to come down and talk to him. She couldn't stay up there forever.

"I'll tell my father."

"Tell him what? About last night?"

She didn't answer.

Rick tried again. "Just what exactly was it about last night that has you crying on a roof?"

Frankie grabbed a tissue and blew her nose. One of the bedroom windows opened and Dorothy Raimondi looked out. "Oh, Rick, hello there."

"Hi, Mrs. Raimondi." He suddenly felt about ten years old. "How are you?"

"I've had better days," she told him. "Get Frankie off the roof so she can get her hair done, will you? We're running out of time. The limousines are here and the photographer just arrived for pictures."

"Yes, ma'am, I'll do my best. Can I come in?"

"Rick, I have seven half-naked women running around this house right now, so you can't come in. Just talk to Frankie out here."

He watched the window close before looking over at the woman he loved, who was still very much ensconced on the roof.

"I'll be back," he told her. He walked back to the front of the house, but couldn't find what he wanted in the garage, so he had no choice but to kidnap one of the waiting limousines. Fifty dollars got him a quick trip to his own childhood home, transportation for the ladder he took from the garage and glowing compliments from his mother, who came outside as he carried the ladder to the car.

"Oh, Ricky, you look so handsome in that fancy tuxedo," she said, kissing him on both cheeks. "Where are you going in a limo, and why do you need the ladder?"

"I have a date," he said, giving his mother a quick hug. "A special date."

"Special?" Her dark eyes gleamed with interest. "Maybe you'd better come to dinner tomorrow and tell me all about it."

"Can I bring a friend?"

"This is a *special* friend?"

"Yes." He grinned. "I have to go, Mom. This is kind of an emergency."

"Well, don't get that fancy tuxedo dirty. That ladder couldn't be clean."

"It's fine, Mom." His mother watched while the limo driver helped him load the ladder into the back end of the car, where it rested on top of three sets of seats. "I have to stay clean for the wedding."

"You're not in some kind of trouble, are you?"

He laughed. "No. I'm a wedding guest. Sort of." He gave her a quick hug. "I'll explain everything tomorrow. Wish me luck."

"With what? Breaking into a bride's house?"

"No, with a bridesmaid named Francesca."

His mother patted his arm. "I knew—never mind, Ricky. Go climb into your girl's window. Just don't let anyone shoot you."

Rick promised he wouldn't and got into the car.

"I'll stand guard," the driver promised, shutting the passenger door. "Don't worry. I've done stranger things than this."

They were back at the Raimondi house in six minutes, the ladder unloaded and the limo driver with a dust rag in his hand to wipe the marks off the upholstery.

"Good luck," the middle-aged driver said, handing him his business card. "If you ever need a limo—"

"Thanks." Rick tucked the card in his pocket, picked up the aluminum ladder, turned toward the house and walked straight into Frankie's father, a man who didn't look pleased to be stuffed into a tuxedo on a hot summer afternoon.

"Hello, Rick. Are you here for Frankie?" Joe Raimondi attempted to loosen his bow tie. "I hate these damn things. Especially in the summer."

"Uh, yes. Is she still on the roof?"

"Unfortunately." Joe's gaze sharpened as he noticed the ladder. "Are you eloping with my daughter?"

"No, sir."

"Damn," he muttered, before he waved Rick on. "I've had just about enough of these extravaganzas. See if you can get her down and then come have a drink with me. I've got a cooler full of beer and ice and a couple of lawn chairs in the garage."

"Frankie's pretty stubborn."

"Runs in the family," the man said, then disappeared into the garage. "Just don't give up too soon."

He didn't, not when the ladder wasn't tall enough to let him see over the gutter or climb above the bedroom windows to the overhang of the roof. Not when the whole thing wobbled as he reached the next-to-the-top rung. Not even when Frankie told him to go away.

"I'm not going anywhere," he yelled, wishing she'd come closer so he could see her. "Why did you leave me last night?"

"I left you this morning."

"Why?"

"Because last night—" She paused and he heard her take a shaky breath. "Because last night was so wonderful."

He clung to the sides of the ladder and prayed that his father had bought the sturdiest brand in Seattle. "It's customary to say that over breakfast the next morning. If you, uh, liked last night, you shouldn't run away and climb up on top of a house. It's real hard on a guy's sensitive ego, you know.''

''Don't make fun.''

Rick stretched, the ladder rattled, and he froze. ''Frankie, I'm risking my life here. I'm not goofing around. Do you think you could lean over so I could see you?''

''No. I'm a mess.''

''I don't care,'' Rick assured her.

''Yes, you do. I'm not Francesca anymore.'' She sniffed and he heard her blow her nose. ''You only wanted Francesca and the black dress with the sexy straps and the makeup and the fancy hair and eye shadow. That's not the real me. I played a trick on you by getting dressed up like that. I wanted you to notice me.''

''I've always noticed you, Frankie.''

''Not like last night. Not like a woman.''

He laughed. He couldn't help it. ''I didn't fall in love with your clothes or your hair, you idiot. I fell in love with *you*, Frankie.'' He heard the sound of scraping wood and almost fell off the ladder when he found himself face-to-face with Mrs. Raimondi, whose freshly curled hair was sticking out of her oldest daughter's bedroom window.

''I'm happy you're in love with my daughter, Rick, but you two are going to have to settle this later,'' she said. ''Get down off that ladder before you kill yourself. And Frankie?" She raised her voice. "Come *off* that roof and *into* your dress before Rosa has a nervous breakdown and I end up drinking in the garage with your father! *Now!*"

Rick made his escape. He knew when a woman meant business. Rosa called to him from another window when he reached the bottom rung and sent something flying toward him.

"Just in case," Frankie's sister said as Frankie climbed off the roof and slipped inside her own window. Rick left the ladder against the house, just in case he needed to talk to Frankie later.

"Rick?"

He'd forgotten about Joe, and when Rick turned, he saw Frankie's father seated in a plastic lawn chair in the garage. The door was open, giving Joe a view of the street and the line of limousines.

"I was only kidding about eloping," the man said. "But I'm real fussy about who marries my daughters. Especially Frankie."

Rick stepped closer. "Yes, sir," he said. "I can understand that you would be."

"You're not going to break my girl's heart, are you?"

"No, sir. Once I make up my mind, that's pretty much it."

The older man nodded. "I'll take your word for it."

FRANKIE CAUGHT A GLIMPSE of Rick at the church when she led the party of bridesmaids down the aisle. He sat in the fourth row, on the bride's side and next to Aunt Gloria, who sniffed into a lace handkerchief and looked overcome with emotion. Rick, easily the best-looking man there, met Frankie's gaze but didn't smile. His eyebrows rose, as if he were asking if she was okay. There was nothing she could do, not without causing a scene. A bridesmaid grabbing a guest and running out of the church was sure to distract attention from the bride's walk down the aisle. No, she decided, holding Rosa's flowers while she fixed her veil, she would stay right here and hope he still wanted to talk to her. She would run into his arms and love him for as long as it lasted. Maybe a brief affair was better than nothing. At least that's what she told herself until Rosa and Donny repeated their wedding vows and Frankie blinked back tears.

After the ceremony, Frankie didn't see Rick while she stood in the informal receiving line at the foot of the church steps. The crowd spilled onto the church lawn and down the sidewalk, and soon the wedding party was whisked away for pictures. The photographer took an endless number of shots in the hotel courtyard, but Rosa's joy was contagious. And Frankie stopped minding the constant order to "smile pretty, ladies" before the blinding flash of the camera.

She didn't spot her "escort" in the receiving line in the ballroom either, though it seemed as if Rosa and Donny knew everyone in Seattle, judging from the number of guests anxious to offer congratulations. The enormous windowed ballroom overlooked Lake Washington, which sparkled and shimmered in the July sunshine, but Frankie didn't really notice. She watched the row of double doors and wished that Rick would appear. She wouldn't blame him for giving up on her. But deep in her heart she didn't think he would.

"In case you're interested, I'm afraid of heights," a familiar voice said behind her, long after the receiving line evaporated and the guests strolled off to help themselves from an elegantly arranged buffet. Frankie turned around to see the most handsome man in the world holding two glasses of champagne.

"You were brave to climb the ladder then." She took the offered glass, but her fingers were shaking too much to attempt taking a sip. Rosa would never forgive her if she stained the rose silk outfit before the rest of the pictures were taken.

"I'm glad you're impressed." He took another sip of champagne and smiled. "Did you really think I'd believe that you were running off to Italy?"

"It was the first thing that came into my head," she confessed. "Silly, huh?"

"Yeah. I'd have followed you to the airport if Rosa wasn't such a bad liar. But I remembered when you were a kid, you'd sit up on that roof like you were in charge of the whole neighborhood." He smiled, so she knew he wasn't angry with her for causing him to climb a ladder and shout "I'm in love with you" while her mother was in the window.

"Rick, Frankie, over here!" Rosa waved at them and pointed to a table of bridesmaids and ushers.

"Is there any way we can be alone?" Now he was pure frustrated male, and Frankie couldn't help laughing.

"In a ballroom with eighty-seven Raimondis and a hundred and fifty other guests? You're joking, right?"

"Soon," Rick said, taking her free hand in his, "you're going to have to hear me out."

"I promise," Frankie replied, but then they were at the table, toasting the bride and groom and trying to listen to eight people talk at once.

Another twenty minutes passed before Rick

leaned over and whispered, "When everyone gets up for the buffet, grab your champagne glass and follow me."

"Okay." Frankie hoped this wasn't going to be a "see you around" conversation. She wanted him to repeat his *I fell in love with you* rooftop declaration, before her mother had interrupted what had to have been one of the most romantic moments of her life. Frankie thought maybe she should apologize for not coming down from the roof, but before she could say a word, Rick took her hand and led her across the room to the privacy of the waterfront deck.

"That's better." He set his glass on the wide railing. "Your family's been watching us."

"They'll be out here soon," she warned. "They heard what you said on the ladder."

"I wasn't finished. Your mother kind of interrupted things."

"I thought you were very romantic." She fought the urge to throw herself into his arms and instead took a shaky sip of champagne.

"Not romantic enough." He took the champagne glass out of her hand before she dropped it, and set it on the railing next to his. "Francesca Raimondi, I promise to love, honor and adore you forever, and if you don't mind marrying a struggling actor, I will do everything I can to make you happy. Everything I have is—and always will be—yours, if you'll say yes.''

"Marry you?" she managed to say. For a second Frankie wondered if she was hearing things, but the look on Rick's face told her he was serious. This was real. *"Marry?"*

"You don't have to look so surprised." He grinned and pulled a small velvet box from inside his jacket. "I already asked your father's permission, which he gave, by the way, with lots of instructions as to what he expected of a son-in-law." Rick took her hand and set the box in her palm. "You have to say yes before you open it. And I hope you do, because I'll love you in denim or in silk, with brown hair or gray, in boots or barefoot. For the rest of our lives, I promise."

Frankie simply stared up at him.

"Say yes, Frankie, and open the box or I'm going to have to drown myself in the lake. Please?"

"Okay."

"Is that a yes?"

She blinked back tears and wanted to laugh. "Yes."

He opened the box for her, displaying a platinum band inset with diamonds. "The jeweler said this style wouldn't interfere with power tools."

"It's beautiful. And I can't believe this. I've loved you since I was eleven, despite everything you did to tease me,'' she confessed as Rick removed the ring from the box. He slid it on the third finger of her left hand, where it fit perfectly.

"How did you know?"

"Rosa told me. She makes a real good paper airplane. I picked out the ring after your mother kicked me off the ladder. The jeweler felt sorry for me and sized it while I was at the wedding. That's why I was late for the reception."

"I still can't believe you did all this." Frankie stared at her hand and then up at him. "Kiss me," she said, lifting her arms to loop around his neck, "so I'll know this is really happening."

He kissed her long and hard, oblivious to the crowd of family members who gathered near the French doors. "Frankie?"

"Hmm?" She rested her forehead on his chest and tried to catch her breath.

"Did I tell you I also guarantee free escort service for the rest of your life?"

"No," she said, laughing against his shirt. "But you're hired anyway."

PROTECTING MARIA
Muriel Jensen

CHAPTER ONE

RAFE PEREZ ignored the elevator and hurried down
the stairs, tugging at the collar on the shirt of his
tuxedo. A sadist must have invented this garment
of torture, he thought. A woman, probably as pay-
back to the man who invented the high heel.

He stopped on the second floor to ask his youngest brother, Rick, for a splash of cologne. As an
actor, Rick had all the gentleman's accoutrements
that Rafe lacked in his work as an engineer. Building bridges and roads in underdeveloped countries
seldom called for a shirt, much less a tuxedo, and
the same went for his sideline specialty of rescuing
kidnapped children held outside of the United
States. God, he couldn't wait for his shoulder to
heal so he could get back to work. Seattle was too
full of memories of Maria and the bleak anguish
he'd felt when he'd come home from Spain to find
she'd married another man.

He made himself dismiss all thoughts of her.
He'd had to do that a lot in the three years she'd
been gone and he'd been overseas, but he had

every confidence that eventually he'd forget about her completely.

When no one answered the door, Rafe continued down to ground level, where his brother Rob shared his apartment with his two young children, Maggie and T.J., and a custom design furniture business. He wasn't even sure Rob owned cologne since he never went anywhere, but it was worth a shot.

A gorilla holding a wriggling toddler in his arms answered the door.

Rafe snatched the child and gave the gorilla a shove backward into the apartment. "If you're here to eat these children," he warned the beast, "they'll give you indigestion. That one doesn't eat her vegetables…" He pointed to a dark-haired little girl watching from a child-size rocking chair in front of the television. "And this one—" he indicated the little boy in his arms "—isn't potty-trained."

The gorilla growled and swiped a paw at Rafe.

Rafe grabbed the beast by the fur at his throat. "You leave this family alone and get back to the zoo before I…"

"No, Uncle Rafe!" Five-year-old Maggie scrambled out of her chair and wrapped her arms around the gorilla's nearest leg. "Don't hurt him. It's Uncle Rick!"

Rafe pretended to look into the gorilla's eyes in surprise. "It is?"

"Show him, Uncle Rick!" she encouraged. "Take off your head."

The large paw reached up and removed the furry head piece. A handsome, square-jawed face emerged. Rick's usually impeccably styled hair stuck up in all directions, his skin was flushed, and the deep, dark eyes that he hoped would one day land him a starring role in Hollywood were filled with disappointment.

"You knew it was me?" he asked.

"Of course," Rafe replied, walking farther into the room. "I wish the zoo would keep better track of you."

"Ha, ha." Rick followed him. "You'll notice I'm not the only one here in a monkey suit."

Rafe had to give him that. "I'm on my way to a formal dinner party. What's your excuse?"

"It's a new gig—Gorilla Greetings delivered in song by yours truly. But, listen! I just landed a part in a community theater Christmas play."

"And won't he be the cutest donkey you've ever seen?" Rick's fiancée, Frankie, emerged from the kitchen with a tray of sandwiches. She was a beautiful, brown-eyed brunette in jeans, a red sweater, and work boots. Usually a very serious tool belt was tied around her hips, befitting her position as second in command in her father's construction business. But she was apparently finished work for the day. She had moved into Rick's apartment since it was bigger than her own, and the two of them often came downstairs to help Rob with dinner and the children.

Rick folded his arms in pretended indignation—a funny sight in the gorilla suit. "Now, that's real loving support." Balancing the tray on one hand, Frankie kissed his cheek. "You could play any role and make it sizzle."

"Congratulations," Rafe said with a grin. "Actually, you have a lot of experience as a donkey."

"Whoa!" Frankie breathed in a dramatically worshipful whisper, noticing Rafe's appearance for the first time.

"Down, woman." Rick snatched the tray from her. "He's too old for you. Rafe, what are you doing here, anyway?"

"I tried to borrow cologne from you," Rafe replied as his nephew, T.J., two and a half, pulled on his earlobe. "But you weren't home, so I thought I'd try Rob."

"Rob doesn't own cologne."

"Yes, I do." Rob appeared from his workshop, wiping his hands on a rag. "Who needs cologne? Oh!" He raised an eyebrow at Rafe's appearance, seeing the answer to his question. "I have Eternity and Drakkar Noir. Mom gave us all cologne last Christmas. Where's yours?''

''I don't know,'' Rafe replied. ''Misplaced it, or something.''

''Or left it in Venice, or wherever you've been.'' Rick had helped himself to a sandwich and pointed at Rafe with it.

''You're not supposed to talk with your mouth full,'' Maggie admonished, shaking her tiny index finger at him.

''Thank you, Maggie,'' Rafe said, following Rob as he headed for his bedroom, then added over his shoulder at Rick, ''In fact, we'd all prefer if you didn't talk at all. And I was in Venezuela.''

When Maria got married, Rafe had sold his classic car garage and taken a job with Overseas Engineering. The cars had always been too much fun to be considered work, anyway. And two of the guys he worked with on the children's rescue team were employed by OE and put in a good word for him.

''Wait until we're reincarnated,'' Rick shouted after him, ''and I come back older than you!''

Rob went into his bathroom and returned with a square bottle.

Rafe went to take it, but Rob seemed to be suddenly distracted. ''Oh, no,'' he said, staring at Rafe's chest and reaching for his son.

"What?" Rafe looked down at his tuxedo jacket and saw a vivid, saucer-size stain on the left side—right where T.J. had been perched in his arm. He was about to say something rude when he saw the toddler's wide hazel eyes studying him. He bit back the oath and groaned instead.

"I'm sorry." Rob put the boy down and shooed him toward the living room. "Frankie volunteered to diaper him while I was busy and she doesn't have the hang of it yet. Come on, take it off and you can borrow the mystery tux."

Rafe didn't see that he had a choice. "I rented my own tux," he said, "because I don't trust the mystery tux. I mean, why would it suddenly appear on your doorstep addressed to us? It's creepy."

Rob tossed the offending jacket into a corner and reached into the back of his closet for the Perry Ellis tuxedo that had arrived at the house without explanation or return address. It had been addressed simply, R. Perez, but no one claimed to know anything about it.

"I thought Rick had it," Rafe said as he pulled the studs out of his shirt and unfastened the cuffs.

Rob nodded as he pulled the fancy tux and its shirt off the hanger and laid them out on the bed for Rafe.

"He stored it down here while he was doing

some painting before Frankie moved in. He just hasn't taken it back up yet.''

Rick had worn the tux when he'd escorted Frankie to her sister's wedding, Rafe recalled.

''I'll leave the cologne on the dresser.'' Rob did so, then turned before pulling the bedroom door closed behind him. ''I'll pay to have your tux dry-cleaned.''

Rafe pulled off the shirt. ''Don't worry about it. But if this tux gets me into trouble in any way, I'm feeding you to that gorilla.''

Rob laughed and closed the door, apparently thinking he was kidding. Actually, Rafe would have happily used the excuse to stay home, but he and his friends on the rescue team, which had been dubbed Angel Rescue, had once recovered the son and daughter of a staff member of Senator Randolph Stanton's. When the senator heard Rafe was home recovering from surgery for an injury ostensibly sustained while bridge building in Venezuela, he'd invited him to a party at his home. It would have reflected negatively on the team not to go.

Although Senator Stanton did make him uncomfortable. The man was the epitome of courtesy and dignity, but Rafe got the impression it was all a facade. Something in his eyes wasn't entirely sincere, as though he spoke a different message than he was thinking.

But Rafe put it down to the fact he spent so much of his own life pretending to be someone he wasn't. It was all part of his job rescuing abducted kids.

On second thought, maybe he *was* qualified to wear the mystery tux. His own life was full of intrigue.

He pulled the shirt on and did the buttons, then fastened the silver and onyx button at the neck and the matching cuff links. The tux had come with a silver-gray vest in a diamond pattern, which he slipped on once he'd changed pants. Finally he pulled on the black jacket.

Checking himself out in the mirror, he decided he looked good enough to open envelopes at the Oscars.

He sprayed a shot of Eternity in the direction of his throat and hurried for the door, trying to remember if he'd switched his keys to the new jacket. There was nothing but a business card for a limo service in the pocket, probably left over from Rick's wedding excursion. He looked around for a trash basket, and finding none, put the card back in his pocket. Once he'd retrieved his keys from the tux jacket on the floor, he raced out.

The family shouted their goodbyes and Maggie insisted on a hug. To protect the mystery tux, he blew T.J. a kiss.

THE PARTY WAS HELD at the home Senator Randolph Stanton shared with his niece. That event was probably great fun for the social and political types who traveled in the senator's circle, but for Rafe, who generally stayed as far away as possible from situations that required small talk and clever repartee, it was torturous and interminable. He drank champagne to dull the pain, and by the time he guessed sufficient time had passed that he could excuse himself without insult, he was feeling somewhat impaired. Not drunk precisely, but not at his sharpest, either. No way would he risk driving home himself.

He looked around the crowd and decided he didn't know anyone well enough to bum a ride home—not that anyone else in the laughing crowd looked ready to leave. He could call Information for the number of a cab company.

Then he remembered the business card in his pocket for the limo service. Why not ride home in style? He found a quiet corner in the hallway and called.

"Fifteen minutes," the dispatcher told him.

When he located Stanton to say his goodbyes, the senator caught his arm and drew him into a kitchen that looked like something that belonged in a hotel restaurant. He opened a freezer against the back wall and produced what had to be a fifty-pound Chinook salmon in a plastic bag.

"Marty Pratt came to the party with six of these tonight. They were just caught this afternoon. They're not quite frozen yet. Tell me, please, that you'll take one."

"Uh..."

"I'd consider it a personal favor. I'm a lobster man, myself."

Rafe loved salmon, especially barbecued, but he wasn't sure how a limo service was going to feel about driving one home. It smelled like a bait barge.

"Sure," he said as the senator forced the end of the bag into his hand. "Thank you."

That small courtesy completed, Randolph Stanton turned him toward the door, seemingly anxious to be rid of him now that he held a smelly, four-foot salmon. "Thanks for coming."

"Thank you for asking me. Do you mind if I leave my car at the end of the drive until tomorrow?"

"Of course not."

"Thanks again."

Then he was alone at the foot of the mansion's steps, holding a salmon in the chilly early October night, and waiting for a limo.

CHAPTER TWO

MARIA CASTILLO readjusted her position behind the wheel of the white Lincoln limousine while waiting for the dispatcher to return to the line. She'd called in delivery of her last client, and was asked to wait as another call came in.

One more month, she thought grimly, and this second job as a limo driver would come to a halt. Her obstetrician had insisted she wasn't having twins. She was just carrying the baby high, and that made her look bigger.

What, she wondered, made her feel bigger? It was as though she was gestating a Buick. Her back ached constantly and she was only at the end of her sixth month. She couldn't imagine what the next three would be like.

Father Sullivan at St. Bartholomew's had promised that she could keep her job at the rectory until she delivered, but she couldn't hold him to that if she was unable to fulfill her duties as cook and housekeeper. It was already getting difficult to bend and reach.

"I have a client for you at…" Charlene Goodman, the boss's secretary and the evening dispatcher at Lawless Limousines, came abruptly back on the line with an exclusive Lake Washington address. "That should be good for a fat tip," she said cheerfully. "We have to get that baby into a classy day care so she can meet some doctor or lawyer's son who'll support you in your old age."

Charlene had been a good friend to Maria since Maria joined the company five months ago.

"That's the plan," Maria teased. "Thanks, Charlie. You and Christopher having a romantic evening in front of the TV?"

"No, I have to work on the books for the shop between dispatches. Night looks quiet so far, but you never know."

Charlene and her husband owned a small antiques and collectibles shop in the Queen Anne district. Charlene worked the shop in the morning, managed the Lawless office in the afternoons and dispatched from her home at night. Christopher worked the shop afternoons and did all the acquiring.

"Can you patch me through to John?" Maria asked. Her boss had left her a message that he wanted to talk to her, but she hadn't been able to reach him at home.

"No, sorry. He left this afternoon to meet a client and said he wasn't coming back. He blocked out the next couple of days." Charlene snickered. "The same days Joanne has off, you'll notice."

"Mmm." Maria pulled away from the curb. Joanne was another driver. "I had noticed. You'd think they'd be more discreet, wouldn't you?"

"You would. I don't care if they have an affair. It's just having to pretend we don't know that makes me uncomfortable."

"Right." It reminded Maria of her mother, who'd remained in a marriage with a man who ran around on her continually.

"Drive safely, sweetie."

"Thanks, Charlie. See you tomorrow."

Maria accelerated, determined not to dwell on the state of John and Joanne's affair, or on what would happen in her own life when the baby was born. She should be concentrating on traffic, but she was used to mulling over her problems and assessing the state of her life as she drove.

The sale of the house she'd shared with her husband had paid for her sister Fernanda's last year at Harvard, and Paloma's next three years at Wellesley. With what little remained, she'd rented a comfortable apartment, then gotten the job at the church.

Things were much better than she'd expected them to be when Emilio died suddenly of an aneurism. He'd had no insurance, and most of his assets belonged to his company. Still, Maria was able to keep her sisters in school, and even learning that she was pregnant only two weeks after her husband's death had been shocking but not impossible to deal with. Her sisters, though a long distance away, were excited, and her friends were supportive.

So she had nothing to complain about.

She could grumble about Rafe Perez taking off without warning one too many times and finally turning her love for him to anger. She could blame him for the fact that she'd married Emilio after one of Rafe's sudden disappearances and ended up less than happy, but that wouldn't be fair. Satisfying, but not fair.

It was better not to think about Rafe. But images of him came to her in her dreams. His hair, black as midnight, and eyes as dark. His handsome, angular face with the formidable, beaky nose and stop-your-heart smile.

As though it were happening now, she remembered the touch of his fingertips on the back of her waist as he drew her to him. The feel of his purposeful mouth on hers with that deadly combination of power tempered by tenderness. She'd been his completely, the cliché of the secretary who fell in love with her boss.

She drove toward her client on automatic pilot, years of experience guiding her as her mind sifted through memories she hadn't allowed herself to explore in ages.

Seven years ago she'd managed the business office in Rafe's classic car repair shop. She'd fallen hard for his good looks and his charm, but even more than that, she'd been taken by his confidence and competence. When he was there, things seldom went wrong, and if they did, they were handled with humor and calm.

At home, her mother had always been in a panic, and she hadn't realized until later that it was probably the result of her philandering husband and her subsequent loss of self-esteem. Life had always felt as though no one was in charge.

Then her parents had died together in a traffic accident when she was nineteen. She'd assumed custody of her sisters, who were then five and eight, and raised them to high school age with little difficulty except that money was always tight.

Then she'd gotten the job with Perez's Classic Car Repair and her financial situation had improved. Rafe paid generously and ran a happy shop. She began to save for her sisters' college education. Fernanda was a genius in math, and Paloma dreamed of a career in journalism.

When she'd fallen in love with Rafe and he with

her, the world took on a rosy glow. She guessed that was why she never questioned his mysterious trips in the beginning.

He would leave suddenly and be gone for several days, sometimes a week. Then he would return, looking tired but somehow invigorated. He'd said the trips were for business, that he was bidding on jobs, repairing cars for a Hollywood studio, a European entrepreneur, a sheikh.

She found it hard to justify these excursions when he had more business at home than he could complete in a reasonable time. Customers sometimes waited months for service, or paid top dollar for rush jobs. The work Rafe did for Emilio Castillo alone probably paid his rent every month.

Emilio was in partnership in several hotels and took pleasure in flaunting his wealth. He flirted openly with Maria every time he came into the shop, and it annoyed her that Rafe never complained about it.

Then Rafe's trips became more frequent, and Maria began to entertain suspicions she didn't like but couldn't seem to ignore. She confronted him in his office one day, insisting that he tell her what was really going on. If there was another woman, she wanted to know. She had experience with such things, she told him, explaining about her father. She would never live as her mother had, never certain from day to day whether or not to expect him home.

He'd assured her that the trips were for business, but that the one from which he'd just returned was his last.

She'd been ecstatic. They'd talked about marriage.

Then she'd come back from grocery shopping one Saturday afternoon to find a message on her answering machine, telling her he had to leave for several days. He knew he'd promised he'd made his last trip, but this client was desperate and he had to go.

While he was gone, Emilio proposed to Maria. She was about to brush him off as she always did, when he added the bonus she couldn't refuse. "I know how worried you are about getting your sisters into college. I'll send them both for you. Anywhere they want to go. I have connections in a few ivy league schools. What do you say? Or are you going to wait around forever for that grease monkey Casanova to get serious? Marry me, give me a son and live the rest of your life in comfort."

Suddenly it was all very clear to her. She could wait for Rafe forever, but there'd always be one more trip. Probably one more woman.

She accepted Emilio's proposal, shocking him

and herself. He'd insisted they marry immediately, before she could change her mind.

They had, and though she'd tried hard to be a good wife, and Emilio had kept his promises about her sisters, she'd failed to get pregnant, and he'd grown disenchanted and morose.

He'd had trouble with the stock market, trouble with his business partners, trouble with the bank. The only trouble he hadn't noticed had been his health. The simple headache he'd had turned out to be an aneurysm, and he'd collapsed one day at the office and never regained consciousness.

And that was how her sisters ended up in prestigious eastern schools, and she became a widow with no prospects.

She groaned aloud as she turned onto the road that would take her to the line-up of mansions on the lake. There'd been something cathartic about reviewing her past three years. It reminded her that while things had come to a sorry pass with Emilio, she'd done her best in the relationship. And though she often wondered what could have been if she'd waited for Rafe, she accepted that she'd simply never know. After her marriage to Emilio, she'd lost complete touch with Rafe. She had no idea if he was dead or alive.

CHAPTER THREE

RAFE WAS GRATEFUL when the long silver-gray
limo appeared out of the darkness. He was about
to reach for the salmon, which he'd rested on the
decorative urn at the bottom of the front steps, then
decided he should probably ask the driver to put it
in the trunk so he didn't "perfume" the interior of
the limo.

He approached the vehicle as it pulled up. The
driver pushed his door open, then stepped out to
open the back door for Rafe.

"Hi," Rafe said. "I've got a package we might
want to put in..." He stopped abruptly, distracted
by the feminine grace of the driver in the silver-
trimmed uniform—and the fact that the jacket
bulged over a high, round middle.

He smiled instinctively at the realization that the
driver was a woman, and pregnant. His father had
taught him and his brothers to revere women, and
despite what one had done to him, he appreciated
their beauty and particularly the lush curves of a
pregnancy. But he couldn't help wondering what

was wrong with the men in this woman's life that she was allowed to drive strangers around in the middle of the night.

"Sir?" She held the door open for him.

"I've got this..." he began again, when the smallest inflection in the voice stopped him cold. A velvet voice like that had once whispered to him in the middle of the night.

No. Couldn't be.

He took a step closer to the car, trying to identify the features on the driver's face, which was in shadow. The breath caught in his lungs when he finally saw them clearly—and watched Maria's mouth fall open when she recognized him.

No. This face was a figment of his imagination and too many glasses of champagne. Maria Escobar had married Emilio Castillo. She was a wealthy matron now, probably living somewhere in this neighborhood, but certainly not driving a limo at night.

The woman took a step back as he took another step closer, needing to know he was wrong. He looked into thickly lashed dark eyes with an exotic upward tilt, beneath straight, delicate brows that exaggerated the shape of her eyes. He saw a small, straight nose, cheekbones that spoke of Native Americans among her ancestors and the mobile mouth he could still feel on his bare flesh when he closed his eyes.

But his mind continued to insist, *It can't be.*

Maria had had yards of thick, glossy black hair that had tickled his nose when she snuggled against him, gotten in his way when he was working on a car and she leaned in to give him a message, shrouded his face when they made love. She'd worn it parted on the side without bangs, and was always pushing it out of her face and tucking it behind her ear.

This woman wore a cap trimmed with silver braid and imprinted with the words Lawless Limousines, but all that was visible under it was bangs. Unable to control the impulse, he took the brim of her cap between thumb and forefinger and swiped it off her head.

Black hair rained down onto her shoulders, over her breast on one side and down her back on the other. The driveway light a small distance away caught the rich strands and danced in them as they tumbled.

Lust roiled inside him with all the old intensity, then knotted itself into an also familiar misery as the expression in her eyes changed from shock to anger.

MARIA WAS SHOCKED to feel a surge of unadulterated delight at the sight of Rafe's gorgeous face.

It was somehow even more appealing with a few extra years sharpening its lines and softening his mouth. And that tuxedo! It had been impossible to hide Rafe's sex appeal under coveralls, but the formality of the tuxedo seemed to underline it, italicize it, punctuate it.

Quickly reminding herself that he'd lied to her and abandoned her to another man, she came down to earth with furious indignation. The best revenge, she thought, would be to show him how little he affected her, how well she'd done without him.

"Where to, Mr. Perez?" she asked, holding the door open and using it as a shield against all the memories that drew her toward him.

His voice was as coolly polite as hers. "Mrs. Castillo. You're as beautiful as I remember. Perhaps even more so."

That was nice to hear, even if it was just patronizing small talk to cover the awkward moment. Emilio, who had always praised her beauty before she agreed to marry him, had seldom noticed how she looked afterward. She'd become just another acquisition, like the cars and the stocks.

"And you're looking well," she replied, determined to be civilized. "How are your mother and your brothers?"

"They're fine. Tom's in California, but Rick and

Rob and I are sharing the building Mom owns in Belltown." He told her about Rob's furniture shop on the bottom floor, and that Rick and his fiancée shared the second floor.

"How are Susanna and Maggie? And wasn't Susanna pregnant when I left?"

"Uh…Maggie's great," he replied, his heightened color belying his attempt to be dispassionate. "She's five. And Susanna had a boy, T.J. He's two and half."

"Wow!" Her smile was genuine. She and Susanna had liked each other. "She must have her hands full."

He hesitated a moment, then said, "Rob has his hands full. Susanna…died."

Her eyes widened in grim disbelief. "What *happened?*"

SHE LOOKED STUNNED. The whole family had felt that way when his sister-in-law's light was taken away.

"She had a rare form of toxemia and died when T.J. was born," he explained.

"I'm so sorry," she whispered.

"Thank you." He wanted to move the conversation in another direction, unwilling to dwell on the sadness of that time. "But Rob's adjusted as well as he can, and with all of us sharing the building, it helps.''

She tossed her head, as though she, too, wanted to talk about something else.

"So, you have the upstairs?'' she asked, then added, her voice betraying a trace of the old quarrelsome Maria he remembered from the times they'd argued about his trips, "*El jefe* always gets the best—or whatever he wants.''

"If there is a chief among the four of us,'' he disputed mildly, "it'd be Tom, the oldest.''

"No. Tom's been gone as long as I've known you. You've been the one everyone turned to, the one whose opinion and approval were always so important.''

That sounded like condemnation. "You're faulting me for assuming responsibility?'' he asked.

"I'm faulting you for thinking it entitled you to have everything the way you wanted it.''

"I wanted you,'' he pointed out without raising his voice, though the gravity of the subject caused a trembling in his gut, "but now you're pregnant with someone else's baby. That sure didn't work out for me.''

"And why should it have?'' she demanded. It never took her long to lose her temper. "You took off on me over and over, and when I called you on it, you promised the trips were finished. Then

you took off again with nothing but a message on
my answering machine. Did you really think I'd
put up with that forever?''

He hadn't, of course, but two little girls had been
kidnapped by their Spanish father, and their American mother had been desperate. The job had required Rafe's command of the Spanish language,
and though he'd resigned from Angel Rescue after
Maria's ultimatum, he'd felt compelled to do this
final job.

He'd stopped by her place to tell her, but she'd
been out, so he'd tried to call her repeatedly. He'd
left the message just before he got on the plane.

''I guess if that was all the trust you had to offer,'' he replied, ''there wasn't much to hold on to
for either of us anyway.''

''Trust!'' she shouted at him. ''I know you lied
about where you were going. Why in God's name
would a woman put up with that?''

The members of Angel Rescue had agreed at the
group's formation that not even wives and sweethearts would know the nature of their work. It was
the only way to keep them safe. When it became
a threat to a member's personal life, he could opt
out and there'd be no questions asked.

''Because you knew me better than to suspect
I'd take up with another woman. You were everything to me.''

"That must be why you kept leaving me."

"You married another man the weekend I was gone. I think that says something about the depth of *your* feelings for me."

"I didn't think you'd care. You never minded that he was always coming on to me."

There was a subtle something in that remark that surprised him—and cast a slightly different light on all that had happened. Had she wanted him to be jealous?

"Men flirted with you all the time," he replied, "but you handled it very well. And Castillo was superficial and avaricious. I guess I thought you saw that. I was also convinced you loved me, so there was no cause for concern. Stupid of me, in retrospect." Really stupid.

The fight went out of her expression and tears puddled in her eyes. She gave her magnificent hair a toss and blinked them back.

"I needed someone I could trust to be there," she said, "and he promised to see that my sisters went on to school."

Rafe could have chided her for marrying for such a reason, but he knew she looked after her sisters with the same devotion he felt for his brothers.

"How are they?" he asked.

She shifted her weight, a hand resting absently on her belly. "Great," she replied with a fleeting smile. "Fernanda's doing her last year at Harvard, and Paloma got into Wellesley."

"All *right*." He was sincerely pleased. He remembered Fernanda as methodical, with a nimble brain and a wry sense of humor, and Paloma as inquisitive and persistent. They'd adored Maria. "Are they excited about the baby?"

She rubbed gently where her hand rested. "Yes, of course."

"First baby?"

"Yes."

This conversation was beginning to cause him pain. And it served no purpose; she was someone else's woman. But he had one more question.

"Why is Emilio letting you drive a limo? And at night?"

MARIO OPENED HER MOUTH to tell him it was none of his business, but his concern for her was distracting. No one had worried about her in a long time. Still, it would be foolish to indulge this explosive return of the old attraction. That part of her life was over. Now she had to deal with the decisions she'd made whcn Rafe left.

She caught her hair in both hands, gave it several efficient twists, then snatched her hat back from him. "I have to explain my time to the dispatcher, Rafe. Your mom's building was in Belltown, wasn't it? Is that where I'm taking you?"

He eyed her steadily for a moment, and it was all she could do not to squirm under his gaze. It was not condemning precisely, but silently reminded her of all she'd rejected when she'd married Emilio.

"Yes," he replied finally. "Number 10 Sandringham Drive. But I have this salmon."

"Pardon me?"

He grabbed a large plastic bag from the decorative urn at the bottom of the steps and held it up. He winced lightly and rubbed his shoulder. "We should probably put this in the trunk."

She caught a whiff of its fishy smell as he approached with the bag.

"I think you're right." She leaned into the limo and popped the trunk for him. Then she held his door open, waiting to give him the full courtesy service Lawless Limousines provided.

"Uh...*chica?*" he said after a prolonged moment, still standing by the open trunk.

She resisted the impulse to smile. She hadn't heard the old endearment in a long time.

"Yes?"

"Well...is this another old boyfriend?"

Confused by the question, she walked the long length to the back of the car and went to stand beside him. Then screamed.

Rafe quickly muffled the sound with his hand.

The scream died in her throat as she stared over

the top of his index finger at the dead man in the trunk of her limo, knitting needles protruding from a hole in the middle of his chest. He lay on his back, legs folded into the trunk in an awkward yoga position. His half-closed eyes stared at her, a permanent cynicism in his frozen expression.

Maria pulled Rafe's hand down and gripped it with hers. "John!" she breathed, shock almost paralyzing her.

"So, you *did* know him?" Rafe asked.

"He's my boss," she whispered in reply. "John Lawless."

"I presume you didn't do this?"

She flung his hand away, annoyed out of her shock. "Of course I didn't do this! He was my boss. I liked him!"

"Then we'll call the police." He'd been pulling out his cell phone as he talked, but she snatched it from him.

"We can't do that," she said, a terrible, dreadful fear overtaking her as she stared at the body. Unconsciously, she rubbed her belly.

"Why not?" he asked.

She pointed an index finger at John and replied in a strangled voice, "Because those are my knitting needles."

CHAPTER FOUR

RAFE NARROWED his eyes at her, feeling a little as though he was trapped in a surreal film. "What do you mean, *your* needles?"

"I mean they belong to me!" she snapped back, her lips trembling. She put both hands over her mouth and groaned. Then she lowered them and pointed again to the needles and the small collection of pink stitches at the end of one needle. Someone had cut off the skein of yarn. "That's the beginning of my baby afghan."

He couldn't believe it. And to think that just ten minutes ago, what to do with the salmon had seemed like a big problem.

They heard voices from the direction of the house as someone opened the door.

"Okay, that's it," he said decisively. He removed the handkerchief from his breast pocket and used it to close the trunk. Grabbing Maria's arm, he hurried her around to the passenger side.

"What are you doing?" she asked when he hustled her inside and handed her the seat belt.

Quickly shutting the door, he ran around to the driver's side, closed the door she'd opened for him, then remembered the salmon. He retrieved it, tossed it into the back, then slipped in behind the wheel, the shock of his discovery in the trunk having a strong, sobering effect on him. He turned the key in the ignition.

"We're getting out of here," he said, heading down the long driveway. "Then we can talk about what to do."

"I can't believe it." Her voice was cracking. "I talked to him just this afternoon before I came on."

"Are the limousines dispatched from his home?"

"No. We have an office on First Avenue. He left me a message this morning, but I haven't been able to reach him all day."

"He wasn't there when you arrived for work?"

"No," she replied. "Just Charlie."

"Who's he?"

"Charlie's a she. Charlene Goodman. Middle thirties. She runs the office in the afternoons and dispatches from her home at night. She said he was meeting with a client, and had blocked off the next few days from his work calendar."

"Who was he meeting?"

"I don't know."

"Could it have been one of the other employees?'' he asked, turning onto a quiet road leading in the general direction of downtown. ''There's always somebody mad at the boss wherever you work.''

''No,'' she said earnestly. ''There are only three other drivers besides me, and everybody liked him. Joanne Collier was fooling around with him, but she adores him. She'd never hurt him.''

''What about the other two?''

''No, they're fine with him.'' She leaned forward, looking uncomfortable, then opened her window and drew a deep breath. ''Sonny Gilette's a struggling novelist always short of money. He resents the fact that I make better tips than he does, but he never blamed John for that. And Keith Shaw fancies himself a ladies' man and is always trying to date Joanne and me. John warned him about sexual harassment, but I don't think that would have led Keith to murder him.''

''This guy didn't care that you were married?''

It was a logical question, so he was confused when it seemed to startle her, then made her look away.

''I'm widowed,'' she replied. Then she asked in a strained voice, ''Could we pull over? I think I'm going to be sick.''

He took the nearest turn into the parking lot of a small strip mall that boasted a gas station, a coffee shop and a few other stores. She moved quickly out of the car and into the bushes. He stared after her a moment, shocked by that announcement. Then he ducked into the coffee shop for a glass of soda and a couple of napkins. His hands full, he let the obliging waitress drop the change into the pocket of his tux.

Maria pulled her hat off as she came back to the car, looking pale and big-eyed.

He offered her the plastic cup and the napkins. She took a sip of the drink, then pressed the napkin to her trembling lips.

"A widow?" he asked gently, opening her door so she could sit down. He leaned on the side of the car near her.

"Emilio died about five months ago," she said with a sigh. "Stress contributed, I think. Things had been going badly for him. You know what the twin towers tragedy did to tourism—even locally. The hotel bookings were down forty percent, he was feuding with his business partners and his tech stocks bottomed out. He died instantly from a brain aneurysm that burst."

"I'm sorry," he said, suppressing a need to say that if he had died on her, he'd have left her better provided for. Instead, he asked quietly, "Is that why you're driving a limo?"

"He had no insurance," she replied, taking deep

breaths. "Most of his assets went to pay off business debts, and I sold the house to keep the girls in school."

"What about the classic cars?"

"He'd used them as collateral on a loan. The bank took them."

"Geez."

"Yeah. Well, I'm fine. I've got a nice apartment, a good job housekeeping at a church and driving helps pay for a few extras. The girls both have jobs at school, but they're always needing something." She stood up suddenly in alarm as a police car, red light flashing, pulled up behind them. "Oh, God," she whispered. "Could somebody know already?"

"No," he said firmly. "Just keep quiet and act pregnant."

"What?"

"Try to look more helpless," he encouraged, then went forward to greet the officer.

"Sir," the officer said, looking from Rafe to Maria, then giving the limo a once-over. "You the driver?"

Rafe shook his head and pointed to Maria. "I'm the passenger. The young lady here is driving. Why? Is there a problem?"

He said something into the crackling radio attached to the shoulder of his jacket, then returned his attention to Rafe. "We got a call that a limo with this license plate was driving erratically."

He saw Maria's frown of confusion. She hadn't been driving erratically when she picked him up, and he'd been very careful not to draw anyone's attention when he'd driven away from Stanton's home after they'd discovered the body.

He wondered idly if whoever had put the body in the trunk had then called the police with that report in the hope the officer would search the car and the trunk for alcohol or drugs and discover the body.

A way out came to him.

"She did get a little erratic, Officer," he said. "She'd just picked me up at Senator Stanton's and began to complain about not feeling well. You can see she's very pregnant. I was trying to convince her to let me take her to the hospital."

He congratulated himself on carrying the story off with just the right suggestion of impending danger to a pregnant woman and her baby, as well as the implication of his own importance—however false—by mentioning the senator's party.

The officer, a true practitioner of the "protect and serve" principle, told Maria that he would provide her with an escort to the hospital. He even offered to take her in the patrol car.

"I'll drive the limo, Officer," Rafe volunteered, "if you'll lead the way."

Maria was on the brink of hyperventilation by the time Rafe had her buckled into the passenger seat. As they followed the officer, Rafe put a hand to Maria's knee. "Stay calm," he advised. "He doesn't suspect a thing. But he will if you look as though you're about to have a stroke. And remember that you're breathing for the baby, too. You get short of breath, it'll be short of breath. And you don't want that."

Maria leaned against the back of the seat and closed her eyes, apparently willing to take him at his word. He wasn't sure about the truth of all he'd said, but it sounded reasonable.

"It's not an it," she corrected. "It's a she."

Trying to distract her from her panic, he asked, "You know it's a girl?"

She seemed to be concentrating on dragging in air and expelling it calmly. "Yes."

"Ultrasound?"

"Intuition."

He laughed lightly and glanced at her. "I wouldn't trust your intuition, *chica*. It was wrong about me."

"Rafe…"

"You've probably got twin boys in there."

"No, my doctor told me it's just one baby," she

corrected. "It just *feels* like twins. Even triplets sometimes."

"What makes you think it's a girl?" he asked, glancing her way.

She smiled. "She kicks when I go shopping. And when I cook."

He liked seeing her with a smile, and tried to inspire another one. "I'm a guy, and I like to cook."

She made a scornful sound. "Adding jalapenos to canned chili isn't cooking, Rafe."

"I thought you liked my chili."

"When you're in love," she replied, "there's no accounting for taste. The officer's turning."

"Remember to stay calm," he advised as he followed the patrol car across the highway and onto the drive that led to Queen City Hospital. "If they have to admit you for a galloping pulse or sky-high blood pressure, I'm not baby-sitting the corpse until you're released."

MARIA WAS WISHED good luck by the police officer, then greeted immediately by a nurse who smilingly assured her not to worry, that she would be fine. She couldn't help but wonder if the woman would change her tune if she showed her the contents of the limo's trunk.

Apparently reading her mind, Rafe warned her

with a look as the nurse frowned over her blood pressure, then decided to take it again to be sure.

The obstetrician, a middle-aged man with a growly disposition, checked her over and ordered a series of tests. By the time she was returned to the room where Rafe waited, Maria was happy to see him.

When he pushed a stool over beside the bed so he could hold her hand, she didn't resist.

"How're you doing?" he asked, smoothing several strands of hair out of her face.

"Fine," she replied, her voice a little high, "for a woman who's knitting a body."

Rafe shushed her. "This place is full of nurses and doctors trained to listen for the smallest sign of distress. Now, come on. I need you to give this some serious thought. I've been thinking about it while waiting for you, and I figure someone set you up tonight, probably called 9-1-1 and gave them your license plate and said you were driving erratically so the police would stop you and check the car—and then the trunk."

"That's crazy!" she whispered harshly. "I don't know anyone who'd do that to me. And I can't imagine it's the result of jealousy over tips, or hurt feelings because of rejected dates."

"But it's happening," he insisted.

The terse obstetrician let himself into the room,

smiling for the first time since he'd arrived. "Good news, Maria," he said, slapping a hand on top of a folder he held. "You're in perfect health, and so is your daughter."

Maria was surprised by his revelation. Hospital staff were usually very careful about revealing gender on the chance the parents didn't want to know. But her surprise was followed instantly by elation that she'd been right. She smiled at Rafe in victory.

He acknowledged her superior intuition with a congratulatory grin.

The doctor noted her expression and asked in alarm, "You didn't know? You didn't want to know?"

She assured him quickly that she'd known all along. She just hadn't had medical confirmation.

"Can't explain what made you so ill," the doctor went on, apparently relieved, "except that it was probably intestinal rather than anything to do with your pregnancy. I'm sure you already know that indigestion's very common, though it's not usually accompanied by vomiting. I'd say be a little more careful what you eat. Avoid fried foods, sandwich meats, chocolate, coffee, alcohol. Sleep with your head elevated six inches, and above all, try to relax." Maria couldn't help the glance in Rafe's direction at that. He kept a straight face, but his eyes warned her to keep it together.

The doctor turned to Rafe, assuming he was her husband. "If she has any trouble at all, bring her back, or call your doctor."

Rafe thanked the doctor and shook hands with him as he left the room.

She swung her legs over the side of the bed and eyed him with a wry smile. "I might be able to relax if you promise to take the rap when I'm arrested."

"You're not going to be picked up," he said, going to the chair over which she'd thrown her clothes. "Here, get dressed."

She hugged the clothes to her, but didn't put them on. "If I get dressed," she said softly, "I'll have to leave here. And I'll have to get in the limo." She hated to say the words, but they were the truth. "And I have no idea what to do."

"You're coming home with me," he said, picking her shoes up off the floor and dropping them in front of her, "so you can get some sleep and we can decide how to handle this."

She liked that idea. The last thing in the world she wanted at this moment was to be alone. But she also wasn't sure she could bear being with him. It made her want things she couldn't have; made her long all over again for the life she was just beginning to accept would never be hers.

"No," she said, reaching behind her to untie the

hospital gown. "I'll take you home, then I'll work out my own problems. I'm sure you'll be off again soon anyway, and you don't need to be involved...."

"Whoever plotted this is clever," he said reasonably, "and obviously ruthless. It was a good plan to get rid of the boss and you in the bargain, by blaming you for his death. But so far, it hasn't worked. My guess is, you're in danger."

"I can take care of myself," she insisted. Then, holding the now loose gown against her, she asked stiffly, "Would you please turn around?"

"Are you serious?" His voice held disbelief.

"Yes, I'm serious," she retorted. "The fact that you've seen me naked a hundred times doesn't qualify you to see me naked now. Your rights as a lover ended when you walked out on me."

"God!" he grumbled under his breath. He turned around and faced a poster-size, month-by-month pregnancy chart. "I meant, are you serious about taking care of yourself? You can't run or bend and you barely fit behind the wheel of a car. Maybe you can still take care of yourself, but can you protect your baby?"

WHEN SHE DIDN'T ANSWER, Rafe finally turned to see her in a lacy black bra, her slacks on, but the jacket still in her hand. She looked genuinely concerned.

He took the jacket from her and held it open. "It doesn't mean you've conceded anything to me," he said briskly, "just that you need a place to stay and someone to help you figure out what to do. And just so you don't think I'm trying to get you back, I'll remind you that I didn't walk out on you, you got married on me."

With a disgusted roll of her eyes, she buttoned her jacket and looked around for her shoes.

He pointed to them, right at her feet.

She grabbed his arm to steady herself as she slipped into them. But apparently that wasn't working very well, so he pushed her lightly onto the edge of the bed and squatted down to ease them on for her.

"Thank you," she said. Then she stood again and added grudgingly, "I appreciate your offer of help, but you're sure you want to get involved?"

He spread his arms. "Seems I already am. I just lied to a cop. Come on."

CHAPTER FIVE

RAFE TOOK HER HOME to his apartment. While she looked doubtfully at the only one of three bedrooms that had furniture, he dug in the linen closet for clean sheets and a blanket and pillow. He had to keep moving. It was somehow unsettling to have her where he'd always wanted her.

Except that in his dreams they'd been in a house in a quiet little town somewhere on the Oregon coast. The yard sloped down to the beach, and behind the house there was a woods of fir and cedar. When he was off on one of his rescue missions, he used to imagine Maria planting flowers in the garden with a couple of children helping her. But he'd always seen boys, not girls.

Still, he was nothing if not adaptable.

Over Maria's protests, he ripped the bedding off the old four-poster Rick had found for him at a garage sale when the doctor told him he'd have to lie low for a while after his shoulder surgery. He made up the bed with the fresh sheets and pillow, then spread the coverlet over it again.

Maria stood in the doorway as though afraid to walk in. "You don't have to fuss for me," she said.

"It's just clean sheets." He wadded up the old bedding, put the sheets in the hallway hamper, then carried the blanket and pillow to the sofa. "I'll sleep out here. Want me to throw your uniform in the wash for tomorrow?"

She looked down at the rumpled, stained suit with a wry twist of her lips. "If you don't, I'm going to look like a refugee from a military school or some old operetta. But please don't put it in the dryer. Just hang it up to dry."

That made him smile. "I probably have some sweats you can borrow."

She nodded noncommittally. Rafe was sure that for a woman who'd always been very interested in fashion, wearing men's sweats was not an exciting prospect.

He went to the closet and dug out a robe he'd been given by the grateful owner of the Casa Guadalajara Hotel in Mexico. He and his group had rescued a nun and a busload of children from a band of revolutionaries. One of the children had been the owner's son.

"You can sleep in this," he said, handing her the thick, midnight blue belted robe with the hotel insignia stitched in gold.

"Did you go to Guadalajara?" she asked interestedly, touching a fingertip to the stitching.

He nodded. "On business." She didn't have to know it had been rescue business. "I've been with an engineering company that works all over the globe."

She smiled wearily. "Still can't stay put?"

When he ignored that, she asked, "What brought you home?"

He flexed his shoulder. "Got hurt building a bridge in Venezuela." That was true. Getting shot was getting hurt.

She frowned. "It must have been serious if they sent you home."

"It was a rotator cuff injury." He flexed his arm again a little more broadly to show that he'd made progress. "I'm doing well. The doctor says a few more weeks of therapy and he can release me."

If only *she* would release him just as quickly. He wanted her with a desperation that was mounting rapidly.

"How nice for you," she said coolly, apparently reminded that all his trips had separated them. That did a lot to quell his ardor. "Well. Thank you." She held the robe against her and asked with renewed gravity, "What are we going to do about the limo?"

"I'll work on that overnight," he said, pulling

the door closed as he left the room. "Don't worry about it. Try to get some sleep. I'll have a plan by morning."

She walked to the door, holding it open as he prepared to shut it completely. "I don't understand," she said softly, "why you're so willing to help me."

He arched an eyebrow. "You mean because I once loved you desperately and you walked out on me?"

With a sigh, she thunked her forehead against the door. "I don't think I can argue that one more time tonight."

"Then stop trying to understand it," he said briskly. "If it wasn't clear to you then, I guess I can't expect it to be clear to you now. Good night."

The door closed softly behind him as he went to put her uniform in the washer.

At about 2:00 a.m. Rafe realized he couldn't remember a night that had been worse than this one. The sofa was lumpy, his shoulder throbbed and his rioting libido was having great difficulty with the fact that the luscious love of his life was only yards away—and in his bed.

Well. Maybe that night outside Kabul had been this bad. He'd shared digs with a flea-infested camel and two companions who'd eaten bad chicken and retched all night. And his heartache over Maria had been only several months old. It had still clung to his back like something with talons and made every breath a misery.

He'd adjusted since then. He'd learned to live without her. He'd learned to stop wanting her, stop remembering her, stop dreaming about her. He'd accepted that she belonged to another man and that he had to make his life without her.

But now that she was in the next room and he knew that Emilio was gone, he longed for her all over again. The old intensity was back full force.

But Maria didn't understand why he was willing to help her.

Apparently nothing in that regard had changed. She had no comprehension of the depth of his feelings, and he couldn't imagine being able to freely give his love again to a woman who didn't trust those feelings.

He turned onto his side, groaned when his shoulder hurt, then turned to the other side. It occurred to him with a sort of fatalistic amusement that "giving his love" was a ridiculous expression anyway.

When she looked at him with those fear-filled velvet eyes, it was as though the feelings were torn from him by the roots.

MARIA AWOKE to a strangely familiar combination of sounds. Water faucet, cupboard doors, cutlery. But then she heard the low rumble of male voices. She looked around, vaguely disoriented. Soft blue room filled with sunlight and sturdy, mismatched furniture.

Not her bedroom.

She glanced down at the big blue robe she wore, sleeves cuffed back several times.

Not her robe.

She heard the unmistakable sound of Rafe's voice, though she couldn't distinguish the words. Old yearning swelled inside her, and for an instant she thought she was back with him, and all the intervening years had been a dream. Then her hand fell to the roundness of her pregnancy under the strained belt of the robe and she had to remind herself of the truth with a demoralizing return to reality.

Not her man.

Was she hearing Rafe's brothers? she wondered. A warm affection rose in her despite the sudden memory of all that had happened last night. She swung her legs out of bed, smoothed the oversize robe, found a comb in the bathroom and ran it through her hair.

Then she followed the sound of the voices to a

bright yellow kitchen where Rafe and his brothers sat around a table drinking coffee.

Rick, who sat by the door, rose at the sight of her and came to her, smile wide, arms open. "Maria," he said as his arms closed around her. "I can't believe you're here. You came back to me, didn't you?" he asked gravely. "Wouldn't you know it. Now that I'm about to be married."

She leaned back to look into his handsome face. All the Perez brothers were handsome, but this one had a face that was perfect. And a visible sweetness rather than the tough cynicism she saw in Rafe.

"I suppose calling it off is out of the question?" she asked, feigning disappointment.

He nodded regretfully. "She's helpless without me."

Rob took Maria from him and wrapped her in his own embrace. This brother was the steady one, the craftsman.

"Hi, sweetheart," he said. "God, it's good to see you. Just ignore Rick. He hasn't matured at all since you…" He was about to say "left," but she leaned away from him to threaten him with a look. "Since you knew him," he amended quickly. "He's the one who'd be helpless without Frankie. I, however, always thought I was the brother you were really meant for."

She hugged him fiercely, then slapped his chest. "Yeah, right. That must be why you were so in love with Susanna." Then realizing what she'd said, she hugged him again. "Rafe told me what happened. I'm sorry."

He shrugged, the sign of acceptance contradicted by the pain visible in his eyes. "We're doing all right." He smiled suddenly. "I have two beautiful children."

"Yes, Rafe told me that, too. That's wonderful, Rob."

Rick pulled a chair out for her and Rob went for the coffeepot and poured her a cup. Rafe took a covered plate out of the oven and put it in front of her. On it was a chorizo omelette and hash browns mixed with jalapenos and cheese—her favorite breakfast.

She had a sudden flash of years ago when she'd been a part of Rafe's life. They'd never lived together, but they'd been involved in each other's families, often sharing riotous parties or picnics by the lake. Her youngest sister had had a terrible crush on Rick.

"Rafe says Fernanda and Paloma are in college." Rick passed her the knife and fork Rafe handed him.

She nodded, inhaling the deliciously rich aromas

of her breakfast. "They've grown up to be very smart and very beautiful."

Rob held his wallet open to show her photos of his children. "Maggie," he said, pointing to an angelic-looking little girl, "and T.J.," a toddler with the devil in his eye.

"Talk about beautiful," she said. "Where are they?"

"Frankie took them to the Children's Museum today, then to visit her parents overnight. They'll be home tomorrow afternoon."

Rafe came to sit opposite her with his coffee, and a sudden tension invaded the easy camaraderie she felt with his brothers. Rick and Rob, too, seemed to sober.

When she'd gone to bed last night, Rafe had said he'd have a plan by morning. His brothers, she guessed, were his consultants.

"You're going to stay downstairs with Rob," he said without preamble, "while I drive the limo to some remote spot so that the police can just discover it out there. Rick will follow me in his car."

She didn't know if that was a good or a bad idea. "What if you get caught?" she asked worriedly.

"Why would I get caught? There's nothing on the morning news about your boss being missing.

It'll just be a limo on its mysterious way some-where.''

"So was I last night, but whoever did this called 9-1-1 to report me driving erratically, remember?''

He nodded patiently. "That's because he knew where you'd be last night. Today, he's not only lost track of the body, but of you, too.''

"So, it has to be someone at the limo service,'' Rob concluded. "Who else would know where she was last night?''

"That's my thought,'' Rafe said.

"I should call the rectory,'' she said, glancing at the clock. "Father will be won—''

"No!'' Rafe shouted, then when she started, he rejected more quietly. "No. Don't call anyone. What if the limo service calls the rectory to find out where you are, or if they've heard from you? Stay away from the phone. Just stay inside with Rob while we're gone.''

"Maria can help me sand spindles.'' Rob grinned at her. "You'd like that, wouldn't you?'' She'd done it for him in the old days because her small fingers could easily fit into the grooves.

Maria punched him playfully. "I was bemoan-ing the fact the other day that I just don't get to sand spindles anymore.''

RAFE ENVIED his brothers' easy relationship with Maria. Of course, all they remembered was that she'd been beautiful and warm and fun to be with. She hadn't broken their hearts, ruined their lives.

He pushed away from the table.

Rick raised a questioning eyebrow.

"I have to find her something to wear," he said. "All Maria has is the uniform she had on last night."

She looked up worriedly. "Did it survive your washer?"

"Yeah." Rafe pushed his chair in. "But you said not to put it in the dryer so I hung it up in the bathroom. It still isn't dry." He topped up everyone's coffee, then went in search of the sweats he wore to physical therapy. His mother had bought him several sets when he'd grumbled about having to go for the sessions.

"You can at least look nice when you go." She'd waggled her eyebrows at him. "Maybe catch the eye of a pretty therapist."

Rafe's therapist was six foot four and answered to the name Rip. A kind and conscientious gentleman, but not one to be impressed with Rafe's co-ordinated sweat suits.

He found a beige set that was particularly soft inside, then searched for an old white shirt he seldom wore, and a couple of pairs of socks. They should fit just fine in the black walking shoes Maria wore with her uniform.

She was standing in the bedroom doorway when he tossed the socks at the stack of clothes on the bed and pushed the drawer closed with his knee.

"Good breakfast," she said. "Thank you."

"Sure." He'd remembered that she used to love chorizo omelettes, and since he cooked for himself a lot, he'd had all the ingredients. He pointed to the bed. "See if those things will work. If not, I'll try to find something else."

She snatched up the sweat bottoms, put her fingers in the waist and pulled as far as she was able. "I think these will go around me. And I can cuff the bottoms." She looked up at him with a grateful smile. "Thank you. Not just for the clothes, but for everything you've done."

Mercifully, she didn't add, "when it really wasn't any of your concern."

"Sure." He headed for the door. "Rick and I are taking off. Rob will wait for you and take you downstairs with him. Just stay there until I get back."

"Okay. Please be careful."

"Careful's my middle name."

She grinned. "No, it isn't. It's Pablo."

"Funny." He responded to her joke with a roll of his eyes and a grudging smile, then left the room.

CHAPTER SIX

AFTER STUDYING her reflection in the full-length mirror on the closet door, Maria cuffed the sweatpants several times to give them a sort of harem look. She topped the pants with the white shirt, also cuffed, its stiff collar sitting primly. It lent a weirdly businesslike air to the whole thing. She looked a little like a CEO doing the Dance of the Seven Veils. But she was dressed, and there was something curiously thrilling about knowing these clothes had touched Rafe's skin.

Impatient with herself for entertaining such thoughts when her boss lay dead in the trunk of her car and her whole world was probably about to fall apart—again—and possibly Rafe's as well, she braided her hair into one long rope, tied it off with a hair clip and went to join Rob.

His workshop was a large square room with tools and supplies hanging from the pegboard walls. Pieces of furniture in various stages of construction were scattered around the room. A workbench with drawers occupied the length of one wall, and the scent of cedar perfumed the room.

"My goodness," she said in amazement. "Your business must have grown since the last time I saw you."

"It has," he confirmed, then pointed to a power cord in her path. "Watch your step, Maria. Wouldn't want you to fall on this concrete floor."

"Right." She stopped where she stood, looking around her in fascination. "Thank you. I just can't believe what you've done." She went to a rocker in a corner. "Safe to sit on?"

He flipped a switch, and an overhead light brightened that corner. "Of course."

She sat in the Bentwood rocker and leaned her head against the high back. With a foot braced on the ground, she rocked herself gently back and forth, closing her eyes. "Oh, my," she said with a little groan of pleasure. "This is so comfortable." She patted her stomach and smiled. "The baby likes it, too, I think. She's settling down."

Rob laughed softly. "I can see you're going to be a lot of help this morning."

Eyes still closed, she held up her index finger in a wait-a-minute gesture. "I'll sand for you in a minute, I promise. Just let me absorb this quiet moment." She rocked several more times then reluctantly opened her eyes and smiled wryly at him.

"In case I get arrested for murder and need to go to a quiet place in my memory to survive incarceration."

"You know Rafe won't let that happen." Rob went around the room, checking the status of various projects.

"I appreciate his help," she admitted, "even though I don't entirely understand it. But I don't see how he can help me, short of taking the blame himself."

She tried to push herself out of the chair, but found it difficult with the rocking motion. Rob came to offer her a hand and indicated a stationary chair in the slatted Mission style.

"Wait." He went to the stool at the workbench, took a pillow from atop it and dropped it onto the chair. "There. Now are you ready to make yourself useful?"

"Yes. Bring it on."

He placed a ragged towel across her lap to protect her clothing, such as it was, and handed her a spindle and a piece of sandpaper. Even in the old days, he'd never used power tools on his spindles, considered some of the most graceful in the business.

"What's to understand?" he asked as he studied a piece of wood on his workbench. "He loves you. He's always loved you."

"He left me," she reminded him, "after he'd promised to stop traveling." She glanced up at him while she worked, something comforting in the old familiar feel of the turned wood in her hands. "I just can't believe there were classic car emergencies all over the globe that required his expertise."

Rob looked up at her to smile, then turned away—almost as though afraid she'd read something in his face he was trying to withhold.

"What?" she asked.

"Nothing." He placed the length of wood in a vice, turning knobs to stabilize it.

"Rob."

"Maria." When he finally looked up at her, his gaze was measured. "He wasn't traveling on business. At least not on automotive business."

The curious look in his eye suggested he was assessing the wisdom of telling her what he knew.

She sat up a little straighter, baby and all. "Then…what was he doing?"

Rob hesitated, frowning. "You're sure you want to know? I mean, it'll change things between you, and if you prefer that things stay as they are—the two of you going your own way—you might not want to touch this."

She was both intrigued and annoyed. "If telling me the truth would have saved our relationship, why wouldn't he have told me himself? And why did he tell you and not me?''

Rob came around the workbench and leaned back against it. ''I think he intended to tell you when he came back from Spain, but you'd run off with Emilio. And,'' he added with a small grin, ''it's seldom that I get anything on him, but he didn't tell me. He doesn't know that Rick and I know.''

She wanted to shout that none of it was her fault, but that would have been counterproductive to finally learning the answer to Rafe's disappearances—trips so mysterious that he hadn't even told his brothers the truth.

''Where was he going?'' she demanded.

''He's part of a group formed during the Gulf War. A bunch of ex-Marines with the fighting skills to locate and rescue children kidnapped and taken overseas, usually by a parent or family member. The fact Rafe speaks Spanish makes him valuable.''

Maria stared at him in openmouthed disbelief. ''What?'' she finally whispered. Emotions were crowding in on her—guilt, shock, guilt, regret, guilt…

''That's why he went to Spain when you were on that shopping trip with your sisters. An American mother had pleaded with them for help be-

cause her husband was about to move into the
Pyrenees with their girls, then they'd have never
been found. He couldn't wait for you to come back
to explain.''

Nausea rolled in Maria's stomach. He'd been
rescuing children!

''Apparently the group made a pact to tell no
one what they were doing,'' Rob went on, ''not
even wives and sweethearts. They figured that
would protect them from possible coercion or re-
taliation.''

The nausea became a knife. Rafe even had a
noble reason for keeping the secret.

''How did you find out?'' she asked, her voice
raspy.

''That weekend you and he went camping in the
North Cascades, remember? Your no-radios, no-
phones, nothing-but-each-other weekend?''

She remembered that clearly. She'd been worried about their relationship, and he'd taken her
camping so they could talk.

''Well, when they couldn't reach Rafe, they sent
a new member of the team to find him while the
pros got ready. The rookie had never seen Rafe,
and when he came here and found me, he pre-
sumed I was Rafe. He started telling me about how
I had to get packed, there was this important mission in Chechnya. He must have seen in my face

that I hadn't a clue what he was talking about, and he went pale. I swore myself to secrecy. Rick had to do the same because he'd been in the kitchen and heard everything." He shook his head at the memory. "The poor kid who came to get Rafe was horrified by his blunder. I told him his secret was safe with us, but that they'd have to handle this mission without Rafe because he was out of touch."

Maria could only gasp, "I can't believe it. And he doesn't know you know?"

"We never told him. Since he sold the garage, he's been working overseas full-time. By all appearances, he and his group are engineers helping to build water treatment plants, sewage treatment plants, bridges, roads. They developed this bond during the war when they took it upon themselves to go into Basra to reclaim the child of one of their translators. Her husband apparently scorned her western ways, kidnapped their daughter and took her to his family. The guys performed so efficiently and without detection that word got around and they were offered other jobs. After the war, they stayed connected for that purpose. So we just let him keep his secret. God knows he's helped us often enough." He folded his arms, his eyes staring, unfocused. "When Susanna died, he came home for a couple of months to help me with the kids. Mom would have taken over out of the goodness of her heart, but I didn't want that. So he came home to help me in the shop, to stay with the kids so I could get out once in a while. Sometimes we left the kids with Mom and took off together. He listened to me talk, didn't press me when I wanted to be quiet. And when I felt I was back on track, he started working overseas again.

"Rick's got stories, too," he went on, crossing his feet at the ankles. "Rafe encouraged him with his acting career, even though he teases Rick about it all the time. Rick was about to give up at one point because he was tired of the endless rejection and having to live near the poverty level. But Rafe told him he was sure he was going to make it, that he had to keep trying, and he gave him a loan to keep him going."

After the shock wore off, Maria became even more furious than she'd been before. It would have been so easy for Rafe to tell her the truth! Despite the group's pact, he had to know she'd have kept any secret for him. And she couldn't believe he'd let his work wedge a rift between them, when he could have set things right so easily.

Rob studied her mutinous expression and smiled thinly. "I shared this to convince you that he's not the rat you believe him to be."

"He should have told me."

"He was trying to keep you safe."

She would have disputed that, but Rob wasn't the one she had to have this out with. She drew a steadying breath. "Thank you for telling me. I appreciate it."

"Sure." He straightened away from the bench and pointed with a grin to the spindle she was sanding. "Careful with that. I want balusters, not toothpicks."

Maria looked down at the spindle in her lap. Its beautiful curvature had almost been flattened by her frantic sanding. She glanced at Rob apologetically. "Sorry. I'll be more careful."

"Relax," he advised. "Hostility's not good for the baby."

"IT'S GREAT to see the two of you together," Rick said as he drove home, "even under these circumstances." They'd left the limo in the woods at Snoqualmie Pass. The limo would be found, Rafe knew, but he was hoping that by then, he'd be able to figure out who'd killed John Lawless and tried to frame Maria for it.

"We're not 'together,'" Rafe insisted, distracted by old images of Maria in his arms. "We're just sharing the same space for a short time. She was never able to completely give me her trust, and I won't live without it."

Rick made a scornful sound and sent him a critical glance. "You mean like the kind of trust you've shown Rob and me by telling us you're spending your time on engineering projects all over the world?"

Hell. He knew. Or did he? Maybe he was just fishing. Rafe could only call his bluff. "I am spending my time on engineering..."

"Oh, please," Rick interrupted. "We know about the rescue team, so you can stop lying about it."

Well, damn it. "I didn't lie," Rafe insisted. "I just didn't tell you. It's a very secret..."

"I know, I know," Rick interrupted again. "We've known for a few years. One of your group came looking for you that weekend you and Maria went to the North Cascades. I think his name was Baker. He was new to the group then, and had never seen you. He mistook Rob for you and started talking about the mission. We promised to keep his secret."

Rafe was both surprised and annoyed that they'd done such a good job of it. He and his brothers were usually so entangled in each other's lives. It had probably helped that he'd been working overseas full-time since Maria married Emilio.

"Does Mom know?" he asked, then realized it

was a stupid question. If she did know, she'd have made him pay for keeping the secret.

"No," Rick replied. "We didn't want to scare her. And we knew she'd make your life miserable for not telling her."

"Well, thanks for that."

"Sure. But don't you think you should have told Maria?"

"The reason I didn't was for her own safety."

There was a moment's hesitation, then Rick asked quietly, "You sure?"

"What does that mean?" Rafe demanded, turning in his seat to give Rick the full benefit of his annoyance.

"It means you should examine your reasons." Rick spared him a glance that told him he wasn't intimidated. "I think when Tom moved away, you got used to being in charge. You had advice and a helping hand for everybody, but nobody could figure out what you needed. Nobody was allowed to try to help you. Until Maria."

"You're crazy."

"She's always been as smart and as strong as you are, and I don't think you liked that. You wanted her to need you. But she knew what she was doing and could have gotten along just fine without you. Though she did seem to love you—

God only knows why. I figure keeping your secret was a way for you to maintain the upper hand.''

　　''If you weren't doing seventy on the freeway,'' Rafe said darkly, ''I'd deck you for that.''

　　''If I wasn't doing seventy on the freeway,'' Rick replied, ''I'd let you try.''

CHAPTER SEVEN

RAFE WAS NOT in a good mood when he arrived home. He was a little sharp when he answered Rob's questions about where and how they'd stashed the limo, then asked him if there'd been anything on the news about John Lawless.

Rob shook his head. "We haven't heard anything."

Maria sat in a chair sanding spindles, just as she'd done for Rob on weekends in the old days when they'd hung out with him and Susanna. For a moment, it was as though the intervening years hadn't happened, and he felt a sense of relief, a soothing second chance.

Then she raised her eyes to look into his, and he knew without anyone saying a word that Rob had told her what he and Rick knew about Rafe's real work abroad.

He turned to Rick, then Rob. "Did you guys wake up this morning and *decide* to make me miserable?"

"You've always been miserable," Rick quipped.

Rob, standing beside Rick, backhanded him in the gut. "Shut up, Rick." He spoke directly to Rafe. "We decided it wasn't fair that she didn't know. And it was time you knew that *we* could be trusted, too."

Maria put the spindle on the table beside her and laboriously pushed herself out of the chair.

Rafe offered her a hand, and she took it until she was upright, then quickly drew it away with a stiff "Thank you." But their hands were in contact long enough for him to feel her anger.

He met her hostile gaze. "You coming with me, or you want to stay and have lunch with Judas and Benedict Arnold?"

"I'm coming with you," she said, while her eyes added, *And I'm going to make you sorry you ever met me.*

She kissed Rob on the cheek. "Thank you for a mostly nice morning," she said, then caught Rick's hand and squeezed it. "See you two later."

Rafe followed her out, but turned at the door to glance back at his brothers and silently promise retribution. Maria headed for the stairs.

"Wouldn't the elevator be easier?" he asked, swearing she looked bigger today than she had yesterday. In view of her mood, he didn't feel particularly solicitous at the moment, but then he didn't want to have to deliver a premature baby, either.

"I have to keep in shape," she said, starting determinedly up the steps. "And maybe if I work off some steam, I'll only be guilty of maiming you rather than murdering you."

"Not funny," he observed, "since some might consider it a repeat offense."

She ignored him and kept going, slowing considerably between the second and third floor. He had to take her hand and haul her up the last five or six steps. He unlocked the door and led the way through the small vestibule to the apartment. Maria marched through the open door, her chin in the air, and Rafe had to suppress a smile. Her affronted dignity was a little comical, given her girth.

In the middle of the living room she stopped to confront him.

"I can't believe you let me *go*," she said, shrieking the last word, "rather than tell me the truth about what you were doing?"

"The group has a pact," he replied evenly. Maria had always hated it when she became angry during an argument and he refused to lose his control. "We tell no one. That way if someone tries to get at us through you, it can't be done."

She waddled toward him and glared at him pugnaciously. "If that was true, you could have told me what you were doing without telling me where or for whom. My God. Fighter pilots tell their wives what they do!''

"That's only because they have to explain away the jumpsuits.''

The color in her cheeks brightened. "I find out that you ruined both our lives for absolutely no reason, and you make jokes?''

"*You* ruined both our lives,'' he corrected. "I just went to rescue a couple of little girls from their father.''

She slapped his chest with an open hand, her fury getting the better of her. "Don't you dare hide behind that! You get to look all noble and persecuted, and I come off as the heavy!''

His eyes ran over her bulbous stomach and she pointed a warning finger at him. "If you dare make a joke…''

"I didn't say a word.''

"You could have told me you had…'' She groped for words she might have believed had he tried to explain. "That it was secret…government…''

"It isn't government.''

"Important…military…''

"It isn't military.''

Impatient with her inability to make her point, she shrieked at him. "Something! Anything! At least I wouldn't have thought you had another woman!''

''If you'd loved and trusted me,'' he retorted loudly, ''you'd have never thought that.''

''And how would *you* trust someone who lies to you?''

''I guess the same way you trust someone who can marry another man the minute your back is turned. Must have been some love you felt for me that you were able to forget it in three days.''

She put both hands to her face and went to the tall, arched window that looked out onto Belltown. She had paled suddenly, and guilt warred with his righteous indignation.

''Emilio promised to send my sisters to college.'' The fight seemed to have gone out of her, and her voice was quiet, her hand resting on the baby as she stared out the window. ''You and I talked about marriage, but you never seemed very serious. I…felt that you loved me, but…I don't know what it was. I couldn't see us going beyond being lovers. I felt as though I knew you, yet there was part of you that you deliberately kept from me. Like the trips.''

''Maybe if I'd known you were serious about Emilio…'' he began.

''I *wasn't* serious about Emilio.'' She turned on him, agitated again. Then she caught herself and lowered her voice, staring back out the window. "And I wanted you to marry me because you wanted to, not because of some ultimatum I made, or some competition between you and another man." She sighed, sounding suddenly weary. "I know you and Emilio disliked each other. I know he felt small around you, because even though he had his own achievements, you had real confidence and self-assurance. His swagger was phoney and he knew it—and so did you. I'd have never played you against each other."

"On those trips, I was never gone more than a week, if that long," he pointed out, unwilling to give ground. "Why couldn't you have waited?"

"Because you did just what you'd promised me you'd never do again—you took off without telling me. There seemed no point in waiting."

"I think the fact that I did something I'd promised not to do would have alerted you that it was something I had no control over. Something I had to do."

When she turned to him again, her eyes were no longer condemning but sad. "All it did was remind me of what my mother went through, and I was determined that wouldn't happen to me."

This argument was going in circles. He wanted desperately to stop it—or to make it reach a conclusion.

"So, if I understand what we're saying here, you're mad at me because you mistrusted me, and on an impulse to hurt me for going away, you married Emilio, which turned out to be a mistake."

She spread her arms helplessly. "I'm angry at you because you continually bring up the fact that I didn't trust you, when there was nothing else I could do when you weren't telling me the truth. And I got what I wanted out of my marriage to Emilio. The girls got—ah!"

Crying out in alarm, she winced and put both hands over the baby.

"What?" he asked worriedly, catching her arm.

She stood still for a moment, holding up a hand for quiet. She seemed to be waiting, assessing. Then she expelled a breath and rubbed her stomach. "She kicked me," she said finally. "But there was real temper in it. Whew! Better now."

He drew her backward toward the sofa. The blanket he'd used last night was folded over the back, so he sat her down and spread it over her legs. "Maybe she's tired of listening to you bad-mouth me and wants some lunch."

MARIA PURSED her lips at him. Trust Rafe to use her discomfort to his advantage.

He disappeared into the kitchen and soon returned with two cups of soup, which he placed on the coffee table. These were followed by a plate of crackers and cheese. Her favorite lunch.

"How is it you happen to have all my favorite things," she asked, taking a cracker, "when you didn't even know I was coming?"

He shrugged. "I spent so much time with you that your favorite things became mine. How do you feel?"

"I'm fine." She took a bite of the cracker, then crumbled the rest into her soup. "The baby's been very restless for a couple of days," she explained. "Sometimes I think she's as aware of me as I am of her. I've been worried about…stuff, and I suppose it affects her somehow."

"What 'stuff'?" he asked, taking the other corner of the sofa and turning toward her.

"You know." She didn't want to be specific, didn't want him to think she was whining or unable to cope. "Just…things."

"The girls?"

"No."

"Delivery?"

She tipped her head from side to side. "Maybe a little." She smiled in self-deprecation. "I hope I don't make a total idiot of myself. But these hips I've always hated should help me out there."

His grin was quick and indulgent. A little thrill shivered between her breasts. She hadn't seen that look in years, and it brought back a whole host of memories she couldn't afford to indulge.

"I've always thought those hips were pretty sensational," he said. "But I'm glad they have a practical purpose as well." The look remained as he sipped at his soup and watched her over the rim of the cup.

"I'm worried about keeping my job," she blurted, needing to talk about something else. "About paying my bills, about being able to maintain my insurance when the baby's born and I'm really going to need it. About being able to afford day care or a baby-sitter so I can stay on at the rectory. About…"

She stopped abruptly, embarrassed as that litany of concerns echoed around her. She didn't know what had possessed her to reveal all that when she'd wanted to appear brave and in control.

"Don't look so horrified," he said, leaning over to reach for a piece of cheese. "You don't have to put on a fearless front for me. I imagine becoming a mother is pretty scary stuff."

"Yeah, it is," she admitted, then added with a touch of hurt feelings, "It's not a front. I thought if I acted brave, I'd feel brave."

His smile was now filled with gentle affection. This was the old Rafe, who knew so much about her. "Is it working?" he teased.

She had to be candid. "Only occasionally. But I expect to get better at it."

"Well, you might convince some people that you're in complete control of your fears," he said, "but I happen to know you're afraid of most insects, even those that *don't* sting, that you don't like the wind, particularly at night and you can't watch horror movies."

She eyed him threateningly. "But you wouldn't mention that to anyone, would you?"

He waggled his eyebrows. "I don't know. What's my silence worth to you?"

In the spirit of their teasing volley, she tried to remember what treats he favored. But all that would come to mind were the sexual ones, and she did something she hadn't done in years. She blushed.

He noted that with the lift of one eyebrow. "Yes," he said, this smile decidedly wicked. "A sexual reward is precisely what I had in mind."

She scolded him with a look as she patted her large stomach. "You wouldn't be able to collect for a long time," she returned, fanning herself with her napkin.

"I remember what making love was like between us," he insisted in a throaty tone, his eyes dusky and lazy with the memory. "I'll wait."

CHAPTER EIGHT

AFTER LUNCH, Rafe insisted Maria stretch out on the sofa, then covered her with the blanket. She dreamed he was pacing her apartment kitchen with a baby in his arms while she stirred something on the stove. He sang a lullaby in Spanish. She felt her own happiness like a little fire in her chest.

She sat up abruptly, not sure if the thought that had awakened her had been part of her dream or part of her reality.

Rafe would never be able to accept Emilio's baby.

Suddenly fully awake, she realized that had to have been a thought formed in her dream. In her real life, there was no evidence of the miracle that would reconcile her with Rafe anyway, so concern over his accepting her baby had no significance.

"Hey!" he said, striding toward her from the kitchen. "You must have really needed that nap. It's been almost three hours."

Guiltily, she swung her legs over the side of the

sofa. "Really? I'm sorry. I'm not being very productive about finding out who killed John, am I?"

"Not to worry. We can't do anything until your limo office is closed anyway. You said your friend Charlene takes the calls from home at night?"

She nodded.

"Okay. Then we're going to stop by the office tonight after dinner at Mom's."

"Dinner at Mom's?" Maria asked warily.

"Yeah. She's rounding up the troops," he said, stopping in front of her, hands relaxed on his hips. "She does that every once in a while to keep us on our toes. You remember. She heard that Frankie had the kids and that you were staying with me...."

She gasped in horror. "She knows about...?"

"No," he assured her quickly. "She has no idea you're a serial killer. She just thinks you've been drawn back to her irresistibly charming and brilliant son to make her dreams come true by finally becoming her daughter-in-law."

Maria closed her eyes against the prospect of Carmen's determined manipulations. "I hope you assured her that wasn't happening," she said.

Rafe nodded with disheartening conviction. "Firmly. I'll find you another shirt to wear since you slept in that one."

Maria watched grimly as Rafe went into his bedroom. Well, that had been a brutally quick and frank denial of any interest in her.

If only she could feel as disconnected from him as she claimed to be. But when she closed her eyes, she could still see that picture of him holding her baby.

RAFE WAS IMPRESSED with Maria's smiling but firm resistance to his mother's attempts to find out why she was staying with him. She explained about picking him up at Senator Stanton's, wisely editing out the body in the trunk.

His mother frowned. "But you married Emilio Castillo. Why are you driving a limo? Particularly while pregnant?"

Maria told her that he'd died suddenly, that she'd had to sell the house to keep her sisters in school and that she was working at St. Bartholomew's rectory during the day and driving limo at night to support herself.

His mother gasped and turned to him, as though expecting him to fix that somehow.

Catching that look, Maria reclaimed his mother's attention with the softly spoken assurance that her apartment was being repainted, and he'd invited her to stay with him to protect her from the fumes.

His mother pretended to believe it. Rafe knew

her better than that, but Maria was still an innocent where his mother was concerned. She didn't understand the devious machinations at work in Carmen's fertile brain.

"Mom!" Rick said, helping himself to another serving of cheese enchiladas. "Frankie has a friend interested in buying your building for a day-care center."

Carmen looked up in pleased surprise. "Really."

He nodded, but his attention was on the food. "Katherine Kinard. Some kind of scandal in her family, but she seems nice and intelligent. Frankie wants you to meet her so you can show her the building."

"Now, that sounds hopeful," she said with a broad smile. "I thought it might be hard to sell. If she likes it, I can go to Reno with my profits so I don't encumber my children with an inheritance."

Rafe laughed. "Thoughtful, Mom."

Carmen stood and went to a table near the door, retrieved a brown leather purse, and brought it to the table. "I just got pictures back today that I took of my vacation with Tom's family. You boys won't believe how the children have grown! Maria, you have to see these."

"Great purse," Maria said, leaning across the

table to touch the cobbled leather. "Whoa. Dooney and Bourke."

"I know!" With a wide smile, his mother clutched the purse to her, then handed it across the table for Maria to admire. "I never thought I'd own one. I could indulge myself, I guess, but I hate to spend that much on a purse. But I was admiring it when I visited them last month, so Tom sent it to me for my birthday."

That was something Maria and his mother had in common—they were both purse junkies. Rafe had once accompanied Maria on a purse-shopping expedition and thought he'd lose his mind while she went from shop to shop and examined every one on the rack for the right number of partitions, the perfectly placed pockets.

"That's the envelope, right there." His mother pointed to the yellow envelope sticking out of the front pocket. Maria took it and handed back the purse.

She smiled over the photographs, passing them on one by one to Rick, who sat beside her. Rafe was looking up, waiting for Rob to pass the next photo to him, when he saw Maria stop abruptly and pale at something in the middle of the stack.

His brothers noticed nothing, but his mother, seemingly interested in finishing off her meal, glanced up with an innocence he guessed was calculated.

"What is it, *cara?*" she asked, straightening up as though trying to see the photo that had stopped Maria from smiling.

When Maria didn't speak, Rick leaned toward her to take a look.

"Well, that's old," he said, snatching the photo from her to inspect it more closely. "This must be the last Christmas you two were together." He handed it to Rafe.

The image stopped Rafe as effectively as it had silenced Maria. It was a photo of the two of them leaning close together at the table in this very dining room. They were looking into each other's eyes and smiling, their hands linked on the tabletop. Love was written on their faces.

"Oh, yes," his mother said with a small laugh. "God knows how long the film was in that camera. I usually use those little throw-away things, but I didn't want to take any chances with photos of my grandchildren, so I took the Minolta you boys gave me that very Christmas, I think, and…"

Her voice drifted away from Rafe as he looked across the table into Maria's eyes, wanting to apologize for his mother's little trick. He was sure she'd known that photo was in there and left it to stir old memories.

But Maria didn't seem angry or hurt. Her eyes brimmed with tears, but there was a sweet expression in them that was just for him, and a faint, sad little smile on her lips. That hurt him more than any of her accusations or recriminations. It said she'd loved him, but she knew it was over.

He tucked the photo into the pocket of his shirt, suddenly and absolutely certain it wasn't.

Rafe helped his mother clear the table, leaving Maria to the attentions of his brothers as they sorted through movies in the living room.

Cornering his mother in the kitchen, he took the photo out of his pocket. "This wasn't on the same roll of film as the photos of the kids," he accused quietly.

She folded her arms. "How do you know it wasn't?"

He turned it so that she could see the printed date on the back—December '98.

"I was looking through pictures," she said without batting an eyelash. "I must have gotten them mixed up."

"Stay out of this, Mom," he warned.

Carmen wasn't impressed with his attempt to be firm. "Or what? You'll stop eating my tamales? You'll stop borrowing my juicer? You'll stop coming over for me to iron your shirts?"

"Mom…"

"I stayed out of it the last time and she married somebody else because you were so busy running around, saving everybody else that you didn't pay enough attention to your own life."

When his mouth fell open at the suggestion that she, too, knew his secret life, she closed her eyes and shook her head. "How stupid do you boys think I am?" she demanded. "You disappear at odd times, your brothers tell me they've just heard from you and you're in Boston, or Cleveland, or San Francisco, but they never seem to know how to reach you. And every time you return, there's something in the news about kidnapped children returned to their mothers. And you wear that macho look our men are so famous for."

"I do not."

"You do. And that's just like you. Always ready to come to the aid of someone who needs you. But they have to really *need* you, and you were never sure Maria did, were you? She's as smart and strong as you are, and you don't know what to do about that."

"God," he exclaimed under his breath. "Set down in a family of Saturday psychoanalysts."

"You get that from your father," she went on, ignoring his groans. "He didn't know what to do with me, either, but we were happy for a long time.

You don't have to be in charge, Rafael, you just
have to be in tune.''

Now completely confused, he helped her finish
the cleanup, sat uncomplainingly through *Casa-
blanca*—the black-and-white version—then saw
that the clock said 9:31. He gathered up Maria and
his brothers and thanked his mother for dinner.

Maria embraced Carmen, his brothers stood in
line for their hug and admonitions, then they all
piled into his car.

"This is exciting," Rick said as Rafe followed
Maria's directions into an alley that led them to the
back of Lawless Limousines, a small storefront at
the north end of Belltown. "We're actually going
to break and enter. A walk on the wild side will
be good for my portrayal of life at the edge of the
law."

Maria held up her keys. "We're not going to
break in. We're going to unlock the door."

Rick groaned with pretended disappointment.

Rob distributed the latex gloves he used to apply
chemicals to furniture. "Wish we had fingerprint-
ing powder," he said, handing a pair to Rafe. "Or
one of those lights that picks up stuff you can't
see."

Rafe snatched the gloves from him. "No more
CSI for you. Come on. On the chance that someone's still around here at this hour, keep the con-

versation down and don't disturb anything. Just look.''

''What are we looking for?'' Rick asked, snapping on his gloves like a character from the television show.

Rafe rolled his eyes heavenward in prayerful supplication. ''We're looking for anything that might tell us what was on John's schedule yesterday. Maria will go through his desk, and we'll check everything else. Be watchful. You might find something where you least expect it.''

CHAPTER NINE

A LAMP on Charlene's desk lit the otherwise dark office. There were three desks in the main room, Charlene's and two others used by the drivers. John's desk was located in a small room at the back.

The ecru walls of Lawless Limousines were decorated with maps of the area, photos of the limo fleet, drivers with satisfied clients and framed letters of appreciation. There were plants here and there, black-and-white polka-dot balloon valances that had been Charlene's idea—a decorating mistake as far as Maria was concerned—and a file cabinet.

Maria pointed to the small office. "That's John's," she whispered.

Rafe shooed her in that direction while he and his brothers dispersed among the other three desks.

With the small flashlight on her keychain propped against the phone to provide light, Maria leaned over John's cluttered desk. In the middle of it was a simple plastic folder that contained a log

Charlene kept of all trips. She recorded them on the computer and made him a printout every day.

Maria opened the book, read the entries for the previous day and found nothing unusual. Her own trip to pick up Rafe was listed on the sheet. Seeing it stopped her for a moment. That meeting had rattled her entire life, yet it appeared on this record as a terse piece of data.

She ran her finger down the morning's log, saw no trips John had taken personally, and nothing listed that was out of the ordinary.

Closing the book, she reached for his calendar. It had been flipped to today's date. That wasn't odd, even though he hadn't been here. Charlene came in every morning before he arrived and prepared his coffeepot, put his mail in the middle of his desk, and turned over the page on his calendar. She'd been mothering him for years.

Maria turned the page back to yesterday's date and put a hand to her mouth to stifle a gasp. Talk to Maria, was written there.

"Rafe!" she whispered loudly.

He appeared out of the shadows of the main office. "Yeah?"

She thrust the calendar at him. He shone his own flashlight on it, then turned to her.

"You said you hadn't seen him yesterday."

"I didn't!"

"Is this his handwriting?"

"Well...I think so."

"Are you sure? Because whoever called 9-1-1 on you last night might have scribbled this to incriminate you."

"I'm not sure, but I can't believe anyone here would do that."

"Find anything else?"

"No. The log for yesterday is very ordinary."

"Okay." He caught her arm and drew her after him, back into the main office. He stopped in front of a locked door near the back of the room. "What's in there?"

"A supply room," she replied. "Everything from office supplies to replacement items for the limos—tissue, champagne, glasses, that sort of stuff. It's always locked. John and Charlene both have a key."

"Do you know where Charlene's is?"

She went to her friend's desk, feeling like a traitor, and opened the middle drawer where she kept personal items. In it was the small makeup bag in which she kept the key.

"Just out of curiosity," he asked as he and his brothers followed her to the supply room door, "what's the point of a locked door if everyone knows where to find the key?"

"We're...trustworthy?"

"Then why is the door locked?"

Maria gave him an impatient look as she turned the key in the lock and pushed the door open. She gasped again as Rob whistled, Rick exclaimed, "Whoa!" and Rafe said darkly, "Apparently one of your colleagues isn't trustworthy."

Stationery and tissue boxes were strewn everywhere, and paper clips spilled from open boxes. A three-step ladder lay on its side, and broken champagne glasses littered the floor. Clear signs of a struggle. Maria stared at the mess in shock.

"No blood," Rob observed as he followed Rafe more deeply into the small room.

"Maybe Lawless was just cornered here," Rick speculated, "then led away at gunpoint."

Maria pushed in a box of envelopes that was teetering on the edge of a shelf. "But he was stabbed with my knitting needles."

"Knitting needles hardly seem like a man's weapon, do they?" Rafe asked his brothers. He turned to Maria. "You said he was having an affair with the other female driver?"

She nodded. "Joanne. We all talked about it. They were always leaving the office at the same time, or were absent on the same days. There were no indiscreet glances or anything, but we were more than a little suspicious." She frowned, thinking about other aspects of the murder weapon.

"But a woman wouldn't have the strength to drive knitting needles into a man's chest, would she? I mean, they're pointed, but they're not sharp."

"A woman could have shot him," he proposed, "then stuck the needles into the bullet hole to frame you."

She groaned, exasperated and exhausted.

"Do you know where this Joanne lives?" Rafe asked.

"Yes," she replied. "Madison Park. Not very far."

"Okay. We'll pay a call on her first thing in the morning and hope no one's found the car yet."

Rob frowned. "So, we're presuming no one's noticed the boss is missing," he asked doubtfully, "and no one's been in this room to notice this mess?"

"It's only been a day and a half," Rafe replied, "and someone in this office did it and is probably covering for his absence. Saying he called in sick, or something."

That was beginning to make chilling sense to Maria. "And sometimes no one goes into the supply room for days at a time. A lot of our clients never touch the champagne, so a bottle and a pair of clean glasses can last several days."

"Everything back the way you found it?" Rafe asked.

His brothers nodded, and Maria locked the supply room door. Once she'd carefully replaced the key, they hurried quietly back to the car.

"Thanks for the help, guys," Rafe said. "I appreciate it."

"Hey, we have a lifetime of experience getting into trouble because of you," Rob said. "All that bonding shouldn't be wasted just because we're adults."

"Yeah," Rick concurred. "But if I'm arrested, I'm giving you up."

Rafe turned a grinning glance on Maria as he drove away. "Family can be such a comfort."

WIDE-AWAKE on the sofa around one in the morning, Rafe heard restless movements from the bedroom. They'd been going on for some time, and he'd been considering the wisdom of seeing if he could do anything to help Maria. She'd been complaining of a backache when she went to bed, and had looked particularly grim.

After her response to their Christmas photograph, he felt reasonably sure she still cared. Still, she'd kept a careful distance from him when they came home. The situation, of course, was hardly conducive to romance or reconciliation.

He heard the sudden crash of something in the bedroom and put all caution aside as he ran to investigate. He found her sitting on the bed in the shadows, the bedside lamp on the floor, casting light on the carpet and the wall.

"I'm sorry." Her voice was high and tight and filled with self-deprecation. "I didn't mean to wake you. I just wanted to read for a while, but I lost my balance and knocked over the light." She indicated her round stomach. "My center of gravity keeps changing."

He felt drawn into the room despite the wariness in her expression. Something about her was sending him a message.

"You okay?" He righted the lamp, then sat on the edge of the bed beside her.

She nodded, rubbing her stomach. Her body drew slightly away from him, though her eyes seemed to be calling him. "The baby's moving a lot and I...can't get comfortable."

"I used to give a pretty good backrub," he said, standing to urge her back toward the pillows. "Remember our first night on the trail on that two-day hike when you insisted we needed an iron frying pan."

Her smile was grudging as he propped the pillows behind her. "You made me carry it."

"It was just a small one," he reminded her, "but along with your hardcover copy of *Shanna,* and your share of our gear, it was too much."

"I'd never been hiking before," she said, her eyes still wary as she watched him walk around the bed and sit on the other side. "I didn't know that what feels comfortable when you first set out feels like ten times the weight a mile into the hike."

"I warned you."

She sighed, her eyes softening a little as she remembered that. "I know. But I always think I know everything."

He was surprised by that admission. Putting a hand to her shoulders, he pitched her slightly forward and ran his palm lightly up and down her spine. "Between the shoulders?" he asked, rubbing lightly there. "Or in the small of your back?" He traced a line down below her waist.

"There," she whispered, her voice choked. She cleared her throat. "I imagine the baby sitting back, with her feet propped up on my second or third lumbar vertebra."

He hitched himself closer so that he could sit up behind her, one arm tipping her sideways into his shoulder while the other worked in gentle circles in that sensitive indentation just below the back of her waist.

She held herself stiffly for the first few moments, then he felt her gradually relax against him until he had her full weight.

"I can't tell you," she said, a little gasp of hedonistic pleasure separating her words, "how—wonderful—that—feels."

"Good. Just let yourself relax."

Maria was quiet for a moment, then she said drowsily, "My name was on his calendar."

"Don't think about that," he said firmly.

"Somebody's going to come across the car."

"We'll have this figured out tomorrow."

With a sigh, she nuzzled her head a little farther into his shoulder. "You always think you know everything, too."

"I guess we're well matched."

"That was the problem, wasn't it?" she asked on a sigh, her voice hardly discernible.

Had she been talking to his mother? Or Rob? Or was it just clear to everyone but him?

"Frankly," he said, still stroking, "I can't figure out the past. I have my hands full of right now."

She shifted sleepily so that she was turned toward him, the backrub apparently having done its job. She leaned into him and seemed about to drift off.

He was wishing he'd turned off the light, but since it didn't seem to be bothering her, he could probably just close his eyes and forget it was there. Because he certainly wasn't moving. She lay heavily against him, the roundness of the baby lying against his waist.

For a moment he just watched Maria, fascinated by her presence in his arms. He'd dreamed of this a thousand times since she'd been gone.

Then his attention was captured by a clear movement in her belly. He saw a very small bulge move from her side to the middle of her stomach. A foot? he wondered. A tiny hand?

Astonished at the sight and completely captivated by the absolute reality of the life she carried, he watched the little bulge start the movement again and, without stopping to think, placed a hand over it.

He wasn't sure if it was the baby's movement or his touch that woke her, but she put a hand over his and looked up at him to smile. "I think that was a *grand jetee*," she said.

He wanted to say something casual or amusing in response, so she wouldn't know his heart was hammering in his chest. But at that moment the three of them had been connected—and the experience stole his voice—his very breath.

MARIA SAW the wonder in his eyes. It was more than wonder, she thought. It was love.

She reached up for him just as he lowered his mouth to hers, and they kissed long and hungrily, the baby still stirring between them. This couldn't be and yet it was, the two of them locked in a familiar embrace despite everything that had gone wrong between them. She held tightly to him, afraid he would evaporate like all the dreams in which she'd held him, only to awaken and find her arms empty.

"I'm sorry I didn't wait for you to come home," she said urgently, pulling away just enough to look into his eyes.

He reached under her hair to cup her head in his hand, his eyes devouring the love in hers. "I'm sorry I didn't tell you the truth."

She traced the inside of his mouth with the tip of her tongue, nipped at his earlobe, dotted kisses down his throat and began to pull at his shirt.

Struggling to hold on to his senses, he caught her hand.

Her eyes, wide and injured, looked into his. "You don't want to?"

He expelled a strangled laugh. "Yeah, right. Of course I want to, but I was worried about the baby."

"Because it's Emilio's?"

He didn't get that for a minute. "What do you mean?"

"I'm carrying another man's baby," she said with deliberate slowness. "Does that...?"

Now that he did understand, he was torn between wanting to shake her, and wanting to prove without further discussion how little it mattered.

He made himself draw a breath. "Who could resent a baby," he demanded quietly, "whoever it belonged to?"

Her look of alarm morphed into a smile. "It's all right. You won't hurt her. We just can't, you know, hang from the chandelier, or anything."

"You're sure it's all right?"

When she began working on his belt buckle, he concluded that she was sure. And after that it was hard to hold on to his concerns because she took charge, and he had to admit that he didn't mind it. She was all-serious tenderness somehow caught in an urgent, almost desperate need to claim his body.

She undressed him—something she'd never done before—and he was surprised that he felt more, rather than less, powerful as he let her do as she pleased with him. She frowned over the wound at his shoulder. He expected recriminations because there was clearly a bullet wound in the middle of the long scar. Instead she put her lips to it.

In the old days, he'd always thought she exemplified the rose—beautiful, fragrant, prickly. Now she was like an armful of orchids, all color and perfume and sophisticated evolution.

She made love to him with the old passion and

charm that had haunted him through the intervening years, but also with a new, generous maturity he sensed rather than understood.

His body went wild and took her with it.

MARIA LAY in Rafe's arms, sated, marveling that their lovemaking was even more dynamic and satisfying than it had been before. She couldn't decide if it was because he'd let her lead, something that had never happened in the old days, or because they were more adult than they'd been, more aware of what the other needed.

"Still okay?" he asked.

"No," she replied. She felt his startled movement.

She laughed lightly, pushing a hand to the middle of his chest to prevent him from sitting up. "I'm not okay. I'm wonderful. I'm marvelous. Magnificent!"

He expelled a relieved breath. "Yes, you are. Let me show you how sincerely I believe that."

She giggled as she wrapped an arm around him. "Didn't you just do that?"

He nipped at her bottom lip. "Yeah, but you did most of the talking."

"Does it matter who's talking?" she asked, kissing him.

"No." He returned the kiss, then nibbled at her

throat. "But I have a different vocabulary than you do."

She dissolved against him as he ran a hand down the middle of her body, over the swell of baby, and into the silky inside of her thigh. "Then, speak to me, Rafe," she whispered.

He'd always been possessive and passionate when he made love to her, but now his confident moves were coupled with unutterable tenderness and care. Every sensor in her body came to full alertness when he touched her. She experienced a host of emotions she'd never be able to find words for, then with her fingertips, tried to express all the same things to him.

They came together with old passion, new devotion and a startling sense of unity she'd never experienced before. She'd loved and adored him, but she'd never felt as though they formed another entity like this.

"Still wonderful, marvelous and magnificent?" he asked as she hooked a leg over him and collapsed against his chest.

"More so," she replied languorously. "You?"

"King of the Hill."

CHAPTER TEN

IN THE LIGHT OF DAY, Maria panicked over what had seemed so right the night before. Last night she'd been tired, emotionally battered by that Christmas photo, horrified that someone among her friends at Lawless Limousines was trying to kill her. When Rafe had put his hand over hers on her baby, she'd fallen under his spell as she had once before.

But even now that she knew about his mysterious trips, she wasn't sure she could live with him placing himself in the direct path of danger time after time. Presuming that he intended something permanent between them—which he'd never mentioned.

Of course, they'd been together again only a day and a half. And fate had forced this togetherness on them; it wasn't a choice they'd made.

Rafe had probably awakened feeling entirely different than he had last night. That was probably why his side of the bed was empty and she could smell coffee and bacon cooking.

She pulled on the ever-present sweat bottoms and topped them this time with the matching shirt. It was huge in the shoulders, but fit comfortably around the baby. She brushed her hair and marched into the kitchen, determined to act unaffected by their lovemaking so that he would think she considered it a reflection of the past, not a portent of the future.

She found him making pancakes, one eye on the small TV in the corner of the counter. He glanced up at her with a smile, then did a double take when his eyes met hers.

She kept her gaze steady and her smile cheerful, though something inside her wanted him with unparalleled desperation. The pretense hurt, but she maintained it.

"Good morning," she said, stopping beside the table. "Anything I can do? Pour coffee? Juice? Warm syrup?"

"YOU CAN GET that damned untouched look off your face for starters," he said, loading the turner with three pancakes and dropping them onto the plate warming in the oven. He was a little surprised he'd said that aloud. At first glance he'd been hurt by that look, and intended to pretend he hadn't noticed. Then he remembered what keeping things to himself had done to them the last time.

Her lips parted in surprise, and she tried to stammer out a response.

"If you're going to lie and tell me last night meant nothing," he interrupted her, "forget it. I know better. It wasn't you needing protection, or me wanting to claim you because you've been Emilio's. I've analyzed it all myself. It was…"

He stopped abruptly when he heard "…body has been found in the trunk of a limousine owned by Lawless Limousines of Belltown. The male, in his late forties, appears to have been stabbed with knitting needles. That is all the detail we have on this breaking news. Stay tuned to…"

Rafe turned off the television, the griddle and the oven.

"Oh, God," Maria said, feeling her life disintegrate around her.

He poured milk into a commuter mug, handed it to her, and dug his keys out of his pocket. "Come on," he said. "We're going to Joanne's right now."

She didn't seem able to move, the enormity of the situation rooting her to the spot. "But they're probably finding out as we speak that I was driving the limo and that the knitting needles are mine! My sisters will have to leave school out of embarrassment. I'll lose my job…go to jail…lose my baby…."

"Hey!" he said, sharply enough to get her attention. When it threatened to waver anyway, he caught her chin between his thumb and forefinger. "You're not going to jail, you're not losing your baby or your job and the girls are staying in school. Trust me on that." Then realizing what he'd said, and her backpedaling approach this morning to their lovemaking last night, he added firmly, "I know that comes hard to you. But do it."

He pulled her after him out to the car.

JOANNE COLLIER was a leggy blonde with worldly hazel eyes and a dark blue towel strategically wrapped around her. She looked surprised to see Maria on her doorstep. She glanced from Maria to Rafe in confusion.

"Joanne," Maria began, before Rafe could speak, "did you see John on Wednesday?"

"Maria," Rafe said in a cautioning tone, "let me..."

"Did you?" Maria demanded, ignoring him.

Joanne continued to look confused. "No. I had three days off in a row this week. I don't go in until tomorrow. Where have you...?"

Maria caught her arm. "Joanne, everyone knows the two of you are having an affair. Please just tell..."

Both Joanne's eyebrows shot up and color

seemed to rise into her throat and face from the top of her towel. "I'm not having an affair with John," she denied.

"Joanne, please. I can't..."

"Hey, babe," a sleepy male voice said from somewhere behind Joanne. Then a handsome middle-aged man appeared beside her, a matching towel wrapped around his hips. "What's going on? I thought you were going to send them away so we...oh, sh—"

Maria's mouth fell open. "Christopher!" she exclaimed loudly before she could stop herself.

"Christopher?" Rafe asked.

"Christopher Goodman," Maria said, indicating the man in the towel. "Charlene's husband."

Maria stared at the two of them, astonished that her suspicions were so off-base.

"Maria, please," Christopher said gravely. "Charlene doesn't have a clue, and the last thing in the world I'd want to do is hurt her."

Maria scorned him with a look for the ridiculousness of that statement, even as she tried to figure out what was wrong here.

She turned to Rafe with a frown. "But John always left the office when Joanne did," she reasoned aloud. "I don't get it."

Rafe frowned with her, then tipped his head back suddenly as he exclaimed, "Of course!"

"What?"

"It didn't mean he was having an affair with Joanne. He knew when she left that it was probably to be with Christopher, and that left Charlene free to be with *him*."

Mouth agape, Maria stared at him and wondered if there would ever be a detail about all this that she'd be able to believe.

"Do you know where she lives?" Rafe asked.

Maria looked fiercely at Christopher. "Is Charlene at the antique shop this morning?"

Christopher looked as shocked as she was. "I don't understand," he admitted. "Are you saying Charlene's having an affair with John?"

"She's not as clueless as you thought, Christopher," Maria replied. "Is she at the shop?"

"Yes."

Maria grabbed Rafe's hand and dragged him with her to the car.

"You know, there's a subtlety to this questioning business," he said as she directed him toward the antique shop. "I think it'd be better if you let me do it. You just jumped in and incriminated yourself when you asked her if…"

SHE WASN'T LISTENING to him. Rafe considered himself fortunate that that was a familiar problem for him. But he was worried that it wouldn't do Maria any good.

"I can't believe it's Charlene!" she said, clearly distressed. "First of all, I can't believe she'd kill anybody, and then I can't believe she'd want to hurt me by making it look like I did it."

"I could be wrong," he said placatingly, handing her the glass of milk she'd put in the cup holder. "Drink. You shouldn't be running around like this on an empty stomach."

He was shocked when she did as he suggested. She lowered the cup to her lap and said grimly, "The really awful thing is—you might be right."

"We'll see when we get there."

She pointed to a side street. "Go down here and we can get in through the rear of the shop. If she's busy in the front of the store, we might be able to look through her desk in the back. Maybe she's still got the gun."

They walked quietly in through the back door of the shop, Rafe insisting on leading the way. Shelving in the back room was cluttered with antiques waiting for repair, and items bearing layaway tags. One shelf held bags and tissue.

A colorful curtain that separated the shop from the back room was not completely closed, and Rafe moved forward to draw the two panels together, wondering where Charlene was and whether or not she was occupied, affording them a little time to look around.

But voices from the front claimed his attention and he peered through the opening when he heard a woman's voice say, "Of course, Officer..."

He saw two uniformed policemen at a glass counter, one of them fiddling with a spinning wheel displayed there.

"And you didn't see him at all that morning," the shorter, older of the two officers asked.

"No," said the woman, who appeared to be in her mid-thirties. She was blond, of medium height and dressed casually, but Rafe could see her heavy makeup from across the room. "He called from home to say that he was going to talk to Maria Castillo that day about her poor performance," she explained, pushing the spinning wheel closer to the younger officer examining it. "That's maple, you know. Grain painted. Pewter Castle design from somewhere in the Vermont countryside. Circa 1835."

The older officer cleared his throat to reclaim her attention. "Poor performance?" he asked.

"Oh, yes. Maria's always late. She's pregnant, you know, and likes to be treated like a little princess. Always had things her way, then her husband died, and she's working a couple of jobs to make ends meet."

"So, you think she really needed this job?"

"Definitely. She counted on it, and the tips she made."

"Then, she might have gotten upset if he called her on the carpet?"

"I'm sure she would have," she said emphatically, "particularly since they had a thing going."

"A thing?"

Rafe heard a small gasp beside him and realized that Maria had stopped searching the desk and was now standing at his elbow, listening to Charlene in wide-eyed shock. She looked up at Rafe helplessly as Charlene went on.

Rafe made a shushing gesture, fearing she might explode at any moment.

"She was always trying to lure him into a relationship," Charlene continued, "but he rejected her over and over."

"You witnessed this at the office?"

As Charlene went on, Rafe turned Maria toward him to force her to refocus on their search for the gun. He made a gun of his forefinger and thumb and pointed to the desk.

She shook her head, telling him she hadn't found it there.

He pointed to the strap of her shoulder purse, silently asking if she'd looked for Charlene's purse.

She shook her head again and pointed to the desk, telling him the purse wasn't there.

Moving soundlessly, Rafe searched the room while Maria drew closer to the curtain to listen, her attention clearly on Charlene's assassination of her character. He went back to her and pointed to the floor where she stood, miming that she was not to move from there.

She nodded absently as she listened to the conversation.

Rafe scanned the shelves he'd noticed when he walked in the door and saw a counter in the corner with a roll of brown paper on a cutter. A desk drawer would be the obvious place to put a purse, so a smart businesswoman protecting herself from back door theft would find another spot.

As he peered over the counter, he saw a series of cubbyholes with a soft fabric purse stuffed into one of them.

Reaching down, he grabbed the purse and opened it—and hit paydirt.

He turned to show Maria—just in time to see her storm through the curtain, shouting, "That's a lie!"

CHAPTER ELEVEN

"THIS IS *NOT* John Lawless's baby!" Maria said to the officers as she confronted Charlene. "I was driving the limo, but she's the one who murdered him! I went to pick up a client, opened the trunk to put away his salmon and found the body!"

The younger officer, whose name tag read Palmer, asked, "His salmon?"

Maria rolled her eyes. "He'd been given a salmon. It's a long story. But that was the first I knew about a body. I did not try to lure John into an affair. We had a strictly business relationship. But *her* husband is having an affair with one of our drivers, and Rafe and I think she was having an affair with John in retribution."

The older officer, McMillan, raised a hand to silence Charlene, who tried to deny Maria's claim. "Who's Rafe?"

"I am." Rafe appeared, the quilted fabric purse in his hands. As he passed it to the officer, Charlene tried to make a grab for it, but the cop was quicker.

He opened the bag and looked inside. Then he took a pen out of his pocket and used it to hook the derringer that Rafe had seen sticking out from under a wallet. It was highly polished stainless steel with an ivory grip. An antique? he wondered.

"I'll bet the autopsy reveals there was a bullet hole in John's chest before the knitting needles were driven in," Rafe said. "And I'll bet the bullet is from the derringer. And if you'll trace the source of a 9-1-1 call made Wednesday night about a limo driving erratically on Bellevue Way, it'll reveal the call was made by this woman. She'd already put John's body in the trunk and wanted Maria to be found with it."

The older officer was on his shoulder radio to the station, asking for another patrol car.

"I think it would be a good idea," he said with world-weary courtesy, "if you all came down to the station so we can sort this out. Another car'll be here in a minute."

"Whoever called 9-1-1," Charlene said, "might not have left his name. In which case it'd be hard to prove who called."

"We have enhanced 9-1-1, ma'am," Palmer said. "Our system tells us who's calling, where they're located and what their telephone number is. It also gives us police and fire department jurisdictions for that number."

Charlene looked stricken, but subdued.

"Put Mrs. Goodman in the car," McMillan advised. "I'll keep the purse."

Palmer grinned. "Looks good on you, Mac."

McMillan threatened him with a look.

Rafe drew Maria to a chair against the wall. He sat her in it, worried that she looked pale and panicky. "It's over," he said, squatting down beside her. "We've got her dead to rights. It's just a matter of waiting around until the autopsy and the forensic evidence prove it."

She folded her arms stubbornly over her rounded stomach. She looked very close to tears. "I am not taking my baby to jail."

"You're not going to jail," he said calmly. "We're going to the station for questioning."

"Same thing."

"Not even close."

She focused on him with new interest, as though he provided distraction from a situation she found upsetting. "I suppose in your life of high adventure, going to jail isn't scary at all."

"That depends on where you are," he replied, happy to keep her thinking about his jail experiences rather than the prospect of her own. "Here, it isn't bad at all. But you don't want it to happen in Mexico."

Her eyes widened. "You were in jail in Mexico?"

"For two days."

"For what?"

"For hitting a cow with my Jeep. I took a corner too fast on a country road and there she was."

"And you can go to jail for that?"

"If the cow belongs to the mayor. Well, I was speeding, but we'd just rescued two American teenagers taken by their father. He was vengeful and on my tail. It seemed important to hurry. At least going to jail got rid of him for me. He wanted no part of the *policía*."

"How did you get out of jail?"

"I paid a fortune for the cow."

She looked at him, that sad expression from the dinner at his mother's coming over her. "There's so much I don't know about you," she said.

That was true. And much of the reason for that, though not deliberate, was his fault. But he no longer felt like defending his position.

"You now know you can trust me," he reminded her.

RAFE WAS INTERROGATED by Officer McMillan, who got a little hot under the collar when Rafe explained about hiding the limousine with John's body so it wouldn't be found until he could prove Maria hadn't killed him.

"That's tampering with evidence," McMillan accused.

Rafe met his eyes unflinchingly. "I know. My woman was in danger."

"Well, you can't go around breaking the law to…to…"

Rafe grinned. "Come on. I just mangled it a little."

McMillan looked from Rafe to Maria, waiting at Palmer's desk, and shook his head. In Rafe's best interest, she did her best to look pathetic, even stroked her large belly in a shameless play to support Rafe's defense of her.

McMillan fell for it with a noisy clearing of his throat. "Okay. I think we can help you out." He drilled Rafe with a look. "But next time you find a body in a trunk, leave it where you found it."

Maria answered questions for Officer Palmer. As Palmer returned, a dark-haired, middle-aged woman with a shoulder holster led Charlene away.

Palmer was kind and considerate of Maria because his own wife was pregnant. He got her a pastry and a cup of tea, then left to check on the ballistics report.

Maria sat in a chair near the officer's desk for what felt like hours. The older officer eventually led Rafe down a hallway, and she watched for his return.

After an eternity, Charlene reappeared in handcuffs, the female officer leading her away. Charlene spotted Maria and stopped in her tracks to shriek at her.

"I *had* John! Christopher was fooling around with Joanne! I knew that! But it didn't matter because I had John. Then you came along with your hair and that walk that says you're better than everybody. John always talked about what a good, brave girl you were. And I just got sick of it. You were *pregnant,* and he still noticed you over me!" She shook her head pityingly, her wild eyes making her unrecognizable as the friend Maria had known. "I was the runt of the litter to my parents, the wife who could help run the shop but who couldn't keep her husband faithful to her. And worst of all, the woman who risked her marriage to have an affair with a man who still noticed a pregnant woman. Pathetic, aren't I?"

Maria stood up, shaking at the evidence of Charlene's hatred as the policewoman led her away. The younger officer arrived just in time to push her back into her chair.

"Ballistics has a match," he said with a broad smile. "Her fingerprints are on the bullet, as well as the gun, and she did make the 9-1-1 call. You're free to go, Mrs. Castillo. Shall I call you a cab?''

''Do you know if Mr. Perez is still around?'' she asked.

''Mac's alone at his desk,'' he answered. ''My guess is your friend's gone. Why don't I take you home?''

She shook her head, a weird sense of unreality taking over. ''Thank you,'' she said. ''I want to walk for a while.''

Strange, she thought as she headed for the big glass double doors, finding a body in the trunk of her limo and almost being considered a suspect in a murder case had become a dark reality for two days. But then, those things had brought Rafe into her life, and that had been a reality she'd been happy to deal with.

Still, he seemed to be gone. She couldn't blame him entirely. In the old days, she'd been selfish and impulsive. And for the past two days, she'd been alternately hostile and clingy. The poor man probably had no idea that she'd fallen madly in love with him all over again, and wanted nothing more than to spend the rest of her life with him, to make her baby his baby.

She'd probably lost him again, she thought, emotion threatening to swallow her as she pushed her way through the doors. She'd altered both their lives beyond redemption so that he was now committed to a life of danger and she'd condemned herself to one of loneliness.

"Except for you, baby," she muttered as she rubbed her stomach.

Carefully she made her way down the stairs, then drew a deep breath of the now early evening air, trying to stabilize her emotions so that she could go on.

She started as a horn blared, then watched, hopeful but uncertain, as Rafe pulled up in his convertible. He had the top down and she couldn't help but notice that the back was filled with a giant teddy bear, a tiny tricycle, a folded-up crib and scores of other baby things.

"It's not a limo," he said, getting out to come around to the passenger side and open the door, "but can I give you a lift home?"

She couldn't help staring at him. He seemed to be enjoying that, because he leaned down to kiss her.

"Do you know where I live?" she asked practically.

"Of course," he said, helping her in and handing her the seat belt. "With me." He closed and locked her door, then went around again to slip in behind the wheel.

HE WAS GOING to commit her expression to memory, he decided as she beamed and cried and held both arms toward him. He leaned over the gear shift to be hugged and have an appendectomy at the same time.

"One thing, though," he said, brushing the hair back from her face and drowning in her love-filled eyes.

"What?" she asked, as though she could now deal with anything.

"We're going to have to name the baby after my mother. Carmen Rafaela Perez."

She leaned against him with a windy little sigh. "That's the most beautiful name I've ever heard," she said.

DISTRACTING DIANA
Kristin Gabriel

CHAPTER ONE

ROB PEREZ was late for the most important date of his life.

"Hurry, Daddy," his five-year-old daughter pleaded as he walked through the front door of their apartment. Maggie wore an ankle-length red velvet dress with a wide silk sash that tied in a big bow at the back. The creamy lace petticoat peeked beneath the hem and rustled when she walked.

He bent down to pick her up, buzzing a kiss on her cheek. "You look like a fairy princess."

She grinned at him. "I know."

Her beautiful smile, so much like her mother's, made his heart contract. His little Maggie was five going on twenty-five, trying so hard to be the lady of the house. Susanna, Rob's wife, had died over two years ago, during their son T.J.'s birth.

Rob set Maggie back on the floor, careful not to dislodge the myriad of pins in her curly brown hair, swept up in some elaborate style of intricate braids and curls. "Did Grandma fix your hair?"

"Yes," she said, grabbing his hand and tugging

him down the hallway. "Come on, Daddy. You have to hurry or we're going to be late."

Rob knew she'd been looking forward to the father-daughter and mother-son dance at her school for the past several weeks. So he didn't even consider suggesting that they skip it tonight, despite the fact that he'd had a lousy day.

First, his power saw went on the blink, then a new customer changed his order for the fifth time this week. That, combined with a heavier than usual demand for his furniture, hadn't given Rob any time to eat lunch, and now his empty stomach growled in protest.

As a custom furniture designer, Rob always tried to make his clients happy. But he'd have to put in a lot of overtime to get all the orders completed in time for Christmas. Which meant less time to spend with his kids.

For the past two years he'd tried to be a good father, tried to fulfill his wife's dying wish that he take good care of the children. But Rob knew he was failing miserably. For one thing, he depended too much on his family for help. With his brothers Rick and Rafe living in the same building, it had been only too easy to rely on them to lend a hand. But things were changing.

Rafe was married to Maria now, with a baby due in a few weeks. Rick and Frankie's wedding was only a week away, and he couldn't ask newlyweds to play baby-sitter. Besides, with his mother putting the building up for sale, they'd all be looking for a new home soon. Then Rob would truly be on his own.

A terrifying proposition.

"Where is Grandma?" Rob asked, glancing around the apartment as Maggie pulled him toward his bedroom.

"She's reading T.J. a story in his room." Maggie turned toward her father. "Okay, now close your eyes for the surprise."

He could hear the tremor of excitement in her voice as he dutifully obliged. "They're closed."

She pulled him through the open door of his bedroom. "Surprise, Daddy!"

He opened his eyes to find himself staring at his bed. Specifically, at the black tuxedo laid out on top of the quilt. "What's this?"

"It's a tuxedo! I saw it in Uncle Rick's closet when me and Grandma went to visit him today."

"Grandma and I," Rob corrected, squatting down on the floor until he was eye-level with his daughter. "And what exactly were you doing in his closet?"

"Playing hide-and-seek with T.J.," she explained, reaching out to caress the diamond pattern on the silver-gray vest. "I told Uncle Rick it would make you look just like Prince Charming, so he said you could borrow it for the dance.''

His daughter loved fairy tales and still insisted he read one to her every night, though she had them all memorized by now. Cinderella was her favorite.

"I thought I'd just wear a suit and tie tonight," he explained. "I'm sure that's what all the other fathers will be wearing."

"But you're not like all the other fathers," she replied, gazing intently at him with those big, dark brown eyes. "You're the best."

How could Rob argue with logic like that? Besides, he didn't have time to argue. If they weren't out the door in the next five minutes, they were going to be late for the dance. There was no time even to shave his five o'clock shadow or grab something to eat from the fridge.

He scooted Maggie out of his bedroom with directions to tell his mother they were about to leave, then hastily stripped out of the blue jeans and flannel shirt he wore to work in the winter.

With a sigh of resignation, he picked up the black pants of the tuxedo. Maggie, or more likely his mother, had laid out everything he would need for the evening. Not only the crisply ironed dress shirt, silver vest and black jacket, but matching shoes and socks. As well as the silver and onyx cuff links that went with the tuxedo and a neatly folded silver-gray pocket handkerchief.

The tuxedo had turned up mysteriously a few months ago in a package addressed to R. Perez. Neither of his brothers had claimed to know anything about it, but both of them had made good use of it. Now, Rob guessed, it was his turn.

By the time he'd slipped on the shoes and run a comb through his hair, his five minutes were up.

"Let's go, Princess," he shouted as he hurried out of his bedroom and down the hallway. He swept his car keys off the kitchen counter, then half slipped on a wet spot on the floor.

"T.J.," he muttered under his breath as his son galloped across the kitchen, naked from the waist down. At two and a half years old, T.J. had a strong aversion to potty-training. Just another sign that Rob was a failure as a single father.

"Don't worry, Rob, I'll clean it up," his mother called as she ushered Maggie into the kitchen. "We just had to add a few sparkles to her hair for the dance and I lost track of T.J."

Carmen Perez never criticized Rob's abilities as a father, though she frequently hinted that it was time he found a wife. Rob knew she was right. Even though he'd never find a woman to replace Susanna in his heart, Maggie and T.J. needed a mother. Someone who could give them the full-time care and attention they deserved.

Tiny dots of silver glitter shone in Maggie's hair as she slowly twirled around the floor. "Like it, Daddy?"

"Very nice," he said.

"And look at you, Roberto," Carmen exclaimed, a smile crinkling the lines around her eyes as she admired him in his tuxedo. "Every bit as handsome as your father."

"Thanks, Mom." Rob leaned over to kiss her cheek, knowing that was the highest compliment she could have paid him. Then he gingerly stepped over T.J.'s latest mess and walked toward the door, where Maggie was waiting impatiently for him. "Thanks for everything."

"Have a wonderful time," Carmen called as they walked out the door.

Twenty minutes later, they finally found a parking spot seven blocks away from the school. Maggie was giddily unaware of the bitter December cold, skipping along the sidewalk, her cheeks rosy from the chill.

"Only six more blocks to go," he said, trying to keep his teeth from chattering.

Then Maggie came to an abrupt stop and pointed. "Look, Daddy, a reindeer!"

DIANA FALCO stood on the street corner, huddled next to the Good Neighbors collection drum, and wondered who would identify her frozen corpse in the morning. With her luck, they'd give up tracking down her parents in Europe and simply carve the name Blitzen on her tombstone.

She'd volunteered to work an extra night for the Good Neighbors charity specifically to avoid the annual Christmas carnival that her accounting firm held for the children of their staff. Her firm was very family oriented, encouraging even the single employees to join in the fun. At Halloween, she'd made the mistake of attending the company party dressed as a clown. Her costume had scared some of the younger children into tears. The older children had expected her to perform tricks, but weren't impressed with her ability to solve complex mathematical equations. A few of them had actually booed her.

So despite the subzero windchill and the fact that she had to wear antlers on her head and bells on her boots, this evening was definitely preferable to another company party. She wasn't in the holiday spirit anyway, since she'd be spending this Christmas alone. Her parents, both college professors, were in Vienna, Austria, participating in a university exchange program. She was housesitting for them and hadn't even put up a Christmas tree. Why bother when she was the only one to see it?

Diana stomped her bell-laden boots on the pavement, trying to jingle some feeling back into her frozen toes. Then a child's voice broke the stillness of the night.

"A reindeer, Daddy! A reindeer!"

Diana turned to see a little girl, not more than five years old, dragging her father across the street toward her.

"Maggie, we're already late for the dance."

"Please, Daddy, I want to see the reindeer."

"You'll freeze out here," he countered.

That will make two of us, Diana thought, flexing her stiff fingers in her gloves.

But the little girl was undaunted by his warning. She waved at Diana as they reached the curb. Diana awkwardly waved back, then turned her attention to the little girl's father.

The first thing she noticed about the man was the stunning black tuxedo under his open wool overcoat. It was an expensive cut and molded to his powerful body in a way that made her bells jingle. Then she looked up into his face and forgot all about the cold.

Wavy black hair that brushed the back of his collar. Deep brown eyes with flecks of gold. The slightest shadow of dark stubble on his jaw. When he smiled at her, the numbness in her toes spread all the way up to her brain.

Diana reached up in a self-conscious gesture to finger-comb her short blond hair, but ended up knocking one of the large brown plastic antlers crooked instead. *Smooth, Falco. Very smooth.*

"Are you one of Santa's reindeers?" the little girl asked, her big brown eyes gleaming with excitement.

"I'm filling in for Blitzen," Diana improvised, all too aware of the man's gaze upon her. "He had to fly off somewhere tonight to help Santa. So I'm helping him collect money for needy kids."

"I can count money," the girl announced proudly. "My uncle Rick taught me."

"I'll let you put some in the kettle, Maggie," her father said, his voice as deep and rich as the starless night above, "but then we need to get inside the school before you catch a cold. I should have dropped you off at the door."

Diana watched the man pat the front of his tuxedo, an odd expression on his handsome face. It finally cleared when he dug one hand into a side pocket and pulled out some loose change.

"Here you go," he said, handing it to his daughter.

The little girl took the coins from his hand, then methodically began to count as she dropped them one by one into the collection drum. "Ten... one...five...one...twenty-five....ten...five." Then she smiled up at Diana. "See. I do know how to count money."

Diana smiled back, remembering how she used to show off counting, too. Only she'd been multiplying fractions at that age, to the thrill of her parents, who were both math professors. They'd often brought her out at parties to compete against their adult guests in solving complex math problems, and she'd often won.

Diana had soon become a favorite at those faculty parties, socializing more with adults than children. Due to skipping several grades in school, she'd never really had a normal childhood. Maybe that's why children were such an enigma to her.

"All right, sweetheart," the man said, steering his daughter toward the brick schoolhouse down the street. "Time to get moving."

Diana watched them walk away, releasing a sigh of disappointment.

A lousy fifty-seven cents.

From a man wearing a tuxedo that had probably cost a thousand times that amount. Not that his stinginess surprised her. Most of the people she met in her business preferred to keep their money rather than give it away—either to a charity or the IRS.

Still, Christmas was the time for giving. It was the time for family, too, and seeing that little girl with her father only reinforced for Diana how lonely this holiday was going to be for her.

Most of her friends had families of their own, and she hadn't even dated anyone since breaking up with her boyfriend last year, preferring to concentrate on her career as a forensic CPA. That's why she worked sixteen-hour days and made little time for a social life.

Then men like Mr. Tuxedo came along and made her start wondering what she was missing. That was the problem with standing alone on a cold street corner. It gave her too much time to think. Too much time to question the choices she'd made in her life.

And to fantasize about a certain sexy cheapskate's smile.

CHAPTER TWO

"TIME TO GET YOU HOME," Rob announced as he and Maggie walked out of the school dance. "Before you turn into a pumpkin."

"Cinderella doesn't turn into a pumpkin," Maggie informed him as they walked the seven long blocks to the car. "Don't you remember the story?"

Rob bit back a smile at the note of exasperation in her voice. "That's right. Maybe we should read it tonight so I don't forget again."

"Let's read both *Cinderella* and *Sleeping Beauty*," Maggie replied, skipping to keep up with his long stride.

"Deal." He reached for her hand, squeezing it through the bulky wool mitten she wore. "Did you have a good time tonight, Maggie May?"

She nodded emphatically, then grinned up at him. "We danced every single dance, Daddy."

"We sure did." Rob smiled as he remembered how often she'd asked him to twirl her. He had been certain she'd eventually become dizzy and want to sit out a dance or two. But not his Maggie.

Every time the music started she pulled him out on the floor, inadvertently keeping him from asking some of the single mothers to dance. One in particular had caught his attention—Lorna Sandoval, head of the PTA and an all-around supermother. Operating a fudge business out of her home, she'd created personalized chocolate fudge Christmas stockings for each one of the children and passed them out at the dance tonight.

When Rob had complimented Lorna on the fudge she'd brought to the dance, she'd given him the recipe, along with her phone number—just in case he had any questions about how to prepare it. Rob knew he'd never attempt making fudge, but he'd try to make time to call Lorna. She was just the kind of woman he needed for his kids.

The cheerful sound of jingle bells made him look toward the corner where the Good Neighbors lady still stood, her antlers silhouetted under the glow of the streetlamp. He knew she must be a Popsicle by now.

You had to admire that kind of dedication, Rob thought to himself as they reached the car. He went to the passenger side first to unlock the door for Maggie.

Only he found it ajar.

In their hurry to get to the dance, she obviously hadn't closed it all the way. The dash light wasn't on either, which wasn't a good sign. Rob swallowed a groan as he bundled Maggie inside the car, then rounded the front fender and slipped into the driver's seat.

But it was no use. The ignition wouldn't even turn over. The car battery, like Jacob Marley in *A Christmas Carol,* was as dead as a doornail.

Maggie's teeth began to chatter. "I'm getting cold, Daddy."

"I know, hon." He reached into his jacket pocket for his cell phone—then realized it wasn't there. He patted down his other pockets, his stomach sinking in dread. No doubt his cell phone was still on the kitchen table at home, along with his wallet.

He hadn't realized he'd left that behind until he'd tried to make a donation to the Good Neighbors lady on their way to the dance. That experience had been more than a little embarrassing, since Rob always made generous donations to charities, both during the holidays and the rest of the year.

This just wasn't his day.

Fortunately, he remembered a pay phone on the same corner as the Good Neighbors lady. He'd call his brother Rick to come down here and give the car battery a boost. Shrugging out of his wool overcoat, he tucked it snugly around his shivering daughter.

"You stay right here, Maggie. See that phone booth next to the lady? I'm going to make a quick phone call to Uncle Rick. I'll be back as soon as I can."

She nodded as she burrowed under his coat, but her breath was coming out in little puffs of frosty air. Without delaying any longer, Rob got out of the car, locking the doors behind him, then jogged half a block to the corner.

The Good Neighbors lady was packing up her collection drum.

"Remember me?" he asked with a smile. If he had to get stranded on a Seattle street, at least he'd done it with a kind and generous good Samaritan nearby. A pretty Samaritan, too. Rob had noticed that three hours ago.

She was petite, barely reaching his shoulder, and had wide blue eyes that made him think of a summer sky. Her blond hair gleamed sleek and silky under the antlers.

"Of course I remember you." She reached up to remove her antlers. "Mr. Fifty-seven cents."

He winced at the subtle note of derision in her tone. "My name is Rob Perez. And you are…?"

She hesitated, as if uncertain about giving her name to a stranger. "Diana."

"Look, Diana, I know it wasn't much money...but the thing is, I need it back."

She blinked. "Need what back?"

"The fifty-seven cents. Or just fifty cents. You can keep the seven pennies."

She placed a hand on her chest and blinked at him in mock wonderment. "Really? The *entire* seven cents? Are you sure you can spare it?"

So much for believing she was kind and generous. Rob was bone-tired, cold and worried about his daughter. "Look, I really don't have time to explain. I need to make a phone call. If you'll just give me my donation back, I promise to make a bigger one later."

She planted her hands on her hips, her blue eyes blazing now. "I can't believe you're standing here asking me for your lousy fifty-seven cents! This money is for kids who won't have any Christmas at all if Scrooges like you start demanding their money back."

Scrooge? Rob loved Christmas. It was his favorite time of year. The wind picked up and he rubbed his hands over the arms of the tuxedo jacket, wishing it was made of warmer material.

"At the moment," he said briskly, "the only kid I'm worried about is my daughter. She's shivering in my car because the battery is dead. I need my lousy fifty-seven cents to make a phone call so I can get her somewhere warm."

"Look, I'm sorry." She lifted her hands in a helpless gesture. "Even if I wanted to, I can't open the drum. And I don't have any money on me."

Rob didn't believe her.

"Merry Christmas," he bit out, then turned and walked away before she could say another word.

DIANA STARED after the man in the tuxedo, wondering what in the world had come over her. She was both tired and cold after standing out here for more than three hours, but that didn't excuse her behavior.

Had she become so focused on her career that she couldn't make simple conversation anymore? Help out a stranger? Shame burned in her cheeks at some of the things she'd said to him—and the way she'd said them.

Diana started after him to apologize and to offer him and his daughter a ride home in her car. But the sound of a car horn made them both turn toward the street.

A young woman leaned out of her open window, smiling broadly at the man. "Hey, Rob, did you forget your coat at the dance?"

Diana assumed there must have been some kind

of dance at the nearby elementary school. She remembered now that he'd been worried about arriving late. That certainly explained why he and his daughter were dressed so nicely.

"Hi, Lorna," he greeted, stepping closer to the curb. "Maggie's wearing it. Seems we have a bit of a problem. My car battery is dead and we're stranded at the moment."

Lorna's face brightened as if she'd just won the lottery. "How awful!"

"I don't suppose you happen to have any battery cables with you?"

"No, I'm sorry, I don't," Lorna replied, not looking the least bit sorry to Diana's eyes. "But I'd be more than happy to give you and Maggie a lift."

He hesitated only a moment. "If you're sure it's no trouble."

"No trouble," she assured him. "No trouble at all."

Diana watched as the woman hastily directed her son to tumble in to the back seat so Rob could join her in the front. Regret pricked her as she watched the woman coyly check her lipstick in her rearview mirror before turning a thousand-watt smile on Rob.

He smiled back and Diana's heart shrank another notch. She saw him point to a car parked at the far end of the street where his little girl huddled inside. Remorse clogged her throat.

Should she run after him and apologize? Try to find some way to explain that she didn't usually antagonize perfect strangers on the street? But what sort of excuse could she possibly offer? Frost-bite of the brain?

The truth was that his sexy smile had magnified the lonely ache inside of her. Made her realize how long it had been since any man had smiled at her like that. Certainly none of the men at work, who saw her more as a competitor than a woman.

So why had she been so willing to think the worst of Rob Perez? Just to keep from dwelling on what was missing in her own life? The family she didn't have around her anymore. The friends she'd all but deserted in pursuit of her career. The love life that simply didn't exist.

Diana swallowed a sigh as she watched Rob place his daughter into the back seat of Lorna's car. The red taillights flashed, then faded into the dark, wintry night as the car made its way down the street. She'd never see the man again. Never have a chance to make amends for the way she'd treated him.

Her shift was over, but part of her wished she could start it all over again. Tomorrow, she'd go in early to work. Try to finish up her most recent financial project before the deadline. Find a way to appease her boss for missing the party.

And volunteer for more hours of community service with the Good Neighbors. Maybe then she'd eventually learn to be one.

CHAPTER THREE

ROB SWORE he'd never put off his Christmas shopping again. The department store was packed with shoppers. He carried T.J. in his arms, his future sister-in-law Frankie Raimondi following behind with Maggie.

"How about a snow-cone machine?" Maggie suggested, admiring the display in front of them. "I bet Uncle Rick would love to make snow cones for Christmas."

"What do you think, Frankie?" Rob had asked her to come along and help them pick out a gift for his brother. The kids loved her and Rob couldn't help but feel a twinge of envy at his brother's good fortune.

"I think you're trying to make me the bad guy," Frankie murmured to Rob. Then she turned to Maggie. "Rick likes snow cones, but I bet he'd like a CD player even better."

Rob shifted T.J. to his other arm, then caught sight of a blond head bobbing in the crowd. *Diana?* As soon as the name entered his head, he pushed it out again. Rob had imagined seeing her in crowds and on street corners for the last three days. Ever since the night of the dance when she'd laid in to him about depriving needy children. No woman had ever talked to him that way before. With such intensity. Such…passion.

But as the crowd shifted, he realized it really was her. She was studying a display of silk ties, her mouth turned down in concentration. Were the ties for a boyfriend? A husband?

His gaze moved to her left hand as it brushed over one of the ties. No ring. He smiled to himself as T.J. began struggling in his arms.

"Down, Daddy. Down!"

Rob looked at his son. "If I let you down, will you stay right next to me?"

T.J. gave him a solemn nod.

"Okay." Rob placed him on the floor as Frankie and Maggie approached them. "Stay right here."

"Look what we found," Frankie exclaimed, holding a dress in her hand.

"Looks a little small for Rick," he said dryly.

Maggie laughed. "It's not for Uncle Rick, Daddy. It's for me to wear to the Christmas concert at school."

"You just got a brand-new dress," he said, as T.J. wove between his legs.

"That was for the dance," Maggie told him, with a plaintive glance at her aunt.

Frankie smiled. "A girl can't wear the same dress to two events in a row. Don't you know anything about women?"

"Apparently not." Then he looked at the price tag. "But I do know that's a ridiculous amount of money to spend on a dress she'll outgrow in a few months."

Maggie visibly wilted.

Frankie leaned closer to Rob. "Do you mind if we make it an early Christmas gift from Rick and I?"

Rob sighed, knowing it was impossible to fight two women at once. "Are you sure you want to spend that much?"

Frankie smiled. "I'm sure."

Then she turned to Maggie. "Let's go try it on and make sure it fits."

Maggie clapped her hands in delight. Then she took Frankie's hand and headed toward the dressing room. "We'll be right back, Daddy."

Rob turned to corral T.J., his gaze falling on Diana once again. She'd moved from the ties to a display of watches, still oblivious to him. Then again, maybe she didn't remember him.

Rob turned back to pick up his son, but didn't see T.J. anywhere. He searched the floor around him, hindered by the crowd of shoppers and the cluttered array of display tables and racks.

"T.J.?" Rob called out, growing more concerned as he searched. But there was no answer.

His son was gone.

DIANA KNEW she should walk straight out the door of the store. As soon as she'd seen Rob with his pretty wife and family, all her forbidden fantasies about the man had gone up in a puff of smoke. Fantasies that had diverted her attention away from her work. Fantasies that had made that night on the street corner with him end very differently.

She watched out of the corner of her eye as the tall brunette leaned forward to whisper something to Rob. Then they both turned and said something to the little girl, who beamed up at them.

A deep ache seared Diana, making her breath catch in her throat. A ridiculous reaction, she told herself, waiting for the ache to subside.

Christmas music wafted over the store speakers and Diana began to hum along, determined to get into the spirit of the season. She turned away from the silk ties, forcing herself not to glance in Rob's direction again. She needed to find a present for her father, a man who was very hard to please.

What would a man like Rob want?

The question came unbidden to her mind. Rob

probably had everything he wanted. A wife. A family. Irritated to find herself thinking about Rob again, Diana turned to a circular rack of dress shirts and began rifling through them.

As she made her way around the rack, she almost tripped over a small white sneaker in her path. She bent down to see that the sneaker belonged to a stocky little boy sitting under the rack, half-hidden by the shirts.

Rob's little boy.

Then she heard his deep voice call out, "T.J.? Where are you?"

Diana straightened and looked around the store, but she couldn't see Rob. No doubt T.J. couldn't see his father either, with the constant ebb and flow of shoppers all around them. But the note of panic in Rob's voice was all too clear.

Diana set down her purse, then knelt on the floor beside the clothing rack. "Are you T.J. Perez?"

He stared at her with big, round hazel eyes, not saying a word.

"Are you lost?" she asked.

He shook his head.

Diana could see the boy was terrified, but she had little experience in dealing with children, terrified or otherwise. She held out her hand. "Come with me and I'll help you find your father."

He shrunk back, his face crumpling as if he was about to cry.

She looked helplessly around her, wanting to go track down Rob, but afraid T.J. would disappear while she was gone. She needed something to tempt him out from under the rack. Digging inside her purse, she pulled out a pocket calculator.

"Look at this," she said, holding it out to him. "See how you can punch the numbers and make them light up?"

He bit his lower lip, his gaze on the calculator. Finally he reached out and punched the keys with one chubby finger.

"Do you want it?" she asked, trying to draw him out.

But he shook his head, staying stubbornly in place.

Diana replaced the calculator and found something even better in the bottom of her purse. An oatmeal cookie wrapped in cellophane that she'd bought with her lunch three days ago.

T.J.'s eyes widened when he saw it. "Cookie."

"You can have it if you come out," she said coaxingly, unwrapping it for him.

His lip quivered as he scrambled out from under the rack. "Daddy's lost."

"I'll help you find him," she promised, giving him the cookie.

T.J. hesitated a moment, then barreled into her arms, almost knocking her off balance. He buried his head against her shoulder as she picked him up off the floor. His hair smelled faintly of soap and his thick arms wrapped snugly around her neck.

For a brief moment, the ache returned and she gave the scared little boy a reassuring hug. Then she turned and headed in Rob's direction.

Maybe she could give him something he wanted after all.

ROB DIDN'T START to panic immediately. T.J. had been at his side just a moment ago. His son had to be somewhere close by. But where?

"T.J.?" Rob called out as shoppers milled around him. He unzipped his jacket, worry making him unbearably warm.

Rob turned toward the dressing room, but there was no sign of Maggie and Frankie. Had T.J. followed them in there? He headed in that direction, then turned back. What if his son had wandered off the opposite way?

Panic began to claw at him as he turned a slow circle. What if someone had carried T.J. off? Child abductions were constantly in the news. How long should he wait before calling for help?

"T.J?" Rob shouted again, louder this time. A

trio of elderly women looked warily at him, then moved on.

What kind of father lost track of his own son? *The kind of father who stared at a pretty blonde. The kind of father who spent his time fantasizing about a complete stranger rather than paying attention to his own child.*

Guilt mingled with his growing panic as he ripped through racks of clothing, looking for his boy.

But Rob couldn't find him anywhere. It was time to get the store involved. Maybe even call the police. If anything happened to his son...

"Merry Christmas."

Rob turned around to see Diana holding a purse in one hand and T.J. in the other.

"Daddy!" T.J. dropped her hand and held out his chubby little arms to his father.

Rob swept his son up into his own arms, his throat contracting. "Hey, T-man."

"You got lost," T.J. accused.

"I know," Rob murmured against his neck, inhaling his familiar scent.

"Maybe you should put jingle bells on T.J.'s shoe laces," Diana suggested with a smile. "In case you get lost again."

"Good idea," Rob replied, wishing he'd thought of something that simple himself. Wishing she didn't look so damn gorgeous. He was doing it again. Lusting after Diana when he should be comforting his son.

What was wrong with him? This was the woman who had refused to return his measly fifty-seven cents. The woman who would have left him and Maggie stranded in the cold, dark night.

"Thanks for finding him," Rob said gruffly. "I appreciate you giving *this* back."

Diana winced at his sharp tone and Rob realized too late that he'd taken his anger at himself out on her.

"I'm sorry," he said hastily, shifting T.J. in his arms. "Look, I didn't mean that. Can I buy you a cup of coffee or something?"

"That's really not necessary." Diana's gaze moved past his shoulder. "And I'm not sure your wife would appreciate it."

Rob glanced back to see Frankie and Maggie standing behind him.

"Hope we're not interrupting anything," Frankie said, then she held out her hand to Diana. "I'm Frankie Raimondi, soon-to-be Rob's sister-in-law."

"Oh," Diana said with a blush, taking her hand. "Nice to meet you. I'm Diana Falco."

Frankie smiled. "Rob's a widower, so no one will mind if he buys you a cup of coffee. In fact,

I'll be happy to watch the kids if you two want to take a break from shopping.''

"Thanks," Diana said briskly, avoiding Rob's gaze. "But I really have to get back to work."

"Merry Christmas!" Maggie called after her.

Diana waved to her as she walked away. "Merry Christmas."

Frankie looked up at Rob with a wry smile. "The Perez charm strikes again."

He sighed. "You heard everything?"

She nodded. "I'm afraid so."

Rob glanced at his daughter, who seemed too absorbed with the new dress in her hands to be following their conversation. He looked back up at his sister-in-law. "I was a jerk."

"Agreed," Frankie replied. "The question is why? Some nice stranger finds T.J. and you almost bite her head off."

Rob cleared his throat. "Diana and I aren't exactly strangers. We've met before. Once," he clarified. "Very briefly."

"She's the reindeer lady," Maggie piped up, obviously paying more attention than Rob had assumed.

"The reindeer lady?" Frankie echoed, arching a brow at Rob.

"It's a long story," Rob said as T.J. struggled in his arms. He wasn't about to make the mistake of putting him down again. At least not until he put some jingle bells on his son's shoelaces.

"I'd like to hear it sometime." Frankie prodded Maggie toward the cash register. "Especially how it ends."

That was the problem. He'd probably never see Diana Falco again, which meant it would end with her thinking he was a complete jerk. Rob couldn't let that happen. He had to apologize to her for his behavior. Had to thank her for rescuing T.J. To do both of those things, he had to find her—and that could be a problem since all he knew about her was her name.

But find her he would. Even if he had to go all the way to the North Pole to do it.

CHAPTER FOUR

"WERE YOU EXPECTING FLOWERS?"

Diana looked up from her desk to see her secretary standing in the office doorway. Beth Haversfield was a fifteen-year veteran of the accounting firm Barney, Beck and Whitney and had shown Diana the ropes when she'd first arrived. As well as let her in on all the company gossip. Now Beth stood with one arm behind her back and a twinkle in her green eyes.

"No," Diana said slowly, setting down her pen. She glanced at the clock, surprised to see that it was almost two o'clock. She'd worked right through lunch again.

"That's good," Beth replied, stepping inside the office. "Because you didn't get flowers. You got…jerky."

Diana watched as Beth swung her arm around to reveal a vase full of beef jerky, all tied together with a big red bow.

"Is this a joke?" Diana asked as Beth set the vase on her desk.

"I can't wait to find out." Beth handed her the card that had been attached to the bow. "The vase is certainly no joke. It looks to me like Baccarat crystal."

The diamond-cut vase was beautiful and the savory aroma of the beef jerky made Diana's mouth water. She looked down at the card to read the short message handwritten in bold, black strokes.

I thought this was appropriate since I acted like such a jerk at the store. Thank you so much for finding my son. Merry Christmas.

Rob Perez

The note was written on the back of his business card. She turned it over to see the words Roberto Perez Woodworks printed on the front of the card, along with an address at 10 Sandringham Drive in Belltown and a telephone number.

"Well, don't keep me in suspense," Beth said at last. "Who is it from?"

"Just a handsome jerk I know," Diana replied with a smile. She picked up the vase and held it out to her friend. "Have one?"

"Don't mind if I do." Beth pulled a stick of jerky out of the vase, then bit off one end. "Hey, this is good. Nice and spicy. So what's the story?"

"Story?" Diana echoed, taking a piece of jerky for herself.

"Who is this guy and how did you meet him?"

"His name is Rob Perez and we met when I was collecting donations for the Good Neighbors."

Beth laughed. "Hey, I guess that would be a great way to meet men. Maybe I'll have to volunteer."

"I'm sure they could use the help." Diana didn't admit that her reason for volunteering every year had nothing to do with men and everything to do with redemption.

At fourteen, she'd made a horrible mistake that still haunted her. She'd been left in charge of a six-year-old boy, the son of another faculty couple. Even then she'd been uncomfortable with children, and had no idea how to keep the boy entertained. She'd finally gotten him interested in a cartoon on television, then pulled out her books to study for final exams at school.

But the sound of shattering glass had pulled her out of geometry and sent her into a panic. Especially when she'd found the boy bleeding all over the floor. He'd accidentally put his arm through the sliding glass door, severing nerves and ligaments. He never regained full use of his arm and Diana had never forgiven herself.

A good friend had suggested that helping others

was a good way to redirect her guilt in a positive way. That's when Diana had first started working with the Good Neighbors. She'd volunteered every year since. Helping others did make her feel better, even if it couldn't erase past mistakes.

"Well, I'd better get back to work," Beth said, grabbing another stick of jerky out of the vase. "By the way, Mr. Beck said the report you turned in on the Harper, Inc. case was perfect, just like always."

"I'm glad he liked it."

Beth headed for the door. "Keep me posted on your romance."

"There is no romance," Diana called after her. "I hardly know the man."

But Beth just laughed as she closed the door behind her.

Diana shook her head, turning her attention back to the project on her desk. But she couldn't seem to concentrate. After several fruitless minutes, she picked up Rob's card and read his message again. She was both surprised and pleased by the fact that he'd taken the time to apologize with such a sweet, unorthodox gift.

On an impulse, she picked up the telephone and dialed the number on the card.

Rob answered on the second ring. "Hello?"

Diana sucked in a deep breath, suddenly nervous. "Hi, Rob, this is Diana. Diana Falco. I just wanted to thank you for the beef jerky bouquet," she continued awkwardly. "I skipped lunch today so it arrived just in time."

His low chuckle sounded over the line. "That's a relief. After I sent it, I worried that you might be a vegetarian."

"Not me," she said, leaning back in her chair. "But how did you know where to send it?"

"I did an Internet search for Diana Falco and found an old *Seattle Post-Intelligencer* article about your job at Barney, Beck and Whitney. There was a photo of you along with the article."

Diana nodded, remembering the publicity photos all the executive trainees had been required to submit during the application process. "Should I be scared it's so easy to find me?"

"There's no reason to be scared of me," he assured her. "Even though I acted like a complete jerk when I made that wisecrack about giving T.J. back. I didn't mean it, Diana, and I never should have said it."

"You were half-frantic with worry about your son," she replied. "I understand."

"That's still no excuse," Rob countered. "I just hope you can find it in your heart to forgive me."

"Only if you'll forgive me for not helping you the night we met. I really couldn't open the collection drum, but I might have at least offered you a lift in my car.''

''Sounds like we both need a chance to start over.''

Diana sat up in the chair, her pulse picking up. ''Oh?''

He hesitated. ''Listen, I know this is short notice, but I was wondering if you might be free tomorrow night?''

''I think so,'' she said, not bothering to check her calendar. Her life consisted of work, work and more work. She couldn't remember the last time she'd spent a Saturday night with a man instead of an adding machine.

''My brother and Frankie, the woman you met at the mall, are getting married,'' he explained. ''Nothing formal, just a simple ceremony at the Sorrento Hotel with family and a few friends. There will be dinner and dancing at the reception afterward.''

''That sounds nice,'' Diana said, a little surprised he wanted to take her to a wedding for their first date. Then again, maybe he hated going solo to those kinds of events as much as she did. ''I'd love to go.''

''Great,'' he replied. ''The wedding is at seven and I told the baby-sitter to be at my place by about six-fifteen. Where do you live?''

She hesitated, pondering the logistics. "I'm staying at my parents' house by Green Lake. If you're in Belltown, why don't I just stop by your place at six-thirty? Then we could go to the Sorrento from there."

"Are you sure you don't mind?"

"Positive," Diana replied, knowing it would be inconvenient for him to drive all the way north just to turn around and go back again. "What's your address?"

"Number 10 Sandringham Drive."

She glanced at the business card. "The same as your business?"

"Yes, my wood shop is right next to my apartment. I'm on the first floor of the building."

"Then I guess I'll see you tomorrow night," she said, feeling a little giddy.

"I'm looking forward to it, Diana."

"Goodbye, Rob." She hung up the telephone, wondering what had come over her. Diana had made it a policy a long time ago never to get involved with a man who had children. She was a perfectionist and her record with children was far from perfect, as any of the kids at that Halloween party could attest.

"Get a grip," she murmured to herself, taking a deep breath to calm her racing heart. "The man asked you for a date, not a lifetime commitment."

Besides, she deserved a night off. She'd already completed most of the projects on the list in front of her, many of them not due until after the holidays. Picking up a pen, she added a new item to the top of the list: *Date with Roberto Perez.*

ROB UNKNOTTED his tie for the third time, wondering why he was having so much trouble getting it on right tonight of all nights. T.J. hung on his leg, aware that something was up. Maggie had left two hours ago with Carmen, eager to perform her flower-girl duties at the wedding.

Something told him he wouldn't be this nervous if Lorna Sandoval was his date for the evening. He'd asked her to the wedding first, finally putting into motion his plan to find a suitable mother for his children. But Lorna had canceled yesterday when her son came down with chicken pox. She'd been so apologetic, though firm in her decision to stay with her sick son. He admired that about her. Hell, he admired all her supermother qualities. He just didn't *feel* anything when he was around her.

Rob hadn't thought that important until he'd met Diana. She'd definitely brought him back to life, making him aware for the first time of the physical numbness that had consumed him since his wife's death over two years ago. Still, he'd surprised himself by asking her when she'd called yesterday. He usually wasn't so impulsive.

"Juice, Daddy," T.J. said, watching his father in the dresser mirror.

"No more juice until Stacie gets here," he said, referring to the teenager down the block who often baby-sat for him when his mother and brothers weren't available.

Threading the tie through the last loop, he cinched it into a perfect knot. Then he picked up a comb and ran it through his hair, wishing he'd taken the time to get a haircut.

The doorbell rang and T.J. climbed off his leg and headed out of the bedroom. "Stacie!"

Rob followed him, taking a quick inventory of the apartment. Maggie had helped him clean it up this morning, but T.J.'s many toys had soon found their way back on the floor. Rob just didn't seem to be able to keep on top of things. Not only in his home, but his business, as well. The invoices were piling up on his desk, the Christmas orders keeping him too busy to handle all the paperwork.

He opened the door to let Stacie inside, T.J. bouncing on the floor behind him.

Only it wasn't Stacie waiting on the other side, but Diana.

A Diana he barely recognized when she stepped into his house and slipped off her coat. She wore a sapphire blue dress that matched her beautiful eyes, and her short blond hair was slicked back in an elegant style. It only took one glance for Rob to realize she'd been hiding an incredible body under her coat the previous times he'd seen her.

"I know I'm a little early," she said, her cheeks pink from the cold. "I thought I might have trouble finding the place."

"No problem," Rob said, trying not to stare. He'd been attracted to her before, but now he felt as if someone had hit him in the head with a two-by-four.

T.J. barreled past him and wrapped his chubby arms around Diana's legs. "Cookie?"

"I'm sorry," she said, regret crinkling her brow. "I don't have any cookies with me tonight."

"I'll get you a cookie," Rob said, peeling his son off her. "Come on in and sit down, Diana. The sitter should be here soon."

She followed him into the kitchen and took a seat at the table while he retrieved a cookie from the cupboard for his son.

"How about a cup of eggnog or a glass of wine?" he offered, walking over to the refrigerator.

"Eggnog sounds wonderful." She looked around the apartment. "You've got a great place."

"Thanks, but I'm not sure how much longer

we'll be here." He poured them each a cup of eggnog. "My mother owns the building and is looking for a buyer."

"Where will you go?"

He shrugged, turning around to find that T.J. had staked a claim on her lap. "I've been thinking about buying a house. One with a big backyard and lots of room to run around in. Maybe even get a dog."

Diana began telling him about the cocker spaniel she'd raised from a puppy, and they chatted until the sitter arrived a few minutes later.

Rob ushered the teenager into the kitchen, telling her he'd be back by midnight, when T.J. interrupted his father by shouting, "Go potty."

"You have to go potty, T.J.?" Rob asked eagerly, still hoping his son would get the hang of it one day soon.

"I think he already did," Diana said with a slight wince.

Rob looked in horror at the dark, wet stain spreading over Diana's lap. "T.J.!"

"Uh-oh," T.J. replied, cookie crumbs dusting his lips.

The baby-sitter wrinkled her nose. "Ewww, that's gross."

"I'm so sorry," Rob said, sweeping his son off Diana's lap.

"That's all right," she replied, rising gingerly to her feet. T.J.'s mess formed a perfect circle on the silk of her blue dress. "I was probably holding him wrong."

T.J. looked from his father to Diana. "Cookie?"

"No more cookies," Rob said sternly. "And definitely no more juice." He handed his son off to the baby-sitter. "Will you please clean him up and help him into his pajamas?"

"Sure." Stacie reached for his hand. "C'mon, T.J."

Rob watched them walk down the hallway, then turned back to Diana. "I think I owe you a year's supply of beef jerky for this."

"It was an accident," she said, looking down at her dress in dismay. "But I can't go to the wedding like this. I'll have to run home and change."

He glanced at his watch. "There's no time. But I might have something you could wear."

She gave him a rueful smile. "I don't think we're the same size."

"I think my wife was about your size. I still have all of her clothes."

Diana hesitated. "Are you sure?"

Rob didn't blame her for asking the question. He'd kept those clothes as a way to deny that Susanna was really gone, though he'd lived every day of the past two and a half years with the knowledge that he was on his own.

But the thought of Diana wearing Susanna's clothes didn't bother him at all. Another sign that he was ready to move on with his life. "I'm sure. Besides, you're probably ready to get out of that dress."

She arched a brow. "Right here?"

That innocent question sent his pulse racing. How long had it been since he'd asked a woman to take off her clothes. Or taken them off himself? Too long, judging by the reaction she was having on his body.

"You can change in my bedroom," he said hastily, hoping he'd remembered to make the bed this morning. "Follow me."

CHAPTER FIVE

THE DRESS FIT PERFECTLY. It was an emerald velvet that hugged her body in a way that had made Rob's eyes flare when she'd stepped out of his bedroom. The price tag had still been attached when she'd pulled it out of the closet, and Rob had explained that Susanna had probably bought it on sale to wear after T.J. was born.

Her shoes didn't match the color of the dress, but all of Susanna's shoes were one size too small, so she'd had to make do with her own.

Diana was a little self-conscious about it as they walked into the Top of the Town, a small European-style ballroom in the Sorrento Hotel where the ceremony and reception were to be held. A crystal chandelier hung from the ornate dome ceiling and the large windows in the round room gave a sweeping panoramic view of downtown Seattle, from the Space Needle to Safeco Field.

Tables were set along the perimeter of the room, while the middle had been cordoned off for the ceremony. A white runner separated two banks of chairs, enough to seat the approximately fifty guests in attendance. The runner led to a white arched bower, threaded with ivy, where the bride and groom would exchange their vows.

Most of the guests were already there, and Rob pointed out his mother and brothers to her. Rick Perez stood off to the side of the room with his best man, Rafe. Diana thought the two of them looked almost as handsome as Rob in their dark gray suits.

A harpist began to play as they took their seats. More than one member of his family cast a speculative glance in their direction, and something told her that they hadn't known he was bringing a date to the wedding. Rob's chair was so close to hers that his knee kept lightly brushing against her leg, the contact making her skin tingle.

"Looks like it's about to begin," Rob whispered to her as Rick and Rafe took their places at the bower with the cleric.

The harpist forcefully strummed a prelude, quieting the guests, then began playing the wedding march. Maggie started up the aisle, carefully scattering red rose petals from her basket. Diana glanced at Rob, seeing the pride on his face as he watched his daughter.

The matron of honor followed behind her, and

Rob leaned over to whisper, "That's Frankie's youngest sister, Rosa."

Then Diana saw the bride herself. Frankie wore an empire gown of champagne silk, her dark hair pulled back in a simple chignon. She carried a bouquet of lush red roses and wore a smile of sheer joy. A smile her groom returned as she walked toward him on the arm of her father.

Rick and Frankie held hands as they exchanged their vows, their eyes only for each other. At twenty-six, Diana had been to her share of weddings, but few had touched her as much as this one.

She saw Rob's mother shed happy tears, dabbing at her eyes with a tissue. Maggie looked over and smiled at her father, her cheeks flushed and her dark eyes wide with excitement as Rick kissed his bride.

"It's my pleasure to introduce to you," the cleric announced, "Mr. and Mrs. Ricardo Perez."

The guests applauded when Frankie and Rick kissed again.

"That was beautiful," Diana said as everyone began to mill around the bride and groom.

Rob nodded and rose to his feet. "Maggie did a good job, too. She was worried that she'd run out of rose petals halfway up the aisle."

Diana laughed. "I thought I saw her silently counting the petals out two by two."

Maggie bounded up to them. "Did you see me?"

"You were the best flower girl ever," Rob said.

Maggie looked up at Diana. "You look beautiful! Just like Cinderella."

"Thank you, Maggie," she replied, touched by the little girl's compliment. "So do you."

As the guests began to fill the tables, they made their way over to Rick and Frankie.

"Welcome to the family," Rob said, kissing Frankie's cheek. Diana saw Rick give her a speculative once-over as Frankie turned to her. "It's so nice to see you again."

"Congratulations," Diana said. "It was a beautiful ceremony."

"This is my husband, Rick Perez," Frankie said, then laughed. "That's the first time I've ever called him my husband!"

"I'm Diana Falco," she said, reaching out to shake his hand.

"I'm glad you could be here," Rick replied, circling his arm around Frankie's waist.

Maggie wedged between Rob and Diana, beaming up at her aunt and uncle. "My dad said I was the best flower girl ever."

"That's right." Rick reached out to tweak her nose. "You'll be the best shepherd girl ever, too."

Rob looked from his daughter to his brother, wondering what he was missing. "Shepherd girl?"

Rick gave him a lopsided grin. "Do you remember that Christmas play I auditioned for a couple of months ago?"

Rob nodded. "Yeah. You said you got the part."

"I did," Rick affirmed. "But they needed some kids for stand-in parts, so I volunteered Maggie."

Rob folded his arms across his chest. "Please tell me she won't need another new dress for this play."

Rick shook his head. "The wardrobe department will send over a costume for her to wear."

"So can I be in the play, Daddy?" Maggie clasped her hands together as she gazed up at her father. "Please."

How could he refuse her? His family would outvote him anyway. "It's fine with me."

Rob watched Rick give Maggie a high five. He could never repay his family for all they did for his children, but sometimes he worried that they spoiled Maggie and T.J. too much.

He understood the desire to shower gifts and attention on his motherless children. He'd done it himself after Susanna's death, trying to make up for the sudden void in their lives. But they needed balance, too. Maybe that was impossible for a single father to provide. Just another reason for him to find someone to help him parent.

He looked at Diana as she chatted with Frankie, realizing he hadn't been thinking about his children at all when he'd asked her out. Following his hormones rather than his head. Hormones that had lain dormant for much too long.

"Earth to Rob," Rick said under his breath. That's when Rob realized he'd been staring at his date.

He turned his attention to his brother. "Yeah?"

"Your daughter is trying to get your attention," Rick said with a grin.

He looked down at Maggie, who was tugging at the hem of his suit coat. "What do you need?"

"Can I go to the slumber party now?"

Frankie's sister had rented a room where the children could eat pizza and watch videos while the adults enjoyed the reception. Maggie had been invited to stay overnight there with the other children and had talked of little else for the last week.

"I don't see why not," Rob said, turning to Frankie. "Do you know the room number?"

"It's in room three hundred," she replied. "And one of Rosa's friends will be there to supervise."

He nodded, then looked at Diana. "Do you mind waiting here while I take Maggie to the party?"

"Not at all," she replied as Rick and Frankie drifted away to talk with other guests.

Diana watched Rob leave the room with his daughter, then accepted a glass of champagne from a passing waiter. Before long, a heavily pregnant woman approached her.

"I'm Maria Perez," she said with a gentle smile. "Rafe's wife."

Diana shook her hand. "Nice to meet you."

"Your dress is stunning," Maria said, "I noticed it as soon as you walked in tonight."

"Oh…thank you." She shifted uncomfortably on her feet. "Actually, it belonged to Rob's wife. There was an accident with my dress and I didn't have time to go home and change and…"

"It's beautiful on you," Maria said, putting her at ease. "Susanna had wonderful taste in both clothes and men."

"Did you know her?" Diana asked, curious about the woman Rob had married.

Maria nodded. "Susanna was a wonderful wife and mother. One of those women who baked her own bread and sewed beautiful dresses for Maggie and had an eye for interior decorating. She put Martha Stewart to shame."

Diana nodded, realizing the dress might be a

perfect fit, but in every other way she was a complete mismatch to the woman he'd married. She didn't bake, didn't sew and her decorating skills consisted of buying colored paper for her computer.

"Susanna and Rob wanted a house full of children," Maria continued. "But that wasn't to be." She laid a hand on her swollen belly. "I just hope I can be half as good a mother as Susanna was. I have to admit I'm getting a little nervous."

"When is your baby due?"

"In just a month," Maria replied, excitement shining in her dark eyes.

Diana smiled. "A new baby for the New Year."

"We can't wait," Maria confided, then noticed her husband waving to her from across the room. "It was so nice to meet you, Diana. I hope we'll be seeing each other again soon."

"I'd like that," Diana said, though she knew that meant seeing Rob, and she was beginning to wonder if that was such a good idea. She liked Rob Perez—maybe too much. He was handsome and charming and sexy. Nice, too. A dangerous combination that was all too rare these days. If she wasn't careful, she could easily fall for him.

"You must be Diana," a voice from behind her said.

Diana turned to see the matron of honor,

Frankie's sister Rosa, beaming at her. "Yes, I am."

"Great dress," Rosa said, then leaned closer. "Frankie told me about you. I'm so glad Rob's finally found someone. A man like that shouldn't stay a bachelor forever."

"This is just our first date," Diana informed her, afraid that Rosa had the wrong idea about them.

But Frankie's sister waved away that trifling detail. "You two look great together. I know Rob's family has been worried about him being on his own for so long, especially trying to raise two little kids. It can't be easy."

"I'm sure it's not."

"Weddings seem to be contagious in the Perez family lately," Rosa told her. "Rafe and Maria last month, and Rick and Frankie tonight. Rob probably won't be far behind."

Something akin to panic washed up the back of her throat. But before she could set Rosa straight, Rob's mother walked up to them.

"I'm Carmen Perez," she said, taking Diana's hand into her own, "and I see my son has abandoned you."

"He'll be right back," Diana assured her, hoping Carmen wouldn't jump to the same wrong conclusions as Rosa. Though Rob's mother didn't strike her as the type of woman who jumped into anything. She radiated a warmth and poise that Diana couldn't help but admire.

"Wasn't the wedding beautiful," Rosa said, turning to Carmen. "I almost cried."

"It was lovely," Carmen concurred. "A dream come true."

Rosa nodded. "I was just telling Diana that weddings seem to be running in the Perez family. First Rafe, then Rick. There must be something in the air where they live."

Carmen's mouth curved into an enigmatic smile. "You never know."

Frankie walked up to them, a tall brunette beside her. "Carmen, I'd like you to meet a good friend of mine, Katherine Kinard. Katherine, this is Rick's mother, Carmen Perez."

The two women shook hands, then Katherine said, "Frankie tells me you own the building where she and Rick live and that it's up for sale. I'm actually looking for a place to open a day-care center here in Seattle."

"Ah, yes," Carmen said, a spark of interest lighting her eyes. "Rick told me about you."

Katherine nodded. "I've been over to visit Frankie a couple of times since she moved in with Rick, and I think that building has a lot of potential."

"I'd like to hear more about this day-care idea

of yours,'' Carmen said, ''I've been a kindergarten teacher for almost thirty years, though with the current budget crunch at our school, the administration has been encouraging me to retire early. Why did you decide to start a day care?''

''It's been a dream of mine for years,'' Katherine began, as she and Carmen drifted away.

Frankie and Rosa got called over to take pictures with the Raimondis, leaving Diana on her own again.

''Miss me?''

She turned around to see Rob standing behind her, and her heart gave a telling leap in her chest. Diana didn't want to be attracted to this man. Not when it was becoming depressingly obvious to her that she was completely wrong for him.

''Your mother and sisters-in-law kept me company,'' Diana replied. ''Your family seems very close.''

''In more ways than one,'' Rob replied, steering her toward a table. ''My brothers and I all live in the same building. Rick and Frankie on the second floor and Rafe and Maria on the third floor.''

''It must be nice to be able to help each other out,'' Diana said, remembering how often she used to wish for a brother or sister. ''To depend on each other.''

He nodded. ''I know Maggie and T.J. love having their aunts and uncles around all the time. I do, too, except..."

"Sometimes it's a little too close for comfort?" she ventured.

"Sometimes." He smiled. "Don't get me wrong. I love my family, but they can be a little overwhelming."

"That's an interesting description."

His smile turned wistful. "I know Susanna was a little intimidated the first time she met all of them. But in the end, I think it gave her comfort to know that Maggie and T.J. and I wouldn't be left alone."

"So she knew she was dying," Diana asked softly.

"I think she sensed it," he admitted. "She suffered from a rare form of toxemia when she was pregnant with Maggie. The doctor said it might be dangerous for her to have another child and I didn't want her to risk it, but Susanna was adamant about having more children. That was more important to her than anything else."

Diana took a sip of her champagne, wondering if any two women could be more different. Susanna had been willing to risk her life for more children, while Diana did her best to avoid them.

"Her blood pressure skyrocketed while she was

carrying T.J.,'' Rob continued. "They had to do an emergency C-section but…she didn't make it.''

"I'm so sorry,'' Diana said, and meant it. She could only imagine the pain and grief he must have endured, on top of the shock at finding himself a single parent.

"It seems like a lifetime ago,'' Rob admitted. "I know Maggie struggles to remember her, and of course T.J. has no memories of Susanna at all. I keep a picture of her in his room, but he's never really had a mother.''

Diana stared down at her glass, tempted to tell him that if he was looking for a mother for his children, she wasn't it. But that would be presumptuous, since he'd never even hinted as much. She was probably projecting her own dreams onto him. Dreams that could never come true. Diana was a perfectionist. She believed if you wanted to do something, you should do it well or not at all. Since children weren't her forte, she'd given up on the dream of having a family of her own a long time ago.

"So tell me about your life,'' Rob said.

"There's not much to tell,'' she replied. "I grew up on the University of Washington campus. My parents are both professors in the math department there, though they're in Europe at the moment on a teaching exchange.''

"Any brothers or sisters?"

She shook her head. "Mom and Dad were both in their forties when they had me. I think I was something of a surprise."

"A nice surprise," he mused.

She smiled. "I hope so. We traveled all over the world together while I was growing up, and I met some fascinating people."

"So how did you become interested in accounting?"

"I've always been good with numbers," she told him. "My godfather was a forensic accountant and told great stories about some of his cases. I love mysteries and thought this was the best way to combine my two interests."

"Mysteries?" Rob queried. "What exactly does a forensic accountant do?"

"Analyze and interpret financial records, looking for evidence of fraud or malfeasance. It can be tricky, because most companies try to hide it. But I seem to have developed a knack for ferreting out clues."

He looked impressed. "Sounds like you love your work."

"I do," she said, wanting to make that very clear to him. "My career is very important to me, Rob. I'm hoping to make partner by the time I'm thirty."

His eyes met hers. "Beauty and brains. A lethal combination."

Her cheeks warmed as she reached for her champagne. He still didn't seem to understand that her work was her life. That she rarely made time for anything or anyone else. *Until tonight.*

He stood up as the band began to play and held out his hand. "Dance with me?"

Diana hesitated for a moment, then rose to her feet, knowing the fairy tale would end all too soon. The clock would strike midnight and she'd turn back into an accountant. So why not enjoy her handsome prince until then?

And imagine what might have been if the shoe had fit.

CHAPTER SIX

ROB DROVE Diana back to his place shortly before midnight, soft jazz playing on the radio. He wasn't ready to end their date, though he knew his babysitter had a curfew. They'd danced all night long, and Diana had fit so perfectly in his arms. Her sweet fragrance still filled his nostrils and his body thrummed with desire for her.

He hadn't expected to enjoy himself this much. Conversation had flowed easily between them and he found himself telling her stories he hadn't told in years. She had a few stories of her own, fascinating adventures of her travels with her parents. Diana Falco was one of the most interesting and intriguing women he'd ever met. As passionate about her career and her ideals as she was about her volunteer work with the Good Neighbors charity. He'd discovered that she was scheduled to stand on that same street corner collecting money every Sunday evening until Christmas, as well as Christmas Eve.

Pulling up behind her car, he shifted into Park

but left the engine running. Neither one of them said a word until the song ended, then Diana turned to him.

"Thank you for a wonderful evening," she said softly.

"Would you like to come in?" Rob saw something flicker in her blue eyes and found himself holding his breath for her answer.

"I'd better go," she said at last. "It's late and I have to work tomorrow."

He nodded, trying to ignore the stab of disappointment inside of him as they climbed out of his Jeep Cherokee. He walked Diana to her car, the cold night breeze fanning the wisps of hair around her face. She unlocked the driver's door, then turned to face him.

"Good night, Rob."

His gaze fell to her mouth and he saw her lips part. That was all the invitation he needed, and he leaned forward to capture her mouth with his own. Something he'd been wanting to do all night long.

He wasn't disappointed. Her lips softened and her arms wrapped around his neck as he deepened the kiss. Desire, hot and fierce, rolled through him as his mouth moved over hers. But there was something more. Something deeper. A connection that went beyond lust. Beyond passion.

She felt it, too. He could see it in her eyes when

he finally broke the kiss. The intensity of this bond between them shook him to the core. Rob didn't say a word as she got into her car and drove away.

Then he took a deep breath, standing in the middle of the street as he tried to regain his equilibrium. Diana Falco had walked into his life and changed it forever. He couldn't go back—but he didn't know exactly how to go forward.

Which meant he should take it slow. Not rush into anything until he was sure his head had caught up with his hormones. He needed to back off for a few days and give himself time to think. He didn't want to embark on a full court press when one of them might not be ready for it.

He'd go nice and easy—even if it killed him.

FIVE DAYS LATER, Diana found herself ringing Rob's doorbell once again. She held the borrowed dress in a dry cleaner's bag in one hand and a sack of cookies from her favorite bakery in the other.

Maggie opened the door, her eyes widening when she saw her. "It's the reindeer lady, Daddy!"

Rob appeared behind his daughter, a dish towel slung over one broad shoulder. A tiny mound of soap suds clung to the front of his faded flannel shirt, the tails hanging out over his blue jeans.

"Diana," he said, his handsome face lighting with surprise.

"Hello." The emerald dress had been back from the dry cleaner for two days but she'd delayed returning it, afraid once she laid eyes on him again that she'd forget all the very good reasons why she couldn't get involved with Rob Perez. Reasons she had to force herself to remember now, as she gazed into his brown eyes.

Then her gaze fell to his mouth, and heat rolled through her at the memory of his good-night kiss. It had been wonderful and terrifying at the same time. Terrifying because it had felt so right when common sense told her that falling for a man like Rob was all wrong.

"Come on in," he said, opening the door wider.

"I can't stay long," she told him. "I just wanted to return the dress and leave these cookies for T.J. since I didn't have any with me the other night."

"Just for T.J.?" Maggie asked, crestfallen. "Don't you have any cookies for me?"

Diana wanted to kick herself for her blunder. "They're for both of you," she amended. "Your dad, too. I hope you all like snickerdoodles."

"I love them," Maggie said, her despair evaporating as Diana handed her the sack. "Can I have one, Daddy? I ate all my supper."

"Just one," Rob allowed. "Why don't you take one in to T.J., too. He's playing in his room."

Maggie scampered off and Diana decided it was time for her to do the same.

"Well, I'd better be going." She turned toward the door. "It was nice to see you again, Rob."

"Wait a minute," he said, searching for a reason for her to stay. He'd picked up the telephone countless times in the last few days, wanting to call her but afraid of scaring her off. Only now she seemed more skittish than ever. "I still owe you for the dry cleaning."

"Please don't worry about it," she said, her hand on the doorknob. "It's no big deal."

"I insist," he replied, not ready to let her go. His day had been chaotic from the moment T.J. had dumped his cereal on the kitchen floor this morning. But the sight of Diana at his door had done more to make him feel better than the two aspirins he'd taken before dinner. "In fact, I want to pay for both dresses. The one you borrowed and the one T.J. soiled."

She shook her head. "That's really not necessary."

"I'll write you a check right now," he said, laying the plastic-covered dress over a chair.

"Rob..." she protested, but he was already

headed toward a small nook off the kitchen that had been converted into an office.

At least, it was supposed to be an office. At the moment, it looked more like a landfill. His desk was hidden under a mountain of papers, file folders and woodworking magazines.

Diana followed him there, staring in disbelief as he searched the drawers for his checkbook.

"I didn't come here for the money," she said, obviously wanting to make that clear.

He met her gaze across the desk and that same spark he'd felt Saturday night sizzled between them. "I know that."

His search disrupted a teetering pile of file folders, starting an avalanche. Diana shot forward to catch them before they hit the floor.

"As you can see, I'm a little disorganized." Rob took the folders out of her hands and placed them back on his desk. "Make that a lot disorganized."

She reached out to straighten a stack of envelopes in front of her. "That's not surprising since you're trying to run both a business and a family all on your own."

"It's too much," he admitted, "at least during Christmas. This is my busiest season."

"Sounds like you need to hire an assistant."

Her words sparked an idea and he spoke before he had time to consider it. "Actually, I was wondering if you'd be interested in the job." He rounded the desk to face her. "Not as an assistant, but just to come over a couple of nights a week to help me straighten up my accounts. As you can probably guess, they're a mess."

Diana stared at him, his offer obviously catching her off guard.

But the more Rob thought about it, the more he liked the idea. He wanted to spend time with her and he really did need some help.

"I'll pay your going rate," he said, trying to convince her. "I'm sure a forensic accountant doesn't come cheap, but it will be worth it to have someone I can trust."

Her eyes softened. "Rob, I'll be happy to help you, but you don't have to pay me."

"I absolutely insist," he replied, not wanting to take advantage of her. "I'm sure I can afford it, as soon as you figure out exactly how much money I have in my bank account."

She laughed. "Then let's compromise by donating my fee to the Good Neighbors charity."

"Deal," he said, touched by her generosity to both him and the Good Neighbors. "And I promise I won't ask for my money back this time."

She rolled up her sleeves as she surveyed the mess on his desk. "What kind of accounting system do you use?"

The doorbell saved him from admitting he didn't have a system. "I'll be right back."

Rob had a new bounce in his step as he walked to the door, feeling more energized than he had in days. Then he opened it and found Lorna Sandoval standing on the other side.

"I come bearing gifts," she announced, walking inside. She wore a red leather coat and carried two foil trays wrapped in plastic. "Two pounds of my homemade fudge, peanut butter and chocolate mint."

"Thanks," he said awkwardly, taking them from her. The trays were cold and he set them on the table as she tugged off her leather gloves.

"It's the least I could do after bailing out on our date Saturday night. How was the wedding?"

He wished Lorna would lower her voice, certain that Diana could hear every word. Now she'd know he had asked someone else to the wedding before her. "Fine. How's your son?"

"Oh, Jason is still covered with spots from head to toe, but at least he's not contagious anymore." She grinned up at him. "Leave it to my son to come down with chicken pox the day before our big date. But you know how kids are when they're sick—I just couldn't leave him with a sitter."

"Of course not," Rob said, feeling a little guilty

that those chicken pox had led to one of the best nights he could remember in a very long time.

"But I'm determined to make it up to you," Lorna said, completely unaware of Diana sitting in the nook and probably hearing every word. "I'd love to make dinner for you this weekend. You can bring the kids over, too. You know how much Jason loves playing with Maggie and T.J."

"I'll have to let you know," he hedged.

"I'll be making chicken enchiladas, Rob," she prodded with an enthusiasm that he found almost annoying. "Maggie told me that's your favorite dish."

"It is," he replied, "but I'm pretty swamped with work right now. It's hard to get away."

"I know what you mean," she replied. "My fudge business has taken off into the stratosphere. But I can't complain since it lets me stay home with my son. I think that's important for good child development, don't you?"

He nodded, relieved to see her finally moving toward the door.

"Well, you let me know about this weekend. And don't forget about the play date I have scheduled for Maggie and Jason next week. We're going to make Christmas ornaments out of dough."

"I'm sure she'll like that," Rob told her, grateful for Lorna's thoughtfulness, even as he realized gratitude wasn't enough to build a relationship on. Meeting Diana had shown him he needed more. Much more.

"Goodbye, Rob," she said, giving him a wave as she headed out the door.

"Goodbye," he called after her. "And thank you again for the fudge."

Then he closed the door and wondered how to get out of this hole he'd dug for himself. Better to face it head-on and explain to Diana before she got the wrong idea.

When he reached the nook, he was impressed by the sizable dent she'd already made in the pile on his desk. But the blush in her cheeks and the way she avoided his gaze made him certain that she'd heard every word.

"I'm sure you must be wondering what that was all about," he began.

She held up one hand. "It's really none of my business."

He moved closer to her, feeling a stiffness between them that hadn't been there before. "Look, Diana, the truth is I asked Lorna out because I admired her as a mother. She's great with kids and I thought maybe she would be good for us. But now I know it was a mistake."

"I don't think so," she said evenly. "Lorna is

the type of woman you need in your life, Rob. I'm...not.''

"I disagree."

She took a deep breath, finally meeting his gaze. ''I'm not mother material, and let's face it, that is what you need. Someone who can fill that role in your family. Your kids are wonderful, Rob, and so are you. But I'm not good with children, I never have been.

''I'm good at accounting,'' she continued, not giving him a chance to reply. ''That's what I do best. So I'll be glad to help you put your business in order, but I think we should just be friends.''

He winced inwardly at the old cliché, a standard line women used when they weren't interested in romance. But the way she'd kissed him Saturday night contradicted her words. Or maybe that was just wishful thinking on his part.

''Friends,'' he said, giving her a slow nod. At least she hadn't walked out the door. ''I'd like us to be friends, Diana.''

He wanted them to be much more than friends, but he wasn't about to push her. Especially when he had Maggie and T.J. to consider. He had to think of them first. If Diana wasn't interested in a family, there could be no future for the two of them.

A possibility he simply wasn't ready to accept.

CHAPTER SEVEN

DESPITE DIANA'S best intentions, she found herself slowly drawn into the Perez family. At first she'd done well at sticking to business, still stung by the knowledge that she'd been Rob's second choice for a date the night of the wedding.

Common sense told her that Lorna Sandoval was perfect for Rob. The woman seemed to possess that natural mothering instinct that Diana was missing. Yet Diana couldn't seem to bring herself to ask Rob whether he'd taken Lorna up on her offer for dinner. It was none of her business anyway, even if the thought did make her feel a little sick inside.

But as the days passed, she found herself letting down her guard. A trip to Rob's apartment to work on his accounts soon included a tea party with Maggie or a shared Chinese take-out with the whole family.

Rob was treating her like a friend, which was exactly what she wanted. At least that's what Diana told herself as she uploaded his accounts onto the computer she'd talked him into buying.

She sat in the office nook as Rob wrestled with T.J. on the living room floor. It was a Tuesday evening and she'd brought pizza for dinner, much to Maggie's delight.

Until the little girl had discovered it was mushroom pizza.

Diana added that mistake to the long list of things she needed to learn about children. Mushroom pizza was out, pepperoni was in. She'd also discovered that her knowledge of Disney movies was woefully lacking, with Maggie filling her in on the names of all the princesses. T.J. had taught her that two-year-olds will eat anything, including a dead cricket on the floor.

Working at Rob's a few evenings a week was definitely an educational experience. Watching him with his kids made her admire him more than ever. In fact, Diana found herself watching him much too often.

While her head knew that keeping their relationship platonic made the most sense, her heart didn't seem to be getting the message. She kept remembering the night he'd kissed her on the street, half-wishing she'd accepted his invitation to come inside.

"What's the matter?" Maggie asked, walking up beside her chair. "Are you stuck again?"

Diana blinked, realizing she'd been staring at a

blank screen for several minutes. Maggie had picked up on her dilemma without realizing it. She was stuck. Caught in a limbo between wanting to be part of Rob's life and walking away.

"I think I just need a break," she said, rubbing a tense knot in the back of her neck.

"Do you want to watch me practice for the play?" Maggie asked.

"Sure," Diana said, following her into the living room.

Rob lay on the floor, T.J. straddling his chest. "What's going on?"

"Maggie's going to practice her line for us," Diana told him.

"Again?" Rob asked, sitting up and gently rolling T.J. off him.

"The play is only two days away," Maggie said, then turned to Diana. "You're coming, right?"

Diana glanced at Rob. "Well, I don't know if there are any tickets left...."

"Daddy will buy you a ticket, won't you, Daddy?" Maggie said, turning to her father.

"Diana's awfully busy with work," Rob told his daughter, then his gaze met hers. "But I think I can rustle one up, if you're free."

He was giving her an out in case she didn't want to come with them to the play. Diana knew she should take it, but she couldn't stand the thought of letting Maggie down. The girl was so excited about her role, practicing her one line every time Diana saw her.

"I'd love to come," she said at last.

"Okay, everybody be quiet now," Maggie ordered, her comment directed at her little brother. He ignored her and began playing with his blocks.

Maggie took a deep breath and pointed to the ceiling. "Look! A star!"

Then she glanced over at her father. "How did that sound?"

"As good as any shepherd girl I've ever heard," Rob replied with a smile.

She turned to Diana. "Did I talk loud enough?"

"Just right," she replied, pleased to be asked for her opinion. The more time she spent around Maggie and T.J., the more she saw them as individuals, with personalities uniquely their own.

Maggie tried so hard to do everything perfectly, a trait that reminded Diana a little of herself. T.J., on the other hand, was like a bulldozer, plowing through the apartment in search of adventure. He tended to destroy anything that got in his path. The latest victim was the potted philodendron that had sat on the computer desk.

Maggie practiced her line several more times before Rob announced it was bedtime for both of them.

Diana went back to work at the computer while he herded his children into their bedrooms to help them change into their pajamas before he read them a story.

Half an hour later, he was back, the apartment now blissfully quiet.

"Join me in a glass of wine?" he asked, holding up a bottle of merlot.

"Sure." She logged off the computer for the night, his offer too tempting to refuse. Or maybe it was Rob himself, dressed in a bulky red pullover sweater and faded blue jeans.

Diana didn't think she could ever get tired of looking at him, although lately her thoughts had taken a decidedly carnal turn whenever they were together. His kiss had set something off in a deep, dormant place inside of her and she just couldn't seem to get it out of her system.

He poured them each a glass of wine, then joined her on the sofa. Every nerve ending went into high alert at his proximity. She took a sip of the merlot, hoping it would relax her.

"You must be exhausted," Rob mused, "working at your office all day, then coming over here in the evenings."

"Look who's talking," she countered. "You put

in a long day at your wood shop, then have to make dinner and entertain the kids. You're on call twenty-four hours a day.''

He shrugged. ''You get used to it.''

She knew that was probably true. When she'd first started working here in the evenings, the noise and activity level had diverted her attention from her work. Now she hardly noticed it.

Rob, on the other hand, distracted her more every day. She'd told him she just wanted to be friends, but she truly didn't know if that was possible. The thought of dating other men didn't appeal to her at all, though she'd made it clear that she wanted Rob to see other women.

''I don't want to intrude on any plans you might have for Thursday night,'' she said, realizing too late that she'd just assumed they'd go there together. ''I can arrange to pick up my ticket at the playhouse.''

''Why don't you meet us here instead?'' Rob suggested. ''Then we can drive over to the theater together. Unless you'd rather go on your own.''

''No, I'll be happy to meet you here.'' It was as if they were always tiptoeing around each other, trying to stay on the friendship path without straying into the romance minefield. She reached up to rub the side of her neck, trying to assuage the ache that had plagued her all day.

"Sit on the floor," Rob ordered.

She looked at him. "What?"

"Sit on the floor," he repeated, spreading his feet wide apart and patting the thick carpet between them. "Right here. I give a great neck massage."

"You don't have to do that," she exclaimed, even as he began nudging her off the sofa.

"I won't take no for an answer," he said, removing the wineglass from her hand and setting it on the coffee table. "Consider it an employee benefit."

She could see he wasn't going to back down, so at last she gave in, sitting on the floor between his legs.

As soon as his fingers began kneading her neck, her eyes fluttered closed, her body melting at the exquisite sensation. "That feels wonderful."

"Good," he said huskily, his thumbs stroking over the base of her skull in a slow, steady rhythm. "Just relax."

She leaned back against the sofa, her arms brushing against his thighs. A small moan of pleasure escaped her when his hands moved to her shoulders, squeezing the taut muscles there.

"I think you went into the wrong business, Rob," she mused, so relaxed she was barely able to string a sentence together. She relished the feel of his broad fingers on her skin, applying just the right pressure.

"I wonder if I could make it as a masseur?"

She smiled dreamily. "I'd hire you full-time."

"I'm available to you twenty-four hours a day, Diana."

Their conversation was veering into dangerous territory and Rob seemed to realize it, too, because he abruptly dropped his hands from her neck.

"Better?" he asked.

"Much better. Thank you." She rose to her feet, her legs feeling a little shaky. "I'd better be going."

He stood up beside her and for one breathtaking moment she thought he was going to kiss her. Then he stepped away. "I'll get your coat."

Diana tried to think of something to say to break the sudden tension between them. "So how's the potty-training going?"

Rob shook his head as he retrieved her coat from the hall closet. "Worse than ever. I must be doing something wrong."

"Maybe T.J.'s just not ready yet."

"Maggie was potty-trained before she was two," Rob told her. "T.J. will be three years old soon. At this rate, I'll be lucky to have him trained by the time he's in kindergarten."

She heard the deep frustration in his voice and

longed to put her arms around Rob and comfort him. But that would only lead to more problems. So she bid him good-night and walked out of the apartment, telling herself that if she was smart, she'd never come back.

Yet the night of the play she was standing outside his door, a book on potty-training that had come highly recommended by one of the young mothers at her office tucked in her coat pocket.

But when Maggie opened the door, tears streaming down her face, Diana forgot all about the potty-training crisis.

"What's wrong?" she asked as she walked into the apartment.

Maggie's lower lip trembled as she turned and pointed to her father, hunched on the sofa with a needle and thread in his hand. "T.J. ruined my costume!"

The little culprit sat on the living room floor, playing with a set of foam blocks. Hearing his name, he looked up and saw Diana. "Cookie!"

"No cookies for you," Maggie cried angrily. "You have to go straight to bed!"

"That's enough, Maggie May," Rob said wearily. "It was an accident." Then he looked up at Diana. "Please tell me you know how to sew?"

He still wore his work clothes, a flannel shirt

that fit snugly over his broad chest and a worn pair
of denim jeans. He looked frazzled and desperate.

"Not a stitch, I'm afraid." She shrugged out of
her coat. "What happened?"

"You know how T.J. likes to traipse around in
Maggie's shepherd costume?"

Diana nodded as she walked into the living
room. She'd seen both children parade around in
the costume, T.J. echoing a fractured version of the
one line Maggie had in the play.

"Well, somehow his shoe got tangled in the hem
and it tore," Rob explained. "The play starts in
less than an hour and I can't reach my mother or
Frankie or Maria. I've been trying to fix it myself,
but I think I've only made it worse."

He held up the costume to confirm his suspicion.
Sure enough, the hem hung at a severely crooked
angle.

"Maybe no one will notice," Rob said hopefully.

"I can't wear it like that!" Maggie exclaimed
in horror. "Everyone will laugh at me."

Rob sighed. "I don't think we have a choice,
honey."

"Let me look at it," Diana said, reaching for
the costume.

Rob handed it to her as Maggie wiped the tears

off her face. She could see the sudden spark of hope in the little girl's big brown eyes.

"Can you fix it?" Maggie asked.

An awareness of her own limitations came back full force. She could solve complex math equations and uncover corporate malfeasance at the highest levels, but making a little girl happy suddenly seemed like the biggest challenge in the world. *What if she failed?*

Looking down at the rip in the hem, she saw that only the stitches had been torn, not the thick polyester material itself. She looked over at Rob. "Do you have any duct tape in that wood shop of yours?"

He wrinkled his brow. "Yes."

"Why don't you get it while I comb Maggie's hair and wash her face. If we have less than an hour to get to that play, we'd better hurry."

Rob sat in the darkened theater, watching as his daughter stood proudly on the stage in her costume. Diana had applied the duct tape to the torn hem like a pro and the quick-fix was invisible to the rest of the audience.

It amazed him that she doubted her own abilities with children. Her methods might be a little unorthodox, but that was one of the things he liked about her. Life with Diana Falco would never be predictable. But most important of all, she seemed to truly care about his kids.

He smiled to himself, remembering how upset she'd been when Maggie had turned her nose up at the mushroom pizza Diana had brought over. His daughter was simply a finicky eater, unlike T.J., who literally ate anything he could put in his mouth. At the moment, T.J. was gnawing on a pocket calculator. Diana held his son on her lap, softly whispering in his ear to keep him quiet.

The rest of his family sat in the row behind them. He knew they were probably bursting with questions about the woman next to him. But his own questions had been answered. Maggie and T.J. seemed to adore her. And Rob knew without a doubt that he and Diana belonged together.

Now he just had to prove it to her.

He turned his attention back to the play just in time to hear Maggie say her line. Her voice rang out loud and true as she proclaimed, "Look, a star!"

"She did it!" Diana whispered to him, sounding as proud as he felt.

He realized that anyone seeing them sitting here together would think they were a family. The thought uncurled a warm sensation inside of him— something he'd never imagined he would experience again.

Rob wanted to reach for her hand, but he held back, knowing this wasn't the time or the place to reveal his feelings.

He'd have to pick just the right moment to tell Diana he was falling in love with her.

CHAPTER EIGHT

FLUSH WITH SUCCESS from her duct tape mending job, Diana began to entertain the possibility that she might fit into Rob's life after all. During the days following the Christmas play, she read the potty-training book and stocked up on other books with topics ranging from child psychology to crafts for kids.

Diana had always been a good student and had finally decided to put this trait to use. Maybe she could educate herself about proper mothering skills since they didn't seem to come naturally to her.

The afternoon sun shone in a cloudless sky as she pulled up to the curb in front of Rob's place. She'd gotten off work early, hoping to input the last formulas into the computer program she'd customized for his business.

Rob and his children were in the front yard of the building, constructing what looked like a wooden snowman.

Maggie saw her and began to wave wildly. Then Rob looked up and met her gaze through the windshield, causing a frisson of desire to spiral through her. He worked without a coat, his sleeves rolled up over his muscular forearms.

The day was unseasonably warm, so she grabbed a light jacket out of the back seat, then climbed out of the car.

T.J. came running up to her as she stepped onto the sidewalk. "Cookie! Cookie! Cookie!"

She swung him up into her arms and gave him a big hug. "No cookies today, T-man."

Maggie skipped over to her. "You're just in time. We're building a snowman!"

"So I see," Diana replied, impressed by the artistry in front of her. The snowman was constructed of wooden crates, piled one on top of the other, each set at an angle. The slats of the crates were all painted different colors, giving the snowman a psychedelic appearance, but somehow it all fit together.

"The Gray Gallery is sponsoring a neighborhood art contest," Rob explained. "I wasn't going to enter, but Maggie got wind of it, and since she believes I'm the best artist in town, how could I let her down?"

Diana smiled. "You *are* the best artist in town."

"That makes a fan club of three," Rob said, returning her smile. Their gazes held for a long moment and a strange warmth washed over her.

She couldn't pretend anymore. She wanted Rob Perez. She wanted the whole package—including Maggie and T.J. Maybe if she tried hard enough she could find a place in their hearts as well as their lives.

"I know we're supposed to go over my new accounting system," Rob said, tying a bright red scarf loosely around the neck of the snowman. "But this project is taking a little longer than I expected."

"Do you want to help us?" Maggie asked Diana, picking up a blue marker off the ground. "Me and T.J. are drawing buttons on the snowman."

"Hey, buttons are my specialty," she replied, reaching for a green marker.

An hour later, the snowman was finished. The four of them stood on the sidewalk to admire the newest art exhibit in the neighborhood.

"Not bad," Rob mused. "The buttons add just the right touch."

"It's wonderful," Diana exclaimed. "You could probably make a fortune just marketing these snowmen."

"I already have more projects than I can handle," Rob replied, adjusting the tool belt slung low on his hips. "Besides, it looks like we'll be moving soon, so I need to clear out the shop."

Diana turned to him. "Moving? Where?"

"I don't know yet," Rob admitted. "But my mother has found someone to buy the building. In fact, I'm supposed to attend a meeting with her tonight to negotiate the contract." He snapped his fingers together. "That reminds me, I need to call Stacie to baby-sit."

"I could watch the kids for you tonight."

"Really?" Rob looked up at her, obviously surprised by the offer. "That would be great. If you're sure you don't mind?"

Diana took a deep breath, ready to put her new skills into action. "I can't think of anything else I'd rather do."

THE MEETING was held on the second floor of the building in Rick's apartment. It was mostly a formality, as Carmen and Katherine Kinard had been in almost daily contact since the wedding and had ironed out most of the details. But Carmen wanted her sons there when she signed the contract.

Rick sat next to Frankie, whose construction company would be in charge of the renovations. Rafe was in the chair beside her, anxious to get back to Maria, who hadn't been feeling well enough to come downstairs.

Katherine Kinard had brought her brother, Drew, along to the meeting. An architect who had already sketched some preliminary changes for the building, Drew was tall like his sister, sharing her brown hair and brown eyes. He studied the blueprints laid out on the table in front of him.

Carmen and Katherine signed the contracts the attorneys had drawn up, the sale now official. Then they began discussing the special demands of caring for a large group of children. Rob's mother had a wealth of experience in that area, having earned her teaching certificate after she and his father had emigrated from Colombia almost forty years ago.

Katherine seemed to love children, too. Their conversation soon evolved into anecdotes about some of their toughest challenges as teachers.

"So have you considered my proposition?" Katherine asked his mother.

"What proposition?" Rob asked, thinking he'd missed something. His thoughts kept straying to Diana, wondering how she was getting along with Maggie and T.J. His kids ran him ragged on a regular basis. No doubt they'd take advantage of Diana's kindness and do the same to her.

Carmen turned to him. "Katherine approached me a couple of weeks ago about becoming a teacher at her day care."

"I thought you wanted to retire," Rick interjected.

"Only because the administration at my current

school wants to decrease the faculty and keeps pushing the idea,'' Carmen explained. ''I'm only fifty-five, but it's hard to stay where you're not wanted.''

''I definitely want you,'' Katherine told her. ''Your experience would be invaluable to me. In fact, I'd like to make you the head teacher at Forrester Square Day Care if you're interested in the job.''

''Is that what you've decided to call it?'' Carmen asked, excitement lighting her dark eyes.

Katherine nodded. ''Yes. In honor of Forrester Square, the neighborhood where I grew up. I made some of my best memories there. Now I want to make new memories and I'd really like you to be a part of it.''

''So would I,'' Carmen said, coming to a decision. ''I'll take the job.''

''Wonderful,'' Katherine exclaimed, clapping her hands together. ''I brought some champagne along to celebrate the sale. Now we have two things to celebrate.''

''Shall we tour the building first?'' Carmen suggested. ''I know Drew mentioned wanting to see it when he first arrived.''

Everyone around the table nodded in agreement.

''Do you mind if we start on the first floor,'' Drew asked, ''then work our way up?''

"I'll lead the way," Rob offered, rising to his feet.

They all followed him down to the first floor, where he gave them a tour of his wood shop. Drew paid special attention to the duct work and electricity, noting the location of all the vents and outlets.

Katherine walked over to admire a rocking chair Rob had recently completed. "This is beautiful," she said, running her hand over the solid oak. "Just what I want for the nursery at the day care."

"That one's taken," Rob told her. "But if you'd like to order one, I'll be more than happy to give you a discount."

"Actually, I'd like to order three," Katherine said as they walked out of the shop. "In fact, I'd like to talk with you about doing all the cabinet work if you're interested."

"Absolutely," Rob said, leading them to his apartment. When he opened the door, he heard a small gasp behind him. Then he looked inside and saw why.

The place was a disaster.

Crumpled newspapers covered the entire living room carpet. Flour coated every inch of his kitchen table and floor. There were pots and pans piled in the sink, and pink frosting fingerprints on the walls and refrigerator door.

"Come on in," he said, wondering what in the hell had happened here. Diana and the children were nowhere in sight. All three of them had probably gone into hiding as soon as they'd heard the key in the door.

"Oh, my," Carmen breathed as they walked inside.

Rob cleared a path through the living room so Drew Kinard could begin inspecting the place.

There was a burnt odor in the air and Rob headed over to the stove, where he saw black cookies inside the oven. Then Drew came out of the bathroom.

"How's the plumbing?" Katherine asked, too polite to comment on the mess surrounding her.

"It looks good." One corner of Drew's mouth kicked up in a smile. "Except for the cereal floating in the toilet bowl."

"What?" Rob exclaimed, going to look for himself. But Drew was right. There was cereal in the toilet. Sugar Loops to be exact.

"Rob?" his mother called out.

He followed her voice down the hallway to his bedroom, where the whole group now stood in the open doorway. Then Carmen smiled and pointed to his bed.

DIANA'S EYES fluttered open and it took her a moment to realize where she was. In Rob's bed, with

Maggie and T.J. snuggled on either side of her. She'd fallen asleep reading them Snow White.

Then she heard a noise and looked up. Seven people, including Rob, his mother and his brothers, all stared at her from the doorway. She sat up, wondering what was going on.

"We were just taking a quick tour," Carmen explained as the group began to file back into the hallway. "Don't let us bother you."

"Oh," she said, looking at Rob. Then she remembered the condition of the apartment. "Oh, no!"

She flew off the bed, but Rob caught her arms. "It's okay. They're just leaving."

"The place is a mess," she cried.

He nodded. "I noticed."

She wanted to sink right into the floor. Not only had Rob seen the disaster she'd created, but his family as well. She covered her face with her hands, emitting a low groan.

"Do you want to tell me what happened?" he asked, sounding more perplexed than angry.

She lowered her hands. "I created a monster. Me."

"Why don't I put the kids to bed?" he said, "then we can talk about it."

She walked into the hallway, relieved to see that

everyone had left. Then she got another look at the mess and groaned again. Her plan had been to put the kids to bed, then clean up. Instead, she'd fallen asleep and awakened to a nightmare. Rob would never trust her with his children again.

Diana was wiping the last of the flour off the kitchen counters when he walked into the room.

"They didn't even twitch when I carried them to their beds," Rob told her. "You must have worn them out."

"Oh, Rob, I had such big plans for tonight." Despair welled in her throat at her failure. "We were going to bake sugar cookies to decorate and make papier-mâché ornaments to paint. I found instructions for the ornaments in the back of a children's magazine. They looked easy enough, but once we got started, everything spun out of control. T.J. kept trying to eat the adhesive and Maggie kept cutting out stars until she'd created the perfect one."

He smiled. "Sounds like they wore you out. There's just one thing I don't understand."

"Just one?" she said wryly, wiping frosting off a cupboard handle.

"There are Sugar Loops floating in the toilet."

"That's right," she admitted. "I put them there."

He blinked in surprise. "Why?"

She sighed. "So T.J. could use them for target practice. According to the book I read it's supposed to be a successful potty-training technique. But he didn't go in there once."

"It's still not a bad idea," he mused.

She shook her head. "Nothing turned out right tonight. I think I forgot to add something to the cookies, because the first three batches just sort of melted onto the pan." Then her eyes flashed. "The cookies!"

"Burned to a crisp," he told her as she flew to the oven and opened the door.

"Oh, no," she exclaimed, tugging an oven mitt on her hand, then pulling out the pan. She dropped it on the stovetop, ready to surrender. If she needed any more proof that she wasn't cut out to be a mother, this was it.

Rob walked up behind her, laying his hands gently on her shoulders. "It's no big deal."

She turned to face him. "It is to me. I wanted tonight to be perfect. But look at this place." She sagged back against the counter. "Don't you see, Rob? I can't do this."

"All I see is a woman trying to be perfect who doesn't realize she already is." He smiled, knowing the right moment had finally arrived. "Perfect for me, anyway."

Before she could say a word, he kissed her, letting his mouth and body convey what was in his heart.

She didn't move for a moment, then a low, hungry moan sounded in the back of her throat and she kissed him back. Rob gathered her in his arms, releasing all the passion inside of him that he'd held back for so long.

"You don't know what you're saying," she breathed when they finally came up for air.

"I'm saying that I want you, Diana. Today. Tomorrow. Forever." Then he kissed her again.

This time Diana's need matched his own, her hands clutching the front of his shirt and her lush body pressed flush against him. She tasted like sugar and nutmeg, and hunger for her roared through his body. They'd each tried to deny the attraction for so long that now it exploded between them, taking on a life of its own.

They found their way to his bedroom without ever breaking the kiss, their hands roaming everywhere. He reached behind him to flip the lock on the bedroom door, then he reached for Diana.

They shed their inhibitions with their clothes, feasting on each other. Rob remembered the condom in his last rational moment. Then he was inside of her, part of her, their bodies moving together in perfect harmony.

"I love you, Diana," he breathed, wanting this moment between them to last forever.

"Rob," she gasped, arching into him.

He shifted slightly, the movement sending her over the edge. He captured her soft cry of release with his mouth. Then he followed her there, knowing she'd captured his heart.

CHAPTER NINE

DIANA AWOKE EARLY the next morning, relishing the sight of Rob sleeping beside her, his face half-buried in the pillow. She let her gaze wander over the curve of his bare, muscular shoulder. Then it moved to the shadow of whiskers on his jaw, and the dark, thick lashes fanning his cheek, before settling on his mouth.

Liquid heat flowed through her when she remembered everything his mouth had done to her last night. The words he'd said to her as they'd made love.

I love you, Diana.

She hugged them to herself as she slipped out of bed, careful not to wake him. Rob wanted her, in spite of her faults. Maybe this relationship could work after all. It had to work, because now she couldn't imagine her life without Rob in it.

Diana pulled on her clothes, then padded out to the kitchen, intending to prove that she wasn't a total disaster there. She used to make pancakes every Sunday morning for her parents. It gave her a warm glow of satisfaction to know she could now do the same for Rob and Maggie and T.J.

She hummed a Christmas carol to herself as she pulled the eggs and milk out of the refrigerator. The white Christmas lights on the tree in the living room cast a warm glow throughout the apartment.

A search of the cupboards uncovered a bottle of maple syrup, and she'd just set it on the table when T.J. appeared in the doorway.

"Good morning," Diana said softly, smiling at the tuft of dark hair sticking straight up on his head.

He stuck a finger in his mouth and leaned against the doorjamb, blinking sleepily at her.

"Are you ready for breakfast?" Diana asked, leaning over to kiss the top of his head.

"Juice," he said, pointing to the refrigerator.

She placed his booster seat on a chair, then set him in it before pulling the bottle of orange juice out of the refrigerator and setting it on the table.

She poured juice into a plastic glass, then placed it in front of him. "I'm making pancakes for breakfast, T.J. How does that sound—good?"

"Cookie," he said, reaching for his glass.

"You'll have to ask your dad about that," she replied, turning back to the counter. She gave the batter one final stir before heading over to the stove.

The skillet was hot and she ladled the first pancake onto it. Digging into a drawer, she found a spatula. As soon as the first bubbles appeared on the top of the pancake, she flipped it over.

"Juice," T.J. said behind her.

She glanced over her shoulder to see him standing atop his booster chair, stretching toward the bottle of juice at the center of the table.

"T.J., be careful," she cried, dropping the spatula.

But it was too late. He lifted one foot off the booster seat, tipping it off balance. Before she could reach him, he fell off the chair, his forehead hitting the edge of the table as he tumbled to the floor.

Her heart stopped in her chest as she rushed over to him. "Oh, my God…"

He didn't move. She saw his eyes roll back in their sockets when she cupped his face in her hands. For a moment she thought he wasn't breathing, and something died inside of her.

Then she saw the almost imperceptible rise of his chest beneath his pajamas and finally found her voice.

"Rob! Help!"

ROB RAN into the emergency room of Seattle Memorial Hospital, carrying a limp T.J. in his arms.

A dark, ugly knot had formed at his son's temple and he'd been unconscious since Diana's screams had brought Rob out of a sound sleep and racing into the kitchen.

He'd seen his son lying on the floor and Diana's stark face, pale with fear. When he'd asked her what had happened, she'd started sobbing, unable to speak a coherent sentence.

But she'd been able to drive them to the hospital while he'd held his son, making the trip in under three minutes. Rob had called Rafe before they left, telling him to go down to his apartment and get Maggie, who was still sound asleep in her bed.

T.J. moaned slightly as they reached the reception desk, and Rob had never been so glad to hear a sound in his life. His son opened dazed eyes as a nurse took him out of Rob's arms and carried him back to an examination room.

Rob started to follow her, but another nurse stopped him. "We need you to wait out here until the doctor sees him," she said. "Can you tell me what happened?"

Diana stepped forward, her arms wrapped around her waist. "T.J. fell off a chair," she said, visibly trembling, "and hit his head on the kitchen table. It was my fault. I shouldn't have left the bottle of juice on the table. If anything happens to him…"

"It won't," Rob said, as much for himself as for her. He pulled Diana into his arms, grateful for the strength her presence gave him.

The nurse asked a few more perfunctory questions, mostly about allergies and T.J.'s medical history. Rob could barely think straight, much less answer her questions. At last she left them alone, promising to report on T.J. as soon as the doctor saw him.

Fear clawed at him as they waited for what seemed an eternity in the reception area. *If he lost T.J....* He closed his eyes, refusing to consider that possibility.

"I'm so sorry, Rob," Diana breathed, hunched over in a chair.

He turned to her, taking her hands in his. "Tell me exactly what happened."

She swallowed. "I was making pancakes when T.J. came into the kitchen and said he wanted some juice. So I poured him a glass, then I just turned around for a minute. The next thing I knew, he was standing on his booster seat and lost his balance. That's when he fell."

"I wish I would have been there," Rob said, then realized it sounded like he was blaming her. But before he could explain himself, the doctor approached them.

He was a young man, barely thirty, with a rubber

Tweety Bird attached to his stethoscope. Rob knew Seattle Memorial had one of the best pediatric centers in the state, but he was ready to demand a specialist if that's what his son needed.

"How is he?" Diana asked, clutching Rob's arm.

The doctor gave them a reassuring smile. "That's one tough kid you've got there, Mr. Perez. T.J.'s got a slight concussion, but he's going to be fine. I want to keep him here a few more hours, just for observation, but I don't anticipate any complications. I'm sure you'll be able to take him home sometime after lunch."

Rob reached out to shake his hand. "Thank you so much, Dr...."

"Dr. Bob," he replied with a boyish grin. "That's what all the kids call me."

"Can we see T.J. now?" Rob asked.

The doctor nodded. "He's awake and hungry. Mentioned something about wanting pancakes for breakfast."

After the doctor left, Rob turned to Diana. "Let's go see him. Then we'll call Rafe so he can let the family know T.J. is all right."

But Diana held back. "I can't do this."

She spoke more to herself than to him, but the tone of her voice sent a chill through his heart.

"What do you mean?"

She met his gaze and he saw the desolation in her blue eyes. "Isn't it obvious? I should have known this would never work. I'm not good around children, Rob. I never have been. I should have known T.J. would try to reach for the juice. I never should have turned my back on him."

He reached out to grasp her shoulders. "That's ridiculous. Accidents happen."

She shook her head, tears flooding her eyes. "You don't understand. A little boy was injured when I fourteen. I was supposed to watch him, but I got distracted." She sucked in a deep breath. "I'll never forget the way his parents looked at me when they walked into the hospital. I couldn't stand it if you ever looked at me that way, Rob."

"Diana, I love you," he said firmly. "Nothing will ever change that."

"I love you," she admitted through her tears. "And I love Maggie and T.J.—too much to ever risk hurting them."

She backed away from him. "I'm sorry, Rob."

Then she was gone.

He stared after her, tempted to chase her down and make her listen to reason. But T.J. was waiting for him. Rob raked his hand through his hair, torn between the woman he loved and the son who needed him.

Diana was upset. Maybe he should give her

some time alone. Time to calm down and see reason. They loved each other and that wasn't going to change. He knew in his gut that the four of them belonged together as a family. Nothing else made sense.

He just hoped Diana knew it, too.

THE NEXT DAY, Diana sat in her office poring over cash flows and financial statements. She intended to bury herself in work, even if she had to take over projects from other accountants in her division. Whatever it took to keep her from thinking about Rob and his children.

A telephone call to the hospital yesterday afternoon had assured her that T.J. was all right. He'd been released and she knew Rob and his mother and brothers would take good care of him. Part of her ached to be there with them, but she told herself a clean break would be for the best. Rob might even be relieved, despite his protests at the hospital.

No matter how Diana looked at it, T.J.'s accident was her fault. She couldn't spend the rest of her life worrying that she was going to look away at just the wrong moment. Endangering T.J. or Maggie because of her deficiencies as a mother simply wasn't worth the risk. They were too precious to her.

A knock on the door broke her reverie. Beth stuck her head inside and said, "There's a call for you on line two. Rob Perez."

She took a deep breath, firming her resolve. "Tell him I'm not available. In fact, I won't be available for any of his phone calls."

Beth crinkled her brow. "Are you sure about that? He sounds tall, dark and handsome. Not to mention very anxious to speak to you."

"I don't want to speak to him," she reiterated, opening the file folder in front of her.

Beth hesitated a moment, then nodded. "All right. I'll get rid of him for you."

Diana watched her close the door, then sagged back in her chair. How long would it take for the pain to go away? Maybe she should leave Seattle for a while. Visit her parents in Austria for Christmas. She had to work the Good Neighbors corner on Christmas Eve, but she might be able to catch a flight to Europe on Christmas day.

She turned to her computer, logging on to the Internet to check flight schedules. Deep down she knew that flying off to a different continent wouldn't be enough to make her forget about Rob. He was part of her heart, part of her soul, and nothing would ever change that.

But at least the distance would prevent her from giving in to the desire to see him again. It burned in her now, making her wish she'd taken his phone call. She longed to hear the sound of his voice. To play tea party with Maggie. To give T.J. a hug.

Diana picked up the telephone and dialed the airport.

CHAPTER TEN

A LIGHT SNOW fell as Diana began her last hour of service for the Good Neighbors. Donations were slow on Christmas Eve, though she'd encountered a few last-minute shoppers. Most people were spending the evening with family or friends.

Diana would be spending Christmas Eve alone, but her plane left for Europe first thing in the morning. Her parents didn't even know she was coming to Austria, since she wanted it to be a surprise.

She just wished she could get excited about the trip. But the thought of who she was leaving behind just left her feeling lonely. Rob had finally stopped trying to call her. The silence almost bothered her more than the incessant ring of the telephone had. She'd let the answering machine pick up at the house, and he'd always just left his name and number, no other message.

Maybe he didn't know what to say. He couldn't deny she was at fault for T.J.'s accident. Or that her mothering skills left a lot to be desired. *So why*

*did she keep trying to convince herself that she was
doing the right thing?*

Pulling her coat more tightly around her, Diana
saw someone walking toward her on the sidewalk.
Sensing a potential donor, she began to ring the
bell in her hand. When the man came into view,
she froze, not believing her eyes.

It was Rob.

He was the last person she expected to see, since
she knew the Perez family had a long-standing tra-
dition of celebrating Christmas Eve together. Diana
had no time to prepare herself as he approached.
No warning to build up her defenses.

"Hello," he said, looking warm and wonderful
in his heavy wool topcoat. The cool breeze ruffled
his dark hair and she longed to run her fingers
through it.

"Hello," Diana replied, her heart racing in her
chest.

"Cold evening."

Surely he wasn't here to make small talk. "What
are you doing here, Rob?"

"I came to make a donation." He reached into
his coat pocket and pulled out a money order. "We
had a deal, remember? The fee for your accounting
services goes to the Good Neighbors charity."

"I remember," she said, a stab of disappointment piercing her heart that he wasn't here to see

her. That reaction told her all she needed to know about her feelings for Rob. Despite everything, their separation had only made her want him more. She missed Maggie and T.J. She missed waking up with Rob in bed beside her.

He dropped the money order into the collection drum. "I guess that completes our contract."

She nodded as the finality of his words sunk in. It took every ounce of strength she had to smile at him. "I hope you have a Merry Christmas."

"I'm afraid that's impossible without you."

She swallowed hard as he moved a step closer to her, her body tingling at his nearness.

"Come back to us, Diana," he said huskily.

Desire battled with apprehension as she gazed into his deep brown eyes. "You need someone like Lorna," she replied, trying to convince herself as well as him. "Someone who understands children. Someone who won't hurt them, even unintentionally."

A muscle flexed in his jaw. "Damn it, Diana, I don't want Lorna or Mary Poppins. I want you. A woman who mends clothes with duct tape and puts cereal in the toilet. A woman who cares about my children so much that she's willing to walk away rather than hurt them."

His words went straight to her heart, threatening to break down the fragile barrier she'd erected.

"And if I do hurt them?" she challenged, wanting him to face that possibility. Diana had made mistakes before. There was no reason to believe she wouldn't do it again.

His face softened. "That's just part of being a parent. It's on-the-job training, and no matter how hard we try, we'll never get it exactly right.

"But there's something you should understand," he continued, a fierceness to his tone she hadn't heard before. "I want you for myself, not just as a mother for my children. I want to make love to you every night and wake up with you every morning. We belong together, Diana. I know I'm right about that."

Everything he said made sense to her, yet once Diana took that step she'd be committed. There'd be no turning back. Her body yearned to fall into his arms, but she couldn't make such a decision lightly. Not when it would affect four lives.

"Take time to think about it," he said, seeing her hesitation. "I'm not going anywhere."

"But I am," she told him, remembering the plane ticket in her purse. "I'm leaving for Austria tomorrow morning to spend the Christmas holidays with my parents."

Disappointment flickered across his face. "Will I see you when you get back?"

"Yes," she promised, determined not to avoid

him again. It was time she stopped running away from life. "I'll give you my answer then."

ON CHRISTMAS MORNING, Rob sat on the sofa in his living room, watching Maggie and T.J. open their presents. Both children still wore their pajamas, whooping with delight as they tore brightly colored wrapping paper off their gifts.

He cradled a cup of coffee in his hands, waiting for the caffeine to kick in. He'd lain awake most of the night, replaying his conversation with Diana over and over in his mind. If he could have only found the right words....

"Is this one from Santa?" Maggie asked, holding up a shiny gold package.

"Let me see it," Rob said, not recognizing the present. When she brought it over, he looked at the gift tag. "It's from Diana."

"Can I open it?" she asked excitedly.

"Sure," he said, assuming Diana had put it under the tree sometime in the past few weeks. He set down his coffee and did a little investigating, finding a present from Diana for T.J., too. It was a fire truck with enough bells and whistles to keep his son occupied for at least five minutes.

Maggie eagerly tore the paper off her gift, then her brown eyes grew as wide as saucers. "It's a crown!"

"I think it's called a tiara," Rob said, moving onto the floor beside her. "Perfect for any princess. Here, let me help you put it on."

Maggie stood completely still as he carefully slipped the shimmering rhinestone tiara on her head. "How does it look?"

"Awesome," Rob replied, touched by Diana's thoughtfulness. She couldn't have picked a better gift for his daughter.

"I wanna go look in the mirror," Maggie said as she raced off toward her bedroom.

The doorbell rang and Rob forged a trail through the gift wrap cluttering the floor to answer it. He expected to find one of his brothers on the other side. Instead, he got the best present of his life when he saw Diana standing there.

She smiled. "Merry Christmas, Rob."

For a moment he didn't say anything, too stunned to speak. "I thought you were going to Austria."

"I decided to reschedule my trip after I realized I'd much rather be here with you and Maggie and T.J. I can't think of a better way to spend Christmas."

Hope flared within him at her words. "Come in," he said, suddenly aware that she was still standing out in the hallway. "The kids are just finishing opening their presents."

As if on cue, Maggie skipped back into the room. She still wore the tiara, as well as a pink feather boa that Rafe and Maria had given her on Christmas Eve. Her face lit up when she saw Diana. "Thank you for the present."

"You're very welcome," Diana said, shrugging out of her coat.

He drank in the sight of her, noting the way her red sweater dress molded to her curves. Rob hoped he wasn't dreaming and that she was really back to stay.

"I have a present for you, too," Maggie told her, racing over to the Christmas tree. She plucked a small, clumsily wrapped gift from underneath the branches. "I made it."

"You did?" Diana said, glancing at Rob. He gave her a small shrug, indicating that it was as much of a surprise to him as it was to her.

They sat down on the sofa together as Maggie walked over to Diana and handed the gift to her.

"T.J. helped me wrap it," Maggie said, "so I guess it's from both of us."

At the sound of his name, T.J. ambled over and stood beside his sister. "Cookie?"

Maggie rolled her eyes. "No, it's not a cookie, you silly. I made it at Lorna's house." She beamed at Diana and Rob. "But it was all my idea."

Diana carefully untied the bow, then peeled

away the paper to find a small box underneath. She opened the lid and saw a hollow circle of shiny baked dough lying on a swatch of cotton.

"It's a ring," Maggie exclaimed, "'cause we want you to marry us." She glanced at her father. "If it's all right with Daddy."

Rob cleared his throat, amazed by his daughter's proposal. Apparently, he wasn't the only one who thought Diana was perfect for them. "Daddy happens to think that's a great idea. But we better make it official."

He took the dough ring from the box and slipped it onto Diana's pinky finger. "Will you marry us?"

Tears pricked her eyes and her mouth curved into a smile. "I'd love to marry you. All of you!"

"Hurray," Maggie shouted.

"Hurray," T.J. echoed, clapping his hands.

Diana held out her hand and admired the ring. "I think this is the best present anyone has ever given me."

Maggie crinkled her brow. "You put it on the wrong finger, Daddy." She pointed to Diana's ring finger. "It's supposed to go on this one."

"I thought my Christmas present to Diana could go there," Rob replied, walking over to the tree and pulling out another present hidden deep under the branches. It was a small black velvet box topped with a shiny silver bow.

Diana's eyes widened when she saw it. He sat back down beside her, then popped open the lid to reveal a one-carat platinum engagement ring.

"Rob," she breathed, meeting his gaze. "Where did this come from?"

He looked a little sheepish. "I bought it yesterday before I came to see you. Call it the power of positive thinking."

She stared down at the platinum ring, tears gleaming in her eyes. "It's absolutely beautiful."

"I know I'm repeating myself," he said, slipping it on her ring finger, "but will you marry me?"

"Yes," she cried, circling her arms around his neck. "I'll marry you."

He kissed her then, while T.J. and Maggie started to giggle. Then Rob and Diana pulled apart and held out their arms to embrace the two children in a family hug.

"I can't wait for the honeymoon," Rob whispered against her ear.

"Then I hope you'll like the Christmas gift I got for you," she said, retrieving an envelope from her purse and handing it to him.

He opened it and pulled out three plane tickets.

"How would the three of you like to go to Austria with me this summer?" she asked hopefully. "I can't wait for my parents to meet you."

"Will you have enough vacation time from work?"

"Plenty," she said, settling down beside him. "In fact, I plan to rearrange my schedule so I can do more work from home. That way I can spend more time with the three of you."

"We'd like that," he said, kissing her again. Then he looked at the tickets in his hand. "I've never been to Europe before."

"Maggie will love Vienna as much as I did when I was a little girl. And if T.J. gets tired of touring the city, he can spend time with his new grandparents."

"What's Vienna?" Maggie asked.

"A place with lots of castles that we can visit," Diana told her. "And we'll hear about all the princesses who lived there."

"Can I wear my tiara?"

"Maybe not on the trip," Rob said, thinking of the metal detectors at the airports. "But you can definitely wear it to breakfast. Who's hungry?"

"Me," Diana said, raising her hand.

"Me, too," Maggie chimed.

They all looked down at T.J. He stared at them for a moment, then said, "Potty."

Rob's eyes widened in surprise. "You have to go potty?"

T.J. nodded, then ran for the bathroom, his father on his heels. Several minutes later, they emerged again, T.J. riding his father's shoulders.

"Success?" Diana asked, already seeing the answer in the proud gleam in Rob's eyes.

"I go potty!" T.J. exclaimed as his father set him on the floor.

"You sure did." Then Rob reached out and pulled Diana into his arms. "Welcome to the Perez family."

She laughed. "Where the excitement never ends."

"Where the love never ends," he promised, then sealed it with a kiss.

EPILOGUE

CARMEN PEREZ laid a holly wreath on the granite stone etched with her husband's name. "I did it, Jose. First Ricardo, then Rafael, and now Roberto. He just called to tell me he's bringing Diana to Christmas dinner today. They're engaged!"

How she wished her husband could be with all of them. But she knew his spirit would be there. It surrounded her daily, giving her the strength she needed to go on without him.

"I know you always told me never to interfere in their love lives, but I was the one who bought that tuxedo and left it on the doorstep," she confided, never able to keep a secret from him for long. "I had to do something to give fate a little nudge."

That was some nudge.

She could almost hear his deep voice in her mind. See the wry smile on his face. He'd been the love of her life and she could see a part of him in each of her sons.

"No woman could resist a Perez man in a tuxedo," she said, remembering her handsome husband on their wedding day so many decades ago. "I know I never could."

And her plan had worked. Today her dining room table would be filled with sons and daughters-in-law and grandchildren. Another sweet baby due any day. Carmen could begin her new career as head teacher at Forrester Square Day Care, knowing her sons were happily settled into their lives.

Her prayers had truly been answered and now a bright future awaited all of them, full of promise and happiness.

And grandchildren. Lots of grandchildren.

A perfect legacy to their love.

Harlequin Books presents

LEGACIES . LIES . LOVE .

An exciting, new, 12-book continuity launching in August 2003.

Forrester Square…the elegant Seattle neighborhood where the Kinards, the Richardses and the Webbers lived… until one fateful night that tore these families apart.

Now, twenty years later, memories and secrets are about to be revealed as the children of these families are reunited. But one person is out to make sure they never remember….

Forrester Square… **Legacies. Lies. Love.**

Look for *Forrester Square,* launching in August 2003 with REINVENTING JULIA by Muriel Jensen.

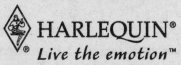

PHFSG

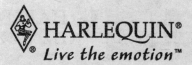

COOPER'S CORNER

The intimacy of
Cooper's Corner...
The high stakes of
Wall Street...

Trade Secrets

Containing two
full-length novels
based on the bestselling
Cooper's Corner continuity!

Jill Shalvis
C.J. Carmichael

Many years ago, a group of
MBA students at Harvard made
a pact—each to become a CEO
of a Fortune 500 company
before reaching age forty.
Now their friendships,
their loves and even their
lives are at stake....

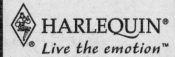

HARLEQUIN®
Live the emotion™

Visit us at www.eHarlequin.com

PHTS